BENEDICT BROWN

A CORPSE AT A WEDDING

IZZY PALMER BOOK EIGHT

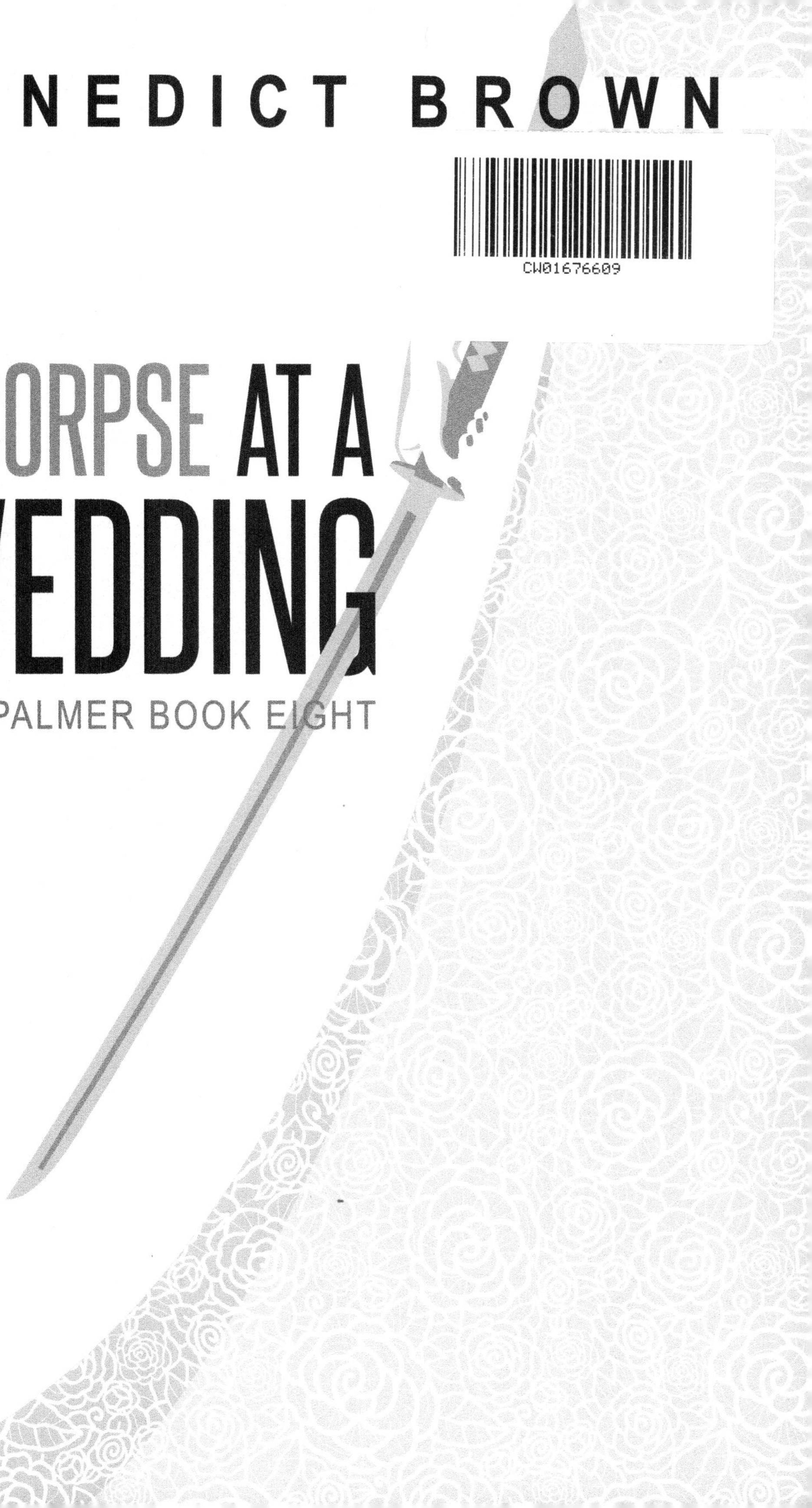

Copyright

First edition May 2022

Cover design by **info@amapopico.com**

To my wife Marion,
my daughter Amelie
and my accomplice Lucy.
(Oh, and Ramesh, of course!)

Author's note

I normally try to write books in a way that people can enjoy them even if they haven't read the rest of the series. This book features no spoilers of previous mysteries but does pick up hundreds of thousands of words into Izzy's story.

So, if you haven't read any other Izzy Palmer Mysteries but are desperate for a juicy slice of murder at a posh wedding populated by eccentric characters, it might take a couple of chapters to get an idea of what's been going on. Oh, and there's a big guest list, but you'll soon learn who everyone is.

All you really need to know is that Ramesh is getting married, and it's going to be fabulous!

Chapter One

On the weekend before my best friend in the world was due to get married, we were knocking back drinks in the office of my very private detective agency. I'd already killed off a two-litre bottle of lemonade like there was no such thing as cavities, while Ramesh was on the strong stuff. He was standing on my desk with a bottle in his hand and had just performed a medley of Cher's biggest hits from the nineties.

"I really think you've had enough Buck's Fizz," I told him when he attempted to do the splits.

"It's not Buck's Fizz, Izzy. It's mimosa." He continued swinging the bottle about even after the music had finished.

"Aren't they identical in every possible way?"

"Of course not." He paused his dancing to consider the distinction. "Mimosa sounds classier!"

As his designated *best woman*, I had offered to organise a more elaborate party to celebrate his approaching nuptials to the beautiful Patricia, but Ramesh had decided that what he really wanted was the chance to sing several hours of karaoke at me. This was not something I would normally have allowed but, as an early wedding present, I decided to make an exception.

It was hard to know whether it was the low-alcohol beverage or the music that was making him so emotional, but he was on his third crying jag of the evening.

"I just think that the world would be a much better place if Cher became president!"

I might have enquired exactly what he thought his beloved diva should be president of, but, at times like this, it's better to let him ramble.

"After what she did for Kaavan, 'The World's Loneliest Elephant', just imagine how easily she could deal with famine, disease and fake news."

I had resigned myself to the fact that I would spend the next few hours nodding along to such deeply philosophical proclamations, when I heard a noise in the tiny reception area of my office. The idea of someone entering the premises of The Private I Detective Agency was strange at the best of times, but this was nine o'clock on a Friday night.

It could be the postwoman, my brain somewhat unconvincingly suggested. *She does seem to arrive later every day.*

Ramesh cleared his throat to speak, but I interrupted him.

"Ra, shhhhh!" I had the unshakable feeling that he was about to break into a version of 'Gypsies, Tramps and Thieves'.

For once, I'd managed to stop him from singing. He even looked a little serious as he jumped down from the improvised stage to listen in the stillness. There was no doubt about it; someone was out there. I could hear a squeaky mumbling coming from the other side of my office door, which could only have been made by another person. Ramesh nervously swallowed the last drop of his drink as we walked closer. He tried to take my hand, but I batted it away.

We were only a few feet from reception now, and the tension around us grew. I could hear a steady scratch, scratch scratching, but it was too dark to see anything through the frosted glass. I looked at my friend in the hope he would change the habit of a lifetime and be the brave one, but he hid behind me and prodded me onwards. I don't like to think of myself as a scaredy-cat, (or whatever word it is that real adults use) but there was something uncanny about that moment that made my tummy turn somersaults.

I reached out towards the door and was just about to open it when…

"Ahhhhhhhhhhh! Plonker!" A man in a wedding dress with fake plastic breasts and poorly applied makeup jumped towards us. "Ahhhh! You should see your face right now!"

He was soon followed into the office by an Oompa Loompa and a man dressed as a giant banana.

"Plonker, Plonker, Plonker!" they chanted, as they circled and pointed at poor Ramesh.

With my heart rate returning to a comparatively healthy level, I tried to make sense of the scene before me. My best guess was that this trio of rowdy idiots provided some sort of insult-a-gram service. Presumably, someone had paid them to dress up and deliver the message that my friend was a 'plonker'.

"We got you!" the drag bride exclaimed with great pride before putting his hand up to high-five the banana.

"You certainly did," Ramesh replied. "I could never have expected any of this."

It finally dawned on me that my Cher-loving friend was acquainted with the morons in our midst.

"We couldn't let you get married without a stag do!" The Oompa Loompa was preparing to stab open a can of lager with a biro, as though he was unfamiliar with the concept of ring-pulls.

"Stag do! Stag do! Stag do!" they sang once more.

"Who's this bloke?" The banana cast his beady eyes over me and, for perhaps the first time that day, I was severely tempted to punch someone.

"I'm not a bloke. I'm *Isobel* Palmer." I used my full name to make sure he got the message. "My friends call me Izzy, whereas you can refrain from speaking to me whenever possible."

"But… but we haven't got a costume for you." He seemed most confused by this point, and the others were too busy to respond.

The bride was removing a collection of accessories from the rucksack on the small orange man's back. They'd soon attached a pair of antlers to Ramesh's head and fixed a tail to his jeans. Oh so cleverly, they'd dressed him as a stag.

"Izzy," he finally explained, "This is Gaz, Tog and Wazza. They're my friends from school."

"Guilty as charged," the one in the dress announced before seizing my hand and charting a path of kisses up my arm. "And you must be the famous detective. Ramesh never said what an absolute babe you were."

"Yeah, what a honey." The Oompa Loompa snorted and then howled like a wolf. The banana thought this was hilarious and stopped blowing up a large plastic human body part to explode with laughter. It's a shame, as I was just about to compliment them on managing to resist bringing any inflatable male appendages. Oh, well.

"We've got so much planned for tonight," Wazza revealed, though this claim would soon be undermined by his friends' next chant.

"Strip club, strip club, strip club!"

I'd love to be one of those people who simply has to sing a phrase for it to be fulfilled. Within ten minutes, they were magically whisked from Leicester Square to a club in Soho. Perhaps even more surprising, however, was the fact that I went with them.

'The Respectful Fellow Gentleman's Club' (not its real name, obviously) was the architectural embodiment of sleaze. Every light was neon. The music pumping through the club was ninety-per cent bass, and the signs for the toilets featured a carrot for the gents' and a pair of melons for the ladies'. On top of all that, I was the only woman there with much in the way of clothes on, and they didn't even sell hot chocolate!

"I personally think that Britney's 2008 album 'Circus' is her underappreciated masterpiece," Ramesh told his own private dancer in a back room of the club as she swayed her hips to 'Oops!...I Did it Again'. Being the sensitive modern man that he was, he'd convinced her to give him a reverse striptease, and she was busy putting her jumper back on.

"Oh, me too!" the erotic artist replied with some excitement. "I consider 'Womanizer' to be a true girl-power anthem. It perfectly skewers the figure of the modern male lothario. It inspired me to leave my crummy ex and start a degree in accountancy."

"Good for you, Sherry!" Ramesh was surprisingly relaxed in the surroundings and was happy to dance in his seat, so long as the charming young woman covered in glitter didn't actually touch him.

I was still in a state of shock at everything that had taken place that evening and was struggling to contribute much to the conversation. The fact that my brain was singing along with the soundtrack didn't help.

When the song had concluded, and we'd both shaken lovely Sherry's hand, I could finally ask the question that I'd been desperate to utter since Ramesh's friends turned up at my office.

"What the heck is going on?"

He was still dancing. "It's a strip club, Izzy. Surely you've heard of them."

"Not this sweat-encrusted den. I'm talking about those men we came with. On the way here in the cab, Wazza told me that he 'doesn't believe in vegetables' and Gaz tried to lick my ear. Who are those people, and why are we with them?"

He looked more nervous now than he had at the sight of all that flesh. "I should have told you before." He took a deep breath. "You see, my friends and family back in Watford don't necessarily know the real me. When I was at school, I was... well, I was different."

I lost my aggressive tone and felt a bit sorry for him. "How do you mean, 'different'?"

"I mean... I don't know how to tell you this, Izzy. But, from an early age, I was... Well, there's only one word for it. I was... popular."

I inhaled rather loudly just then, and he raced to explain himself.

"It's not my fault. I never meant to end up like that, but I was good at football, I mean shockingly good – junior trial at Arsenal good – and the boys at school loved me. Plenty of girls fancied me too, and even the teachers used to go on about how talented and charming I was."

"How is this possible?" I fought to get my words out. "I thought you were like me."

He placed his hands on mine. "I know Izzy. I knew it the first day we met. You told me how bad your clothes were when you were a teenager, and how your only friend was a book." His recollection wasn't totally accurate but close enough. "I felt so bad for you that I couldn't bring myself to tell the truth."

I took a swig of my fruity cocktail and tried to adjust to this unsettling new reality. "I can't believe this is happening."

"You have to understand; that wasn't the real me. I didn't want to have my picture in the paper for being the fastest hundred-metre sprinter in Hertfordshire or win the vote for the most adored boy in school. I was living a double life and, locked away in my bedroom, I would binge on Abba records, celebrity gossip magazines and classic recordings of Broadway musicals. I come from a traditional family, and my friends thought I was some kind of macho superhero. I could never be myself around them."

His confession still hadn't sunk in, but I tried to look at it from his perspective. "So you haven't told anyone in Watford about your Shania Twain fan site?"

He shook his head.

"Or the time you dressed up as Freddie Mercury and made half of London sing 'Crazy Little Thing Called Love?'"

"It would kill them if they knew!" His words came out in a howl wrought with sorrow.

"You're about to spend a whole weekend with these people for your wedding. Surely they'll get an inkling of your eccentricities when you sashay down the aisle in a bright orange, feathered headdress with an illuminated tailcoat."

He didn't say anything then. In fact, he grew incredibly quiet and wouldn't look at me. Luckily, my brain is a psychic.

O... M... G! He's planning to hide his inner peacock! Don't let him do it, Izzy.

I sucked in a loud breath. "Is it true, Ramesh?"

Understandably, he looked puzzled. "Is what true?"

Oops, I sometimes forget that people can't hear my inner monologue. "Are you really planning to disguise yourself at your own wedding?"

His eyes fell to the sticky carpet, and I knew he wouldn't answer my question.

"You can't do this, Ra. You'll regret it for the rest of your life."

I thought he would find the courage to respond, but we were interrupted once more by the band of travelling idiots.

"Ramesh!" the banana yelled. "Did you have a lovely dance?"

"We had some delicious chicken wings!" Tog, the Oompa Loompa, still had the sauce all over his face to prove it.

Gaz plumped down beside me in the heart-shaped booth. He was the slimiest of the lot. "So, young lady, I'll be going to the wedding *solo* next week." He raised his eyebrows suggestively and adjusted his veil. "Any chance of a smoochy late-night dance with yours truly?" He pointed at me as he said this, so he apparently didn't know the meaning of the phrase *yours truly.*

"Urmmm…" I tried to come up with a reason why this would be categorically impossible. "I think I have a cold sore coming on."

He leered a little more pronouncedly and shuffled along the bench towards me. "Herpes doesn't bother me."

Quick Izzy, make up a fake boyfriend. It wouldn't be the first time.

How dare you! My pen pal Jake was a real boy who really loved me. It's not my fault he lived in New Zealand and was afraid of flying.

I was referring to the last family party you went to. Now hurry up before this idiot tries to kiss you.

"I'm so sorry, Gaz." I didn't sound it. "But I already have a boyfriend."

"Do you?" Ramesh sounded surprised so that his friend didn't have to.

"Uhuh."

Gaz did not look as though he believed me. "Go on then. What's his name?"

Just say the first name that comes into your head. Anything will do, so long as you don't say Danny. My brain had a good laugh then. *Claiming you were still going out with your recently dumped ex would be really awkward.*

"It's…" I tried to sound confident and not like someone who was picking a name from thin air. "Nigel."

Nigel!?

"Nigel?" Everyone in the room queried at the same moment, as though they'd never heard the name. Wazza and Tog even stopped sliding down the stripper pole to listen.

"Yes, Nigel. And we're very much in love."

Not Nigel! Anyone but Nigel!

But you said I could say anyone but Danny.

"Miaow, Izzy." Ramesh sounded proud of me. "What happened to the guy you were seeing in December?"

I'd rather he hadn't mentioned that. "Well, he was lovely and everything but, sadly, he believed he was Father Christmas."

"I had no idea that you and Nigel were back together." My friend punched me on the arm and gave me a wink. "You dark horse."

"That's right. I grabbed the pink cocktail from the pink cocktail table beside me and tipped it down my throat. Memories of my ex-ex-ex-boyfriend came rushing through my head and I leaned over to steal Ramesh's drink. "Nigel and I are very much in love."

Gaz was still staring at me. "You already said that."

"Yeah. Well, if you knew Nigel, you'd understand why I like to restate my love for him on a regular basis."

The room had fallen quiet and, aware of the situation I'd got myself into, I knew there was only one thing for it. In a single stealthy, fishlike movement, my hand shot out to grab hold of Gaz's outfit. I whipped a part of it free and jumped to my feet. The boys looked on in confusion as I darted around an Oompa Loompa and a tall banana and escaped from the soundproof bunker we'd been trapped within. I felt guilty for leaving Ramesh with them, but I got the impression he knew how to handle himself. Despite the name-calling, they clearly still looked up to him like a celebrity.

Out in the main room of the club, two tired-looking women with fake tans that were almost exactly the same shade as Tog's face paint were dressed as sexy traffic wardens. They were wagging their notebooks and pens at the assorted oglers, but I wouldn't let myself get distracted. I threaded a path through the club, made it past the two giant bouncers at the door and escaped into the cool night.

I don't know if it was the alcohol that had gone to my head or the fact that I was standing up for women after centuries of objectification, but I felt immortal just then. I held up Gaz's fake plastic breasts in the air and roared with all my might.

Don't get carried away, my brain told me. *You've just told Ramesh that you'll be attending his wedding with Nigel "I only tried your shoes on to see how they would look on my feet" Perkins.*

So then I didn't feel so powerful after all.

Chapter Two

I freely admit that I do not have the best track record when it comes to *l'amour*.

"It's not that I have bad taste exactly, it's more that the men I fall in love with turn out to be different from how they first seem."

My friend Dean was standing on the table in my lounge with his arms out. "Izzy, that is the textbook definition of bad taste in men."

"Hey, I didn't fancy you at least." I thought this was a sterling argument until I remembered that he was a tech genius millionaire.

Mother draped a piece of pink chiffon over one of his arms and a square of blue, zebra-print velvet over the other, but he remained focused on our conversation.

"Don't remind me. I haven't slept since your cruel rejection."

"So, will you do it?"

He emitted a particularly heavy breath. "As tempting as it is to call myself Nigel all weekend and pretend to be your boyfriend…" He hesitated, and I actually thought he would agree. "… I can't."

Before I could complain, my mother ran from the room waving a rainbow-coloured machine gun about the place, screaming, "I thought I said I wanted ammunition in this thing?"

I ignored her and focussed on the issue at hand. "Seriously, Dean? Why not? You did it last time."

"I can't go with you to Ramesh's wedding because I'm already taking my girlfriend, who, as it happens, is a real person."

Now that is a good argument!

I was tempted to huff and moan, but my heart wasn't in it, and he kept talking. "Why don't you say that imaginary Nigel has to work next weekend? You could invent a really high-powered fictional job for him so that everyone is impressed by what an incredible fake boyfriend you have."

"If I go to the wedding alone, Ramesh's scuzzy, lager-lout friends will be all over me. Being in the same room as Gaz, Wazza and Tog is like going scuba diving in a sea of Calvin Klein Obsession."

"Izzy?" my father interrupted, tapping me on the shoulder most insistently. "Izzy, I'm really rather worried about your mother's performance at the wedding. She has a whole 'Soldier of Love' routine planned, but none of us are ready. I think it could be a disaster."

I made a sympathetic face and tried to get rid of him. "Sorry, Dad, but I've already told her that I'm having no part in whatever she has planned. I have enough to deal with as Ramesh's best woman."

My poor, lovely father looked sad and shuffled away, dragging the stuffed crocodile he'd been carrying behind him like a rather bedraggled teddy bear. I stared after him for some seconds and fell into a bit of a trance.

"Izzy, what's got into you?" Dean asked, but I was busy trying not to think about my last proper boyfriend.

Danny, Danny, Danny!

It wasn't working.

"Izzy?" Dean tried again. "Is the real reason you don't want to go to the wedding alone because Danny's bringing a new girlfriend?"

"Is he? How interesting."

The truth is that Dr Danny Fields was perfect. He was my dream man: an Adonis made flesh, but ridiculously sweet with it. I'd ended the relationship six months earlier because… because… Oh, there was definitely a reason. I just couldn't quite remember what it was.

"Yes, Izzy. He is. And I know that because you told me."

"Did I?"

"That's right. And I also know you haven't seen him since you broke up."

"Do you?"

I could have continued like that for hours, so I was rather glad that my stepfather Greg rushed into the room just then, shouting, "We'll never pull this off! We were fools to even think we could get away with something so bold. The guests at the wedding will eat us for breakfast."

Dean and I were desensitised to such drama from my family and continued with the conversation as though a man in his sixties hadn't just run around the room in a circle, dressed as a bear with its paws in the air.

"You'd better get used to the idea," Dean said in that wise voice of his. "You're going to have to spend the weekend with your ex and his new Mrs. I've heard she's rather lovely."

"Oh, have you? And who told you that?" I got a bit angry then, but it didn't last long. "Wait. It was me, wasn't it?"

I'd accidentally spent an hour searching online for a photo of "a girl called Eliza Fairhurst who worked in the Department for International Development and spent a gap year volunteering in Tanzania," (which was all Mum had been able to learn about her on my behalf.)

"That's right, Isobel. And it sounds to me as though a little green monster called envy has–" Thank goodness my mother reappeared at this moment to drape a third piece of lurid material over my friend's face.

"Yes, I think that's the combination we need." She stood back to admire the colour palette. "Passionate puce, diesel zebra and, spring-fresh lime."

I had to feel a little guilty that Dean was being used as a human clothes horse – a clothes centaur? – but he was the one who enjoyed hanging out with my melodramatic parents so much. I never forced him to come to my house and assist with one of my mother's elaborate productions. If anything, he seemed to take an inexplicable thrill from the chaos that my family created.

"I'm still not telling you what I have planned for next weekend," she sang in a taunting voice.

I looked her in the eyes and responded with all the compassion I could inject into my voice. "And I'm still not asking. But I'm sure that whatever you do will be brilliant."

Mum had been in full theatrical-diva mode for more than a year by this point. She'd always lived her life in an over-the-top fashion, but since a theatrical agent had discovered her, and the West End musical of her life had become such a hit, every day was a new chance to shine. She seemed to suck everyone around her into this otherworldly vortex, so that my previously sane fathers (numbers one and three) walked about the place like they were minor characters in a Victorian melodrama.

"Oh, it will be, Izzy. It will be..." She walked away chuckling to herself, and I removed the veil from poor Dean's face.

"Fine," I told him when he breathed loudly in my direction. "You've convinced me. I'll have to take matters into my own hands."

My still reassuringly geeky friend didn't have a large range of facial expressions but now went from looking mildly disgruntled to mildly bewildered. "What on earth are you talking–" I did not hear the inevitable conclusion to this question as I'd already left the room.

I marched straight out of the house and down Hawes Lane to a cul-de-sac I hadn't set foot in for what seemed like decades. Little Court felt like some distant land that I'd visited on a school trip many years before. It was hard to comprehend that it was only a minute's walk from my house. I peered up at the detached, red-brick buildings as though they were ancient temples but, the further along the road I walked, the more tangled and knotted my intestines became.

Nigel's house was the only one with a crumbling wall in front of it and a yellow 1970s Ford Cortina with no wheels in the drive. Failing to repair that rusting car was one of his many hobbies, and the sight of it was almost enough to make me turn and run to safety. A couple of days with Nigel would still be preferable to a lonely weekend avoiding Ramesh's friends while Danny and his beautiful girlfriend elegantly tangoed around me.

Are you sure about that? This is Nigel Perkins we're talking about. You do remember who that is, don't you?

Vaguely.

Perhaps I should explain something before I step through that door. You see, I was only twenty-five when I started going out with Nigel. We met in West Wickham library, and he seemed so much older and more experienced than me. He had a job in the city – though I never discovered what he actually did – and a lot of exotic-sounding interests, like Japanese industrial noise music and Russian politics. In reality, he was the biggest bore Southern England has ever produced but, sadly for me, I didn't have the self-confidence to realise it, and we went out for two long years.

As my brain rushed to remind me of all this, I rang the bell to number seventeen. There was no reply at first and a sense of great calm descended upon me as I came to believe that the decision would be taken off my hands. If he wasn't home, he couldn't come to the wedding, and I wouldn't be forced to–

"Hello, Izzy," a feeble voice said through the cracked-open letter box. He did not sound surprised to see me.

"Hi Nigel."

As he put his eyes up close to the flap, I finally realised what a mistake I'd made returning to the place of so many nightmares.

When he said no more, I finally had to ask, "Why don't you open the door?"

He let out a high-pitched grunt. "I want to make sure you're not carrying any potatoes first. Show me your hands."

"Why would I be carrying any–"

"The last time you were here, you threw a potato at me."

"Was that the time I found you trying on my shoes?" I felt the same old arguments rearing up within me. "Or the time you said that I should give up my job and earn my living as a guinea pig in medical trials?"

"Show me your hands, Izzy." He sounded like my old headmaster.

Remembering that I needed a favour from him, I did as instructed. It was a good thing I hadn't brought any potatoes with me.

I heard the chain sliding back before the door swung open. And there he was, standing in silence, staring back at me. He was wearing his favourite black t-shirt with a picture of a crow eating a heart on it, and he still had that slightly constipated expression on his face. He was an odd-looking chap at the best of times, and the fact he'd grown a beard since we'd last met didn't help. It seemed that what little hair he'd gained on his chin had disappeared from the top of his head. The small clumps of fluff that circled his cranium gave him a rather monk-like appearance.

"So… Izzy Palmer. I was wondering when you'd show up." He clicked his tongue and shook his head like he'd said something hilarious.

"I'm sorry to bother you, Nigel, but I need a–" Before I could finish the sentence, he'd turned to walk into the house.

Don't follow him! He'll trap you in there and steal your shoes!

I ignored every last instinct and stepped inside with all the trepidation that twelve-year-old Izzy would have had entering a ghost house at a funfair. Come to think of it, I'm still not much a fan of ghost houses… or funfairs for that matter.

"Nigel?" my voice echoed back to me. "Hello, Nigel, are you–" A sudden explosion made me jump a foot off the ground. For a moment, I wondered whether he'd spent the time since we'd broken up booby trapping his house on the off-chance I'd return.

I walked into the lounge to find him, just as I should have expected, sitting in front of the thousand-inch TV with a video game control in his hand. Images of exploding brains and angry old ladies with swinging handbags flashed across the screen and, quite involuntarily, I took up my old place on the armchair next to his own.

"The great thing about Zombie Death Squad V," he began, as I knew he would, "is that you get to be the zombies, the soldiers or old ladies with handbags. It's so funny when the biddies get eaten, and yet, I can't help rooting for them."

As bad as it was that I'd spent the two years we dated sitting in that chair, watching him play computer games, that wasn't nearly so painful as having to listen to him talk about them as if they were great works of art. I crossed my fingers that he wouldn't use the word pathos.

"The true pathos of the game…" Too late! "…is the way in which it shows the ultimate futility of the human struggle when faced with an irrepressible foe. Think of the Irish peasants at the massacre of Drogheda before the might of the British army, or the Aztecs bowing down before their conquistadors." As I'm sure you can imagine, he put on a Spanish accent when he said this word and made sure to roll the R. "Those are the images that run through my mind when I witness an old lady swinging her leather purse through the air before the zombie hordes descend upon her."

I had fallen under his spell and found myself nodding along with his analysis. I desperately needed something to snap me out of it, but that chair was just so comfy. It was quite evident that no one had sat in it since I'd last been there; my bottom fitted into the grooves just perfectly.

Snap out of it, Izzy. You're better than this.

Oh, come on. He owns his own house and has most of a car. It's not as if any suitable bachelors have been sniffing around me recently. Would it really be so bad to get married to Nigel and watch him playing computer games every night for the rest of my life?

Yes, it would!

"I'm a detective," I blurted, to break free from the sleepy haze that had consumed me. "A damn good one, in fact. I've solved all the murders. Every last one of them." I wasn't entirely sure what I was talking about, but if it saved me from the Emerald City poppy field I'd just entered, I'd say whatever it took. "I have a case to work next weekend, and I need your help."

He diverted his attention from the screen for approximately three seconds, and it was long enough for the zombie he was controlling to be crushed by a steamroller.

"Seriously, Izzy! I was about to complete level seven! I knew I shouldn't have let you in here. It would have been better if you'd thrown a potato at me through the window."

"Forget the game for one minute." I'd found my voice (and my spine) and hurled the words at him like a stick of dynamite from an old lady's purse. "I'm going to a wedding and I'm worried that my friend is in danger." This was all complete nonsense, but what else could I say? "I need you to pretend to be my boyfriend and I'll–"

"I thought you hated me. I thought you said I was a shoe-stealing weirdo!"

I couldn't hold in my resentment. "You are, but that's not why I broke up with you. You never listened to a word I said and only wanted me around as a mirror to remind you how great you are. It wasn't your foot fetish that made me leave. It was the two years I spent feeling worthless." All the things I wished I'd been able to say to him back then came pouring out and, I have to admit, it felt amazing!

He looked at the television and then at me, before crumpling a little in his seat. "Then I should probably say I'm sorry." I thought this would be one of those fake apologies, but he surprised me. "I'm sorry you felt like that. It's been brought to my attention that I'm not always the most confident person, and I take that out on the people around me."

Now I felt bad for being so harsh on him.

It's a real rollercoaster in your head today.

I decided to provide some more context. "The truth is my ex-boyfriend will be at the wedding with his new girlfriend and I don't want to go alone. So… will you come with me?"

"Fine, but only if I can try on your shoes."

I bolted from my chair, disgusted once more, not just with the oddball man-child in front of me, but my younger self for going out with him. "Not a chance."

He pressed a button on the control and the sound of death and destruction fired up again. "So, enjoy the wedding alone, mademoiselle."

I let out an aggressive huff to let him know that I meant business, then whimpered and gave in. "If you come with me next weekend, I'll let you borrow an old pair of my slippers for one evening."

"Deal." The room fell silent, and he unleashed a diabolical laugh. "Oh, Izzy… you pretty little fool, you never were much of a negotiator. I would have settled for a pair of flip flops."

Chapter Three

It's hard to know if I was more nervous about the speech I had to give as best woman or the thought of Nigel Perkins ruining the wedding with endless boring stories about cricket or his remote-controlled drone or the correct way to ferment beer. I was struggling to understand what possessed me to curse that happy event by inviting him. And yet, some part of me must have known.

In truth, it was all about Danny.

I like to think of myself as a self-aware, rational sort of person, and I hadn't forgotten that I was the one who had ended our relationship when it turned out that kissing my oldest friend in the world felt a bit too fraternal. But none of that changed the fact that the thought of him dating someone who was perkier, prettier and more successful than me was enough to interrupt my normally sensational sleeping patterns. I didn't want to be *one of those women* who lost their mind over an ex, but that's exactly what had happened, and I wasn't sure why.

"Perhaps it's your age," my mother helpfully suggested as we packed up the car the following Friday to head to the wedding. "You're thirty-one now Izzy. Perhaps you're broody for a baby and you know you've given up your best chance of happiness."

I ignored her and climbed aboard.

My biological father was busy attaching a trailer to the back of my mum's hairdresser, Fernando's, limousine, and my stepfather was busy sipping Prosecco.

It was down to Fernando to come up with a more suitable answer. "I've got a question for you, Izzy." He turned around in the driver's seat and lowered the electric screen to be able to see me. "Am I right in saying that Danny is the best boyfriend you've had, even if you decided to call it a day?"

Another name popped to the front of my mind, but I batted it away because he was in prison. "I suppose you could make such a case, yes."

"Well, there you go then." Fernando nodded confidently. I always enjoyed his perspective on things. "If you look back over the men you've dated, there've been some real trolls."

Nigel was sitting beside me, playing a game on his phone. "How rude. I'm right here."

"And I told you not to be obnoxious if you want me to keep my end of the bargain." I had to be tough to keep him in line. "Please, Fernando, continue when you're ready."

"I'm saying that this is a new experience for you. You've never had to look back on a relationship and worry who your ex might be seeing because you were better off without every bloke you dated."

Or they were surrounded by men in orange jumpsuits.

"And this is why I employ you as my hairdresser/chauffeur/life coach, Fernando." Poking her head through the window, my mother beamed with pride and started a slow clap that Nigel decided to join in with.

"So, I'm not a terrible person for being jealous of Danny's new saintly humanitarian girlfriend?"

Fernando released a warm chuckle. "No, of course you're not. It's a stage that most people will go through at some point in their lives. You're just unlucky that you've been out with a bunch of stinkers and didn't get past it when you were a teenager."

Nigel sneered and pointed. "You really do have the worst taste in men, Izzy."

I grabbed his phone and tossed it into the boot. I would have thrown a potato at him, but I didn't have any to hand.

"Righty ho! Off we go!" Dad sang as he jumped into the front passenger seat. "I've secured the Trojan horse!" He gave my mother a theatrical wink and, as theatrical winks are the only kind she can do, she returned the gesture.

I peered back through the rear window of the car to confirm that he was not speaking metaphorically. There was an oversized papier mâché horse attached to the trailer behind us and, as Fernando pulled away, it seemed to nod at me through the glass.

"Wagons roll!" Greg shouted and made a honking horn gesture. For my stepdad, one glass of Prosecco was clearly one too many.

We had to pick up Ramesh first, as he'd refused to tell anyone where the wedding was being held. In fact, he'd been surprisingly reticent about the whole thing. Normally, I would have expected my exuberant bestie to have been singing about his plans non-stop. To be honest, when I'd agreed to be his best woman, I'd imagined that it would be a full-time job, but he'd done most of the work himself. Perhaps it was my detective's instinct, but I was suspicious, to say the least.

"I know, darling," he said into his phone as he placed one pet carrier after another into the car. Apparently his cats, Elton and Kiki, would be included in the wedding. "I completely understand how you're feeling. If Izzy did that to me, I'd never speak to her again."

No one made a sound as Ramesh got in, and Fernando started the car. We were all trying to work out what the problem was.

"It'll be fine," he continued. He was obviously talking to his fiancée, but the exact details of what was troubling her would have to wait until he'd finished the call. "Absolutely, my angel. I'll be there soon. I love you."

He hung up and looked at the audience he had amassed. We did nothing to hide the fact we'd been eavesdropping, and he didn't seem upset either way.

"So?" I had to be the one to ask when no one else would. "What's happened?"

He put the back of his hand to his head in a typically Ramesh-like manner. "Horror, Izzy! Shock and horror; that's what's happened."

"You poor thing," my mother replied, when it was clear that he intended to milk the situation for all the sympathy he could get.

He gave a dejected huff and finally explained the situation. "It's Patricia's bridesmaid, Sindy. The woman is an ogre. The pair of them were best friends at school but have hardly spoken for years. That didn't stop Sindy inviting herself to the wedding and deciding that she should be the head bridesmaid, though. My dear sweet fiancée was too polite to say no and has spent the last month having to referee her friends, who can't stand the obnoxious interloper. It's a disaster."

"That's terrible, Ramesh," my father began. "But are you going to tell us where you're getting married now?"

A smile broke out across his handsome face. "You'll be lucky."

"How about which direction we should drive?"

"Not until I have a glass of bubbly in my hand." He snapped his fingers. "Greg! Prosecco me! This is my wedding, and I expect to enjoy it at just the right level of tipsiness."

My friend was eventually persuaded to tell us that the ceremony would be taking place to the north of London, but he would reveal nothing more until we'd spent several hours sitting in traffic on the M25.

"Bloody Fridays!" Fernando bellowed as he hunched over the wheel. Though normally an impressively calm man, he did not deal well with queueing. "I'll give you a *Friday feeling*… Damn traffic!"

I had all sorts of ideas in my head for what Ramesh's dream wedding would look like. I thought that there was a good chance he had built his own venue – I pictured some sort of space dome with all members of the wedding in shiny silver outfits like extras from 'Barbarella'. As for the officiant… well, what with Ramesh's family living in Watford, there really was no doubt in my mind that Elton John had been drafted in to do the honours.

I still hadn't had the briefest glimpse of Ramesh's suit, the dress he'd bought me or even the floral centrepieces, though it seemed inevitable there would be a theme to the whole thing. Knowing my dear friend as I did, I was fairly confident that it would be popstar based.

Despite all this, I really wasn't prepared for what we discovered when we arrived at our destination. We pulled off a country road through a set of grand golden gates. I was on the wrong side of the car to see the name of the place, but I could tell it was posh from the fact that the security guard on duty looked down his nose at us even though we were arriving in a stretch limousine. He tapped the top of the vehicle, and Fernando rolled us onto the property down a moodily lit avenue of topiary animals. It brought back bad memories of the time my boss was murdered – the second one, not the first.

"Bleeding heck!" my father marvelled with his mouth open. This was quite the rudest swearword I'd ever heard him use, and I leaned into the front of the vehicle to see what the fuss was about.

"Bloody hell!" I cawed. "Ra, you're getting married in a castle!"

"Blooming heavens!" My mother chimed in. It was not the most natural of responses, but it fit the pattern my father had established. "That's not a castle! It's a school of wizardry."

Like excited golden retrievers, my fathers stuck their heads out of their windows, and I couldn't blame them. The up-lit turrets of the immense edifice towered above the car, and we were still a minute's drive away. As a detective who'd investigated more than… well, I couldn't remember exactly how many murders I'd solved, though there'd been a lot. As an experienced detective with a love of classic crime fiction, I'd seen my fair share of stately homes. But nothing had prepared me for this place. I was fairly certain that Fernando's disproportionate road rage had led to a car accident, and I was now dead, because we were clearly in heaven.

The building was immense with the grandest wing in the centre and four tall towers around the outside. The place was built in pale grey stone and, despite its age, it was in immaculate condition. It looked as though it had been hosed down daily, like Dad does with his 1940s Spitfire motorbike. I spotted a church spire at the back of the property, which I could only imagine would host the wedding itself and, in the centre of the impressive gardens, a helicopter was taking off from a designated helipad.

"Welcome to Hartford House, everybody." Ramesh lounged back on the white leather upholstery. "Our home for the weekend. And don't worry about the hoi polloi bothering us. I've booked every last room."

"We've got this whole place to ourselves?" My voice was so high, I sounded like someone had just punched me in the kidneys.

"That's right." He could no longer play it cool, and an explanation came pouring out of him. "I've been saving up for this since I saw it in an episode of 'The Clothes Show' when I was eleven years old."

Every last person in that car – except Nigel who was singing the jingle from an advert – was stunned into absolute silence.

"Carpets at the right price! Carpets at a nice price!"

My eyes grew wider as Fernando pulled the car to a stop on the perfectly neat gravel courtyard in front of the main entrance. Without a word, a team of staff surrounded the car, wheeled the trailer with my mum's horse away and removed our bags from the boot to take them to the exact places they needed to go. How they possessed such knowledge was a mystery.

Ramesh exited the limousine while the rest of us sat there, our mouths agape, except for Nigel, who had produced a bag of smoky bacon crisps and was tossing handful after handful into his mouth.

"It's not my kind of place," he told us, as though anyone cared. "I hate old buildings. Give me concrete and glass any day."

I decided to follow Ramesh then, mainly because I'd been a witness in a number of court cases and didn't fancy going on trial for Nigel's murder.

Izzy! Izzy! My brain was even more excited than I was. *I think they filmed an episode of Miss Marple here!*

I crunched my way up the drive, wishing that I'd worn something other than jogging bottoms and a jumper with a Christmas tree on it – yes, I know it was June, but, in my defence, I normally do my washing on a Sunday morning, and it was the only clean one I had. How stupid would I have looked turning up there in slightly musty knitwear?

"Welcome to Hartford House, Miss Palmer," the posh doorman said. He was better dressed than me, obviously, but was well enough trained not to show that he had realised. "Mr Khatri has gone ahead to the ballroom, where his betrothed, Miss Green, will soon join you. If you'd like a hot chocolate, your personal assistant Cheryl is on call twenty-four hours a day."

I wondered if Hartford House hired psychics, as he appeared to know absolutely everything about me – well, my name and my favourite drink, at least, so all the important stuff.

I squeaked my thanks and wandered inside to feel even more out of place than I normally did. The expression *entrance hall* really didn't do that room justice. They should invent new vocabulary for such luxurious surroundings and, knowing rich people, they probably already have. What can I even say about it? Immense, stunning, transcendental, wooden; all these words would figure in a description, but before I could put them into any useful order, a chap in a top hat had ushered me through it, along a hallway lined with portraits of horsey women and men on horses, and into the ballroom.

The ballroom itself was immense, stunning and transcendental (excuse my limited vocabulary). The floor was made of marble, the walls were mirrored glass, and the ceiling was quite literally heavenly. A scene of cherubs, angels and silver-lined clouds made the Sistine Chapel look pretty paltry in comparison.

My enjoyment of it was only cut short by a blood-freezing scream, as the bride-to-be ran into the room.

Chapter Four

Patricia Octavia Green remains, to this day, one of the most sensationally beautiful women I've ever met. Thanks to her French-Italian mother and Senegalese father, she had an unplaceable look about her that I can only imagine modelling agents would lose their minds over. Slim, elegant and, I would normally have said, composed, it was a shock to see her come screaming across the checkerboard floor to crash into her fiancé. Ramesh caught her in his arms like an unexpectedly virile romantic hero.

"What's the matter, my darling?" He even sounded like a leading man. I was having a hard time making sense of the world.

Patricia couldn't reply as she was playing the part of a pathetic heroine and sobbed into his shoulder. "I… It's…"

My normally soppy friend pulled his bride closer and wrapped his muscly arms around her back.

Huh… He does have muscly arms. How did we not notice that before?

Strolling in behind us was a duo of laddish chaps who immediately started clapping and cheering as Ramesh dipped Patricia backwards and planted a gentle kiss upon her lips. Though they were out of costume, I recognised Gaz and Tog from the stag night.

The sillier of the two let out a sound like a gorilla and shouted, "You're the boss, Ra!"

Mum and Dads were the next to arrive, and my mother looked genuinely surprised at the scene. "I'm not going to lie," she whispered under her breath to her companions. "I was still half-expecting Patricia to turn out to be a man."

There were two women standing in the doorway that the fiancée had emerged from, but I paid them little attention and went to see the blubbering bride.

"Is everything okay?"

Ramesh was whispering words of comfort into her ear and, when she finally looked up at me, she had to take a deep breath before she could speak.

"I'm being emotional over nothing." The woman voted *Southeast*

England's Most Promising Businesswoman of 2018 was the last person I'd describe as excessively emotional but, rather than contradict her, I listened to what she had to say.

She looked around the ballroom as though seeing it for the first time. "It's just the pressure of all this. I'll be fine once I've had a cup of tea."

Before she'd finished the sentence, a woman pushing a shiny silver trolley had bustled into the room. "Rooibos, Earl Grey, Assam? What can I get you, Miss Green?"

I had to assume this was our personal assistant, Cheryl. She was neatly dressed in the same green uniform as the reception staff, though she could have picked a better moment to be omniscient.

"Are you sure you're alright?" I persisted, as Patricia opted for Moroccan Mint.

Still in his assertive mood, Ramesh must have realised that his fiancée wasn't going to admit to anything with such a large audience present, and so he made an announcement to the room. "Nothing to see here, everyone. If you head to your suites, we'll catch up at dinner."

There was some not-so-subtle mumbling as the other guests speculated over what had upset the poor woman, but almost everyone shuffled away. The only lingerer was a middle-aged woman in a floral frock. I couldn't tell if she was part of the wedding party or a nosy member of staff, but she hung in space for a minute longer than everyone else and only left the room when I stared at her.

I suppose, if I'm being honest, I was equally guilty of outstaying my welcome. In my defence, it is my job to be nosy.

"You can tell us the truth," Ramesh whispered in a reassuring voice. "Was it Sindy again?" He was unusually serious. It was rare for him to go five minutes without mentioning Dolly Parton's pop-crossover years or breaking out into a lesser-known Janet Jackson B-side.

Patricia instantly scanned the room at the mention of her bridesmaid's name. "I told you, I was just–"

He interrupted before she could cover up her true feelings. "This is our wedding, Patri-tri. If something has upset you, I need to know about it so that Izzy can put it right."

That's the Ramesh we all know and love.

I should probably have been annoyed by this, but I knew what he meant. "I am the best woman after all. If I can't solve the problem, who can?"

Patri-tri… I mean, Patricia took a step away from her betrothed and blew on her steaming mug. "Yes, it was Sindy who upset me. You know what she's like; I shouldn't have been so sensitive."

"What did she do?" Ramesh wouldn't let her get away with papering over her feelings and angled his head to look her straight in the eyes. "Tell me right now, or Izzy is going to storm over to her room and turf her out."

"No, don't do that." She laughed then, and it made everything seem better. "Sindy just told me that her boyfriend is coming."

I failed to see how this was a problem, but Ramesh let out a yelp that was probably heard in Aberdeen. "Not Anfony! I thought they broke up?"

Patricia could do little but nod as she peered hopelessly into her tea.

I didn't understand what was happening but still felt terrible for her. "Who's Anfony?"

Ramesh has a special voice for when he's pressed for time but needs to recap a major movie or TV show. It goes something like this… "Sindy, Particia and I were all at school with Sindy's boyfriend Toby. Toby left Sindy at the altar, and so Sindy tried to get her own back by dating Anfony. And Anfony…" It was not often that Ramesh ran out of words but, to my surprise, Patricia had to finish the sentence for him.

"Anfony makes Sindy seem quite pleasant, but only because he's the single worst person I've ever met." She had to pause to let out an anguished groan. "I once saw him try to kick a dog."

It sounds as though he'll get on with Nigel at least, I thought but didn't say, as I was supposed to be dating the guy.

"I heard him describe wearing shoes without socks as a 'life philosophy'," Ramesh was quick to add. "And he thinks that Lindsay Lohan is overrated."

"Ra? He tried to kick a dog!" Patricia looked at him as though she was seriously reconsidering this whole *marriage* idea. "And don't forget that he hit on me in front of his girlfriend, and you, at our engagement party!" The panic had risen in her voice again. "I only said Sindy could bring a guest with her because she promised they'd broken up. She didn't tell me until tonight who she was bringing. If

Anfony is here this weekend, I don't see how I'll be able to enjoy my own wedding."

They both turned to me then, but I no longer felt so confident in my abilities to deal with the horrendous Sindy and her psychopathic boyfriend. It was a bit like in Jurassic Park, when you hear all about the T-Rex, but you don't see it until it's too late, and the gigantic toothy beast is reaching down to bite some poor schmo's head off.

Ha! Great film!

"So you're sure you want me to tell Sindy that this Anfony guy can't come?" This was my last gasp attempt to get out of my task.

They grinned serenely, and Patricia held out the key card. "She's up in the bridal suite. She insisted that she and the other bridesmaids have a sleepover together tonight. 'A sleepover'! She's thirty-three, and that's the word she used. Urghhh."

Ramesh could see that his girlfriend was becoming teary again, so he gave her another hug and motioned for me to get on with it.

"The bridal suite is in the east tower," Cheryl the super-assistant appeared from behind a pillar to explain. She no longer had her trolley but walked briskly past to lead me from the ballroom. "Hartford House was built for the first Earl of Edgington in the Jacobean style popular of the early seventeenth century. Some years later, the Edgington family fell out of favour with the king, and the estate was passed to the Marquess of Berkeley, whose family has retained possession of Hartford ever since."

She rattled off this history lesson in a schoolmarmish tone, but I was too nervous to concentrate. Every step through those stunning hallways and galleries that we navigated took me closer to the mysterious Sindy. I'd been staking out a catnapping on the night of Ramesh's engagement party and hadn't met any of Patricia's friends before. In fact, I knew very little about the happy couple's lives before they moved to South London except that they had known one another at school, hated one another with a passion, and met again by chance in London a few years later. I hadn't even met Patricia's mum before.

"The Queen Mary suite is so called for the visit soon after the house's inauguration by the Queen herself and it is now used as the bridal and honeymoon suite of this marvellous wedding venue-slash-conference centre." Cheryl had switched from a teacherly voice to full-on salesperson. Perhaps she thought I might be in the market for a wedding venue myself.

Ha!

Little did she know that I only had a fake boyfriend, whom I appeared to have mislaid.

Coming to a stop on the upstairs landing, she pointed me down the corridor then vanished into thin air. Well, that's how it seemed anyway. In truth, she had scurried off down the stairs while my back was turned, but there was something very *Good Witch of the South* about her.

I was tempted to call her back and ask for a drink of my own, but I knew that even hot chocolate couldn't help me now. I forced myself onwards, down that oddly gloomy corridor. The floor was made of ancient, polished wood. There were gold brocaded tapestries hanging from every wall and, if I'd stretched an arm out, I would have knocked over a year's salary worth of pottery. Still, gloomy is just the word for it. No light penetrated the narrow hallway, and a faint sheen of melancholy overlaid the glamour. This was just the kind of place I would haunt if I were a ghost, and the hairs on my arms and were vertical, like sunflowers in a field.

I made it to the end of that grim hallway and followed the right-hand turn to discover I was not alone there. Two middle-aged women were sitting with their backs to the door of the bridal suite.

"Izzy?" the woman I'd noticed downstairs in the excessively flowery attire enquired. "Are you Izzy Palmer? Thank goodness you're here."

Both were crouched down, but I noticed that the other woman had her hand to the handle, as though trying to make sure that no one could escape.

"Oh, Izzy," the chicer of the two screeched, all a fluster. "Patricia said you'd be the one to sort out this mess. I don't know what my daughter was thinking, allowing Sindy within a hundred miles of her wedding. You'll have to talk to her."

Though Mrs Julia Green had lived in Britain most of her life, she still had a noticeably European twang to her voice. Already in her sixties, she was an attractive woman with brown hair piled high on her head and a figure that most thirty somethings (including myself) would murder for. Unlike her frumpy, chintzy friend, she was dressed ever so fashionably in a tight-fitting bodycon dress.

"I'm Deidre," the friend explained, blowing a disobedient curl from her eye as she spoke. "Julia's close friend and official Sindy wrangler for the weekend."

"That's right," the mother hesitantly agreed. "Deidre has been a great help to me ever since my husband died. But even she can't stop the wicked schemes of Sindy Braithwaite."

I realised then that I still hadn't said anything. "Okey dokey!" I began, as that seemed like an appropriately nonsensical response to a perfectly ridiculous situation. "Are you keeping Sindy prisoner, or should I go in and have a word with her?"

Julia got to her feet in one smooth movement then had to tug Deidre out of the way as her knee was giving her trouble.

"I really appreciate this, Izzy," the mother of the bride said with a sigh. "I've tried to talk sense into the woman, but she's like a creature from another planet. There's no reasoning with her, there really isn't. Patricia thinks terribly highly of you, and I know you'll do what it takes."

The two women nodded appreciatively and stood side by side, as though they'd just cut the ribbon on a new supermarket or were waiting to show me the facilities of a gym I was joining.

Ha! Izzy in a gym. Hilarious.

Shhh!

"I'll give it my best shot," I told them and, with a stoic look on my face, turned the handle to enter the bridal suite.

Five minutes later, I raced back out, panting and terrified. I slammed the door behind me and stood with my back to it, desperately searching for something to seal that terrible portal so that it might never be opened again.

"She's a monster!" I yelled like a villager in every Frankenstein film ever made. "A monster!"

Chapter Five

Sindy Braithwaite was truly unlike any other person I'd come across in all my year and a half as a full-time detective. On entering that frankly gorgeous suite which was decorated with quite the most tasteful period furniture, harking right back to the–

Izzy, focus!

Right. Sorry. As I entered the suite, a disembodied voice struck up.

"Tut, tut, tut, young lady. You're not a bride or a bridesmaid. Are you sure you should be in here?" It seemed to come from all around me and I thought at first someone was talking to me through a speaker system.

"Urmmm, I think so?"

I looked about, but there was nobody there. It didn't make sense. Whoever was speaking must at least have been able to see the door to work out I was a "young lady". Unperturbed, (though also entirely perturbed) I pressed on through that exquisite lounge towards a small antechamber, where I assumed the bedrooms must be. The door to the right was open a crack and, when that oddly childlike voice struck up once more, I understood what was happening.

"I don't think so, little miss. In fact, I think you've been very naughty, coming in here when you weren't supposed to."

The voice was coming from an echoey bathroom, and whoever was inside was watching me in the mirror. (Well, it was Sindy obviously, but if you'd told me it was the ghost of a spurned lover who haunted the east tower, I would also have believed you.)

"I'm Izzy Palmer," I said, kicking the door open with one foot in case she had a gun. Evidently, if she had possessed a firearm, she could have still shot me, but at least I'd have looked like a cool American cop from a TV show as I died.

"I know who you are, young lady." Her head jerked away from the mirror, and she looked straight at me. I was afraid for a moment that her gaze alone could turn me to stone.

And what a gaze it was. She said nothing more, as her eyes etched a pattern into my skin, and I attempted to make sense of the scene before me. If you've ever seen one of those puffy, pink meringues they sell in bakeries, you'll have a good idea what I was looking at. Dressed in a near transparent gown with feathers on the sleeves, she appeared somehow bigger than the room that contained her. I don't mean she was obese, but that her aura or essence, or some such nonsense I would never normally believe in, filled the space.

She was one of those people who I wanted to tell to wear less makeup if it weren't for the fact that it's a very judgy thing to say. Her face appeared as though someone had recreated it on canvas with big black stains for eyes, luminous red lips and two perfect crescent eyebrows. To maintain this appearance, she'd colonised the bathroom. On every spare inch of surface, bottles, tins and tubes were scattered. Five matching yellow toilet bags had been emptied indiscriminately, and her clothes covered the rest of the space. Unlike me, I think it's fair to say she was a girly-girl.

I didn't have a voice anymore. I suppose I was still capable of speaking, but whatever part of my brain was responsible for such a function was cowering before this terrifying, yet oddly impressive character.

Finishing her eye makeup with a flick of a pencil, she threw it down in the sink and thundered from the room. "So, the famous detective has come to save the day. Is that it?"

"Gzzzzzzz…" This was the best I could do. At least my legs were still working. I managed to follow her into a bedroom, where she proceeded to stretch herself out upon a chaise longue like Botticelli's muse.

"You have to see it from my perspective, little one." She spoke as though she were decades older than me and had all the wisdom of the world in her bright blonde head. "The man I love has agreed to take me back into his life, despite all my failings. I obviously want him here to celebrate my best friend's wedding. How sad would I be all on my lonesome?"

Her voice occasionally shifted between Trans-Atlantic influences, and she delivered this last question as a true southern belle.

I shook my fingers out and rolled my shoulders in the hope that it would loosen me up. With one deep breath to calm the nerves I was ready to do my job. "The thing is…" I began. "You see, Sindy, what I'm trying to say is… your boyfriend…"

Good work, Izzy. Those were definitely words. Now, if you could put them into sentences, we'll be motoring!

"My boyfriend was invited to the wedding." Her eyes drilled into me and, without shifting them for a moment, she produced a piece of heavy-bonded, champagne-coloured card from the back of her hand like a stage magician. "This invitation says Lusinda Braithwaite plus one. It didn't specify who that one could be or when exactly I would have to reveal his identity. I am well within my rights, therefore, to invite the man of my heart, Anfony LeQuinn."

Far from bowling me over with the force of her words, her arrogant tone served to steady my nerves. "I'm sure that Anfony is a wonderful partner and the man of your dreams, but have you considered your best friend in all of this? It is Patricia's wedding after all."

She smiled smugly and batted her eyelids. "But that's just it; if Patricia really is my friend, she should try to accommodate me as much as possible on her special day. Or are you saying that she doesn't want me here after all?"

Her power was hard to describe. I'd met people with incredible skills of manipulation before, both murderers and victims, in fact, but Sindy was different. It wasn't as though she possessed such great intellect or linguistic ability that she could break down any argument that was presented to her. It was more that she simply didn't care what anyone thought, which was a rare and unique gift. If I could stop wondering whether everyone around me thinks I look like a court jester, my life would be so much better.

She peered at me curiously, and I finally remembered to answer. "This isn't about you, Sindy. You're the head bridesmaid, so obviously Patricia cares about you very much. Ramesh was just telling me that the pair of you were inseparable when you were at school."

This half-truth seemed to appease her, and she glanced down casually at her bright blue nails. "Oh, my dear, dear Patricia. How lucky she is to have a friend like me." She let out a dreamy sigh of approval before her tone grew harder once more. "If she only took the time to get to know Anfony, I'm sure they'd be the best of friends."

"She told me that he hit on her in front of you."

She had a laugh like a woodpecker's peck. "Oh, that's just my little man's funny way. He squeezes every girl's bottom. You should see him with my mum."

Yaeegghhhurrr! I think I'm going to be sick.

"He tried to kick a dog!" I managed to replicate the sheer disbelief that Patricia had invested in these words.

"Yes, but perhaps he's allergic to them."

"He described Lindsay Lohan as overrated!" I didn't mean to say this, but when you spend a long time around Ramesh, such slights really sting.

This had at least given Sindy pause for thought. "And I told him off for that but, in Anfony's defence, he's only seen a few of Lilo's later films and is yet to enjoy the joyous work she did in 'Mean Girls' and 'Freaky Friday'."

I was tempted to say that the remake of 'The Parent Trap' was surely Lohan's finest hour, but it really wasn't the moment.

She narrowed her eyes and studied me once more with a singularly spiteful look on her face. "I heard that you have a lovely boyfriend. A doctor, isn't he?"

She's trolling you, Izzy! There's only one thing for it. Just open your hand and give her a slap.

"No, that's my *ex*-boyfriend. Danny and I broke up."

She pouted even more than normal. "Oh, how sad. I heard he was quite perfect. A real hunk of burning love."

"Did Patricia tell you about–"

"Not Patricia… Ramesh." Oops, obviously. "He said he was happy to see you with someone with a kind heart."

"Things don't always pan out the way we expect," I growled, uncertain how the conversation had turned in my direction.

"Very true. So I assume you've come to the wedding alone?"

I wanted to scream then because I knew what she was trying to do, and I was powerless to stop her.

"Not exactly."

Her fake eyebrows lurched towards one another, and she turned her head to the side in mock surprise. "You surely wouldn't want to inflict a total stranger on poor Patricia on the happiest day of her life. He must at least be a very special friend?"

Grrrrrrr! went my brain, and I wished I'd never volunteered to speak to her.

"Something like that."

"What a relief." She let out a long breath to underline this point.

"I'd hate to think of you bringing the wrong sort of person to the wedding."

And that was when I came to understand just how conniving a creature she was. I could have yelled and complained, but it would have done no good. I didn't know exactly what she was up to, but I could tell she had a plan of her own to complete.

With a look of pure steel, she rose from the chair to fix her thickly mascaraed eyes upon me. "You should be running along, little lady. I'm sure you'll want to make yourself presentable before dinner."

Chapter Six

"She's a monster!" I whisper screamed, slamming the door behind me as hard as I could. "A monster!"

Julia and Deidre looked even more crestfallen now that I'd failed in my quest.

"Perhaps we could call security and have her removed," flowery Deidre suggested.

"That can be arranged." Cheryl, the luxury assistant, popped her head around the end of the corridor with a silver tray bearing three hot towels and a finger bowl. "The Hartford House security guards can deal with any problem guests in the most discreet manner imaginable."

Julia considered the possibility for a moment before shaking her head. "No, Patricia would never forgive us. She doesn't want to cause any more problems for Sindy than she already has. The poor girl is a bit of a mess, and we should be more sympathetic."

I doubted the logic behind this but, having dealt with Sindy myself, I very much doubted that even a squad of burly security guards would be able to extract her from the hotel.

Cheryl nodded with her usual supernatural efficiency, handed us the refreshing flannelettes and retreated from the scene.

"Oh, that does feel so much better!" Deidre chirped as she dabbed her brow. She was sucking on a boiled sweet and occasionally made a tutting noise, as though disapproving of everything around her.

The scent of magnolia filled the air, and I felt as though I'd just had a thirty-second spa treatment. This shot of refreshment served to clear away the doubt from my brain, and I delivered my verdict.

"She's up to something. I thought at first that I'd be able to talk her round but couldn't have been more wrong. That woman is an evil genius."

Patricia's mother still looked shaken. "You're right. Sindy's much smarter than she lets on. It was the same when she was a child. She was a real little gang leader but acted like an angel in front of her teachers. More often than not, it was my daughter who got into trouble for the things that weasel got up to." There was a flash of fury in Julia's eyes then, and Deidre swished over to calm her down.

Before I could hear more about the misdemeanours of Sindy's youth, the self-appointed head bridesmaid emerged from the bridal suite.

"Izzy, it'll be dinner soon. I thought you were going back to your room to get changed." She threaded her arm through mine and dragged me along the corridor as the mother of the bride silently glared. "I'll tell you what, we'll have a look what clothes you brought and choose you something nice. It's a wedding, deary. You don't want to look like a total slob." She let out that high, monotonous laugh of hers, and I considered sticking my fingers in my ears and saying *la la la* until it had subsided.

Cheryl appeared shortly after to direct us to my room, the location of which Sindy apparently already knew. I was to be in the west tower, on the same floor as the groom. Luckily, I'd planned ahead this time and would not be sharing a room with my fake boyfriend. Less happily, Nigel had the one next to mine and there was no lock on the adjoining door.

"Where did you go?" he barked as I entered. He was lying on my bed with his shoes on. "And who's this?"

He looked at Sindy; she looked back. I think that a moment of understanding passed between them as they realised that they were two covers of the same book. Loud, grumpy, aggressive people who were used to getting their own way and complained incessantly at the slightest disappointment. Presumably sensing that he was no longer the top toad in the swamp, Nigel became very quiet, grabbed a dinner jacket and exited the room.

"So that's your boyfriend?" Sindy looked quite amused by the discovery. "Patricia will not be happy."

I felt a sudden surge of loyalty to Nigel just then. Such instincts were the only reason that I dated the man for as long as I did. My old friends from back when we were dating used to warn me that he was no good. The more they criticised him, the more I felt the need to defend him and, soon after we got together, I ended up breaking up with them instead of Nigel.

I might well have married the man if I hadn't caught him naked in his kitchen, trying on a pair of my trainers. It triggered something deep within me and I finally saw everything that was wrong with him. I mean, if he'd gone for some stilettos or a nice pair of leather boots, I could understand, but sports shoes? That's just weird.

Before I could come to his defence, Sindy had rolled off towards the walk-in wardrobe of my luxury suite. It wasn't as nice as the bride's rooms, of course, but it still made most places I'd visited before look like poorly maintained slums.

Perhaps inevitably, my clothes had already been put away by the superhuman staff. As always, I'd packed extremely poorly and ended up with a selection of slightly damp loungewear (which I'd pulled straight out of the washing machine) and my very fanciest evening dresses.

"This one!" Sindy screamed, on walking her fingers along the rack of hanging items.

"No chance." I was resolute in my response, and there was no way she was going to convince me otherwise.

"Okay, then how about a moist onesie covered in pictures of jumping dolphins, or an extra-large Paddington Bear t-shirt and a pair of orange jeggings with a hole in both knees..." She held up the offending article. "... and the crotch."

I looked at the sparkly monstrosity that my mother had given me for my last birthday. Covered in chainmail-esque sequins, it was blinding and should have come with a health warning.

"Not that. I only brought it with me so that my mum wouldn't accuse me of being ungrateful that she gives me such nice things." As I said these words, I realised just how desperate I was to move out of my childhood home, if only to avoid such teenage arguments with my parents.

"So, Paddington it is then?" She held the adorable little bear out to me. I felt sorry for him as much as myself but, inevitably, gave in.

Like in every teen movie from the nineties, Sindy inflicted one of those awful makeover scenes on me then. I'd like to tell you how we bonded over the way she combed my hair and ultimately came to see that we weren't so different after all, but it would be a massive lie. She spent the twenty minutes waving around a set of curling tongs, telling me... Actually, wait. She can say it herself...

"What people don't understand Izzy," she began in her most distressed manner, "is that blonde jokes are actually a form of racism."

I had to watch her in the mirror to make sure she wasn't trying to wind me up. Fairly confident that she was as mad as she seemed, I cleared my throat and, in the politest tone I could muster, attempted to set her straight.

"I understand where you're coming from, Sindy. But I don't think that racism is the right word for it, because blondes aren't a race of people."

She held three fingers up to stop me, and I thought she was going to recite the scouting creed. "Well, yeah, but let me ask you this; have you ever met a blonde Spaniard? No, of course you haven't." She closed her eyes then, as if to say, *I rest my case.*

I wanted to laugh (or scream) but was left quite speechless. If she didn't understand the difference between a race and a nationality, I had no hope that she'd understand my main argument.

I sat there looking slightly comatose as she found my makeup bag and did her worst. She'd turned me away from the mirror, and I could only imagine I looked like a drunken panda. But, when she'd finished and I got to see her handiwork, I was speechless for a whole different reason. Her technique was impeccable and, to my genuine surprise, she hadn't gone overboard with the makeup.

"Where do you work, Sindy?" I had to ask.

"At The Cut Above Salon in Watford. I'm a makeup artist." Which explained her skills with a brush, but not her desire to make her face look like a discarded painting by Joan Miró. "Now, let's get you in that dress and down to dinner so that you can wow everybody."

She was very excited about the transformation, and I had to stop her pulling my clothes off and dressing me herself. Once I'd discreetly popped into my stately bathroom and pulled the presumably radioactive gown over my head, I was ready to go.

Sindy linked arms with me once more, and I felt like an old person in a residential home, being escorted about by an overeager volunteer. "I see a lot of myself in you, Izzy." Though I imagine this was supposed to be encouraging, nearly every word she spoke came across as a thinly veiled insult. "I didn't use to know how to do my hair or look so beautiful, but we all have to learn sometime."

"That's so kind," I managed to say without scratching her eyes out.

We did not encounter anyone else in that part of the hotel. Clearly, everyone had heard that Sindy was about, and they'd all gone into hiding. Ramesh is normally quite toddlerish in his devotion to me, and even he'd kept his distance.

By the time we got down to our own private dining room, more guests had arrived. In fact, it was a who's who of significant names from my previous cases. (Sort of Princess) Penelope Gravely-Swans was there with her entourage, several Porter siblings had turned up, my ex-ex boyfriend's auntie had made an appearance, and the Akerele family had brought an assortment of London theatre's brightest stars. I had no idea that Ramesh had stayed in touch with any of these people and could only imagine how disappointed he would be that Julie Andrews was yet to make an appearance. I know they'd only met briefly at a funeral, but I was fairly certain he would have invited her.

Sindy ran to find someone else to torment and, from the top of the stairs, I scanned the mingling group in the hope that the man of my dreams (who I'd recently dumped) would have arrived. For once, thanks to the work of the pink monstrosity, I didn't feel out of place in the outfit I was wearing; everyone there was dressed to the tens. I actually thought I looked rather ravishing and descended that incredible staircase with all the grace I possessed, only to run straight into Nigel.

"You look…" His gaunt face scrunched together as he searched for a suitable word. "…appetising."

Yuck! I thought, and then…

"Yuck," I said. "I'm not a starter. Thank you, Nigel. And I hope you haven't developed an interest in cannibalism since we broke up."

Admiring the slit in my spangly dress, he leered with his nostrils aflare. "Depends who's asking."

I felt queasy and, yet again, regretted inviting him. "Okay, buddy. Take it easy. Why don't you find our seats, and then play your computer game without talking to anyone?" He was not the only man in my life who I had to speak to as though he were a child.

He was happy with the plan and immediately pulled out his phone as he cut through the crowd.

"What happened with Sindy?" Dressed in a rather fetching white tuxedo, Ramesh grabbed me by the shoulder and pulled me into an alcove under the stairs. "Have you sorted the problem?"

I think I started humming the theme tune from 'Friends' just then, as I wasn't desperate to tell him the truth.

"Izzy?"

"Urmmm… Sindy curled my hair. Don't you think it suits me?"

"Isobel Palmer?"

"I tried my best. Really, I did. I told her that she should think about how Patricia feels and tell Anfony he can't come."

"And what did she say?"

I tried to recall the scene in the bridal suite, but it was all a blur. "Something about how I was selfish for bringing Nigel and how Patricia should be happy that her best friend has found love."

"But they're not best friends!" Ramesh threw his hands in the air. "Patricia doesn't even like her. And if she wasn't the saintliest woman since Joan of Arc, she'd kick her out."

"That's just it." I considered hiding my suspicions, but Ramesh is a person who functions best when there is a certain amount of panic at play. "I'm pretty sure that Sindy realises she isn't wanted here. I think she engineered this whole scenario."

He groaned, tipped his glass of champagne down his throat and went to headbutt the wall. "Brilliant! Just brilliant. *The greatest day of my life* will only be the third or maybe even fourth greatest because some crazy person has a nefarious plan to enact."

"So perhaps you can convince Patricia that, for the sake of the happy stories you will tell your grandchildren, Sindy has to leave."

He turned back to me, and his eyes were as wide as the Dartford Tunnel. "It's not going to happen, Iz. We're talking about the woman who has not only dated me for the last decade but actually agreed to marry me. She's clearly not the kind of person to get rid of weirdos!"

I put one hand on his nicely tailored sleeve. "It'll be alright, Ra. You'll just have slightly less happy stories to tell your grandchildren."

Cheryl came by then with a glass of bubbly for Ramesh and a can of orange Fanta for me. The woman was a mind reader! Once she'd moved on, I looked around to check that Ramesh's stupidest mates were out of earshot. "I was meaning to talk to you about something, actually. Are you sure this is what you want for your wedding? Don't get me wrong, it's absolutely beautiful, but it's not exactly you."

He looked up at the domed ceiling, with its endless display of ornate wooden carvings, and then over to the string quartet, who were playing sedately in the corner. "It's just for one weekend, Izzy. I can keep my eccentricities in check for that long. We'll have the rest of our lives together for me to be me."

I took a swig of the fizzy orange drink, and the bubbles went up my nose.

Dang! That stuff is gooooood.

I was hoping to have a frank discussion with him, but I ended up laughing like a baby on YouTube. "Sorry. I'm so sorry..." I waited for the sugary hit to subside and tried again. "You shouldn't have to hide who you really are. If you don't inject a bit more Ramesh into this wedding, I think you're going to regret it."

He stared at the bubbles in his glass. "Have you got *any* good news to share with me?"

I had a think. "Well... Sindy seems to be under the impression we're best friends now. She says she's taking me to brunch on Sunday in Watford."

"Please tell me I'm not invited."

Despite the happy event we were attending, he looked so glum that I felt genuinely sorry for him. "There you go, some good news at last! You are not invited to brunch with Sindy. It'll just be the two of us and our supposedly eligible boyfriends."

"Well, at least that's something."

Somewhat bizarrely, it was harder to take him seriously in a sharp dinner jacket than the t-shirt he sometimes wears with Mariah Carey's body and his head superimposed on top. "Cheer up, Ra. Sindy and her boyfriend might not be our sort of people, but what's the absolute worst that can happen?"

Idiot! You know that, if you ask a question like that, the hotel will burn down, we'll be taken hostage by terrorists and Mum will insist on singing a duet with you. You've just cursed this wedding.

I waited to see if this was true and, five minutes later, after I'd finished my drink and got over my hiccups, I was pretty sure that there was nothing to worry about.

"Ladies and gentlemen?" Feedback screeched out of the P.A. system and the pre-dinner drinkers herded over to the far corner where Sindy had got hold of a microphone. "Good evening, ladies and gentlemen. My name is Sindy Braithwaite and, before we sit down to eat, I'd like to make a speech."

Chapter Seven

"Izzy, normally when I go places with you, people die," Ramesh whimpered as we went to join the crowd. "Why can't it happen today?"

"Where are you, Ramesh? Don't be shy." Sindy had a voice like an air-raid siren. "Don't leave your blushing bride up here on her own to face the music."

My friend let out a brief, fake cry, and we moved through the other guests so that he could be included in this magic moment.

"Here he comes, here he comes." Everything Sindy said was followed by an excited giggle as she looked around her audience.

Cheryl, the clairvoyant, omnipresent assistant, was manning the sound desk and had quickly addressed the technical issues. She had also hooked up a projector so that images from the bride's childhood morphed into one another.

"I met Patricia when we were just five years old," our emcee continued. "I never knew on our first day of school that we would still be so close all these years later, and that I would be here as she marries her lovely man."

For Patricia's sake, Ramesh put a brave face on things and shook his floppy brown fringe as if to say, *Me? Lovely? Oh, you're too kind!* It was obvious what he was really thinking, but there were other faces there that were harder to read. The bride herself was clearly still on edge from Sindy's revelation before we arrived and had her fingers crossed at her side. It was hard to know whether she was thinking, *please don't say anything offensive,* or, *please say something terrible so that I have an excuse to throw you out.*

Standing next to her, her mother's stare was as sharp as broken crystal, and she could feign no joy at the maid of honour's cloying speech. Julia Green's right-hand woman, Deidre, seemed similarly infuriated and rocked from side to side, like a lid on a boiling pot. She looked as though she might punch the mic from Sindy's hand.

I noticed that Ramesh's three amigos had fallen quiet too. As Gaz, Tog and Wazza had been at school with Sindy, they presumably already knew what she was capable of. In fact, the atmosphere suggested that they weren't the only ones waiting for her to say something nasty. The air in that room was suddenly as cold as the champagne.

"The truth is that Patricia was always the clever one between us. She was the one who would study a master's in business and end up working in project management."

Huh, so that's what Patricia does.

"I, meanwhile, would stay where we grew up and work in a salon above a dog grooming parlour. She has achieved more in the last ten years than I ever will, and do you know how I feel about that?" Her voice had become shaky and fragile, and her bottom lip was shaking. This was it. This was the moment when she would unleash her anger on the world. "Do you know how I feel when I see all that she's done? When I see her in this castle, preparing for the biggest party that a Watford girl has thrown since Geri "Ginger Spice" Halliwell got married?"

She waited so long that I had to hold my breath as I imagined what the answer would be. Someone was running a finger around the rim of a glass, and an eery hum consumed the scene.

"I am simply so happy for her."

I let out a relieved puff of air when she said this, and it seemed to trigger those around me to do the same. The sound of tiny exhalations travelled around the room like falling dominos.

Sindy raised her glass and smiled at the happy couple. "Patricia, I just want to say that I hope you and Ramesh will always be as happy as you are right at this moment."

Patricia was in tears, and so Sindy rushed over to wrap her up in a tight hug. Ramesh looked a bit left out, but his family arrived just then, and his beloved Uncle Kabir came sprinting over, shouting, "My boy! My beautiful Ramu. I can't believe you're getting married."

The two embraced, and everyone in the room seemed to relax. Ramesh's parents were far less effusive but looked pleased for their elegant son and his exquisite fiancée.

A buzz of conversation ignited, and the string quartet started playing 'Pachelbel's Canon' for at least the second time. Perhaps it was my suspicious nature, but I couldn't help thinking that Sindy's display had more to it than she wanted the audience to believe. Patricia's tears weren't just out of happiness or relief; she looked terrified. And, though I couldn't hear what was said, I watched the look on her face as Sindy whispered some parting words into her ear.

This moment would have lasted some time longer if another of the bridesmaids hadn't come to call Patricia away. The poor woman practically had to pull the bride and her supposed friend apart. This newcomer did not look like she was a fan of Sindy Braithwaite's, but then I'd yet to meet anyone who was.

"Where's my barbie doll?" a voice from the grand medieval entrance to the room called. A man in a bright yellow suit with turned up trousers, black brogues and no socks was standing with his arms out.

Anfony had arrived.

"Daddy!" Sindy yelled, as she went shooting across the room to see her boyfriend. She looked like a large, pink meteorite.

I was tempted to go off into a corner and discreetly throw up. The feeling was only enhanced when the peculiar couple pushed one another against an ancient portrait of a fox hunt and began to make passionate love to one another.

Izzy, they're only kissing.

That's what I said!

Their arms worked up and down one another's backs, and I was amazed they could go so long without breathing. There was something quite animalistic about them. After approximately two minutes of staring in bemused wonder, I began to wonder if they had become involuntarily attached. Did they, perhaps, have easily tangled braces on their teeth? Was Anfony trying to eat Sindy's tongue? I was unable to answer these questions but was relieved when Cheryl appeared with a wooden beater and struck a gigantic gong that was hanging from a frame beside the head table of the dining room.

"Ladies and gentlemen, dinner is served."

"About bloody time," Anfony said, as though he'd been waiting for hours. His face was covered in lipstick by this point, and Super-Cheryl did not look impressed by his rude attitude.

He's even managed to upset Cheryl!

There was a seating plan for the pre-wedding dinner printed on a large silhouette of Ramesh and Patricia's heads. I didn't have to consult it as my date for the weekend had already taken his seat and was stuffing bread down his gullet. To my disappointment, Anfony would also be sitting with us, but at least Sindy had a place at the top table.

Ramesh had told me in advance that there was no room for me, as he needed to put his cats Elton and Kiki somewhere. He claimed they couldn't be away from him for too long without being sad. I was pretty sure that the reverse was true, but, either way, I was happy to see the two large pet carriers had secured a prime spot between Ramesh and the mother of the bride.

I'd never met Ramesh's own parents before, and it was true what he'd told me about them being quite unlike their son. They sat quietly at the long rectangular table, looking perfectly befuddled by everything that was going on around them. If I hadn't seen photos of them over the years, I would have thought that Ramesh had hired stand-ins for the weekend or pulled two age-appropriate strangers off the street.

"Hello Izzy," a voice said to break me from my ever-so-subtle surveillance of the other guests.

I turned to see my lovely ex, Dr Danny 'Hunk of Burning Love' Fields. I hadn't seen him since we'd broken up, which meant there was a painful hole in my life which his sudden presence filled. Inevitably, this left me mumbling inanely, though he wasn't doing much better himself.

"You look…" he had to clear his throat. "That dress is…"

"I'm Lizzy!" a simply gorgeous brunette, with an exceedingly posh voice, leaned around him to introduce herself. "Danny and I met through his work with *Medicins Sans Frontières*."

Her French accent was just perfect, of course, which told me she'd almost certainly spent a good few winter seasons at Chamonix and tried out for the British Olympic skiing team. She probably went to Oxford University and was, no doubt, an excellent lacrosse player, spoke four languages and owned a (supposedly modest) apartment in Notting Hill.

How did you get all that from just two sentences? You're better than Sherlock Holmes!

"I'm so glad you're here!" I said in quite the phoniest, bubbliest voice I've ever used. "You must sit down next to me and tell me all about yourself. I've been just dying to meet you ever since I found out that Danny would be bringing a little friend."

The poor girl clearly didn't realise that I'd lost my mind. She immediately did as requested and began to chatter away like a sparrow. As it happens, my predictions weren't too far off. If I'd swapped out lacrosse for show jumping, I would have been spot on.

"I had to wait until I was eleven before my parents bought me my first horse," she explained. "His name was Charade, and I was just so in love with him. I can't tell you what it feels like to a form a bond with such a clever animal."

"I know just what you mean," I said, sounding far more like the Queen than I had intended. Oh, well. Too late now! "I just adore horses, they're so... horsey!" I let out a cackling laugh for some reason. Clearly, the Fanta had gone to my head.

"Oh, so you ride yourself?"

"No, darling, I pay someone else to do it for me!" Yet more guffawing ensued. I have no idea if this joke even made sense, but Lizzy seemed to enjoy it.

"We should go out together some time. My father has his own stables in Kent."

Nigel looked up from his phone for just long enough to suggest I was a liar. "As if you know how to ride a horse, Izzy."

Damn, I'd forgotten I'd brought a fake boyfriend with me. "Of course, I do. There's nothing so exhilarating as going out for an early morning hack. Isn't that right, Lizzy?"

"Absolutely!" She was overjoyed with the conversation and clearly thought I was wonderful.

Danny had been staring at me across the round table this whole time. "So you had horse riding lessons? On an actual horse?"

Damn, I'd forgotten that he'd known me since we were children. "That's right. I used to go every Thursday night with my father."

"Ted never told me he took you for horse riding lessons!" Damn, I'd forgotten that my mother was sitting within earshot.

At least my father wasn't close enough to contradict the next ridiculous fabrication I was about to vomit out. "Of course he didn't. He had to pretend he was taking me bowling."

Leaning over from the neighbouring table, my mother looked totally bewildered. "So you had *secret* horse-riding lessons? Why on earth didn't he tell me?"

I glanced around the faces of everyone at that table in the hope that someone would be able to save me from myself. Anfony was drinking in my pain (though none of the drinks Sindy kept stopping by to offer him). Danny looked as though he might have to perform emergency brain surgery upon me at any moment, and Gemma and Peter (two friends of Patricia who hadn't got a word in because I was having some sort of jealousy-induced mental breakdown) could do nothing but smile nervously.

"Obviously he didn't tell you, Mother," I began, stalling for time until my brain did its job. Sadly, it was a bit busy singing an old song at that moment.

"It's a long way to Tipperary,
It's a long way to go.
It's a long way to Tipperary,
To the sweetest girl I know!"

"Of course he didn't tell you, Mother," I tried once more. "Because he knew you'd react like this."

She seemed, if not appeased by my words, then at least discombobulated enough that she turned around and concentrated on eating her starter until the most embarrassing conversation I'd had in literally weeks was finally over.

Thankfully, it was Danny's turn to act like a moron. "So you're Nigel, are you?" He puffed his chest up as he said this and fired the words out in the direction of my plus-one.

"Last time I checked." My temporary amour didn't look up from his game but waited until he'd finished the level of Killer Car Ninja Robots 49 (or whatever he was playing) before acknowledging Danny's presence. "Who's asking?"

Though I was pleased to escape the spotlight, this frosty standoff only made things worse. As the two not exactly alpha dogs (what's the Greek letter for N or perhaps T?) glared at one another, I tried to calm things down.

"Nigel works in the city." I thought this sounded rather impressive.

"Yeah, I do!" So did Nigel.

"Oh, really?" Danny was no good at hiding his feelings. He was the human equivalent of a Care Bear. "Cleaning the streets or washing floors?"

Nigel glared a little harder.

"Actually, he's a…" I began, before remembering that I hadn't a clue what his job was. "Nigel's a very important…"

"I'm a Senior Resonance Diversification Specialist for a major wealth management firm." Which was obviously ultra-swanky, but I had no idea what such a role entailed.

Danny didn't have much to say to that, but Anfony certainly did. "I, meanwhile, am a vision clearance engineer, not that anyone thought to ask."

"How interesting," Gemma the bridesmaid began. "And what exactly does that involve?" I knew she was a bridesmaid thanks to the badges Sindy had stuck on every member of the wedding party.

The woman's a monster!

Sadly, I'd accidentally dropped mine in a bin.

Anfony's lip curled in response to the cheery question. "I wash windows for a living." He let out a huff through both nostrils like a small, grumpy dragon with terrible hair.

Sitting next to me, poor Lizzy (or Izzy Mk 2, as I instantly thought of her) let out a laugh and received a stern look in reply. She must have thought that Anfony was joking.

"It is a perfectly respectable job, thank you very much." He banged his fist down on the table so that everybody's cutlery shuddered, and the emptiness of our wine glasses became apparent. Luckily, Cheryl arrived at just the right moment to fill them. I'm not a big fan of squished up grapes that have been left to rot for years on end, but she knew this and had a bottle of fizzy apple juice just for me.

With this distraction over, and our main course delivered by someone other than Cheryl – she couldn't do everything after all – a silence set in across the table. Danny, Nigel and now Anfony shot aggressive expressions at one another over their pork a l'orange. Nigel's angry sipping eventually got so loud that I had to do something to make things less awkward.

There's a rather wise saying by which I choose to live my life. It's like one of those slogans pasted over a sunset on a meme, or a motto from a fortune cookie. I'd like to say that it had been passed down from generation to generation, but, in actual fact, I came up with it myself. It simply states, *when in doubt, make a fool of yourself.*

"Lizzy, have I told you about my love of yachting?"

This kept the conversation going for a good half hour and at least it stopped Danny from challenging Nigel to a duel. He was too busy staring at me, presumably wondering whether he should call for a psychologist.

To my credit, it turned out I knew a lot more boating terms than expected, thanks in no small part to my love of mystery novels set on cruise ships. Why I couldn't have talked to her about my taste in fiction, instead of desperately trying to convince her that I knew anything about sailing, is beyond me, but I succeeded in my plan. I made it through dinner without anyone getting stabbed, and then removed myself as soon as was humanly possible.

Chapter Eight

"Izzy, can I sleep in your room tonight?" Ramesh knocked on my door to ask. "I'm scared."

I'd been reading Christie's 'Death on the Nile' to have something to discuss with Lizzy the following day and hadn't gone to sleep yet. "Won't Patricia be upset that you're spending the night before you get married in another woman's bed?"

"No, of course not. Quite the opposite, in fact." He strolled past me into my room. "She thinks of you as one of those really hopeless people who casinos pay to hang around blackjack tables in the hope their bad luck will rub off on the other players. I'm far less likely to go off with another woman when you're around."

I'd like to have extracted some sort of compliment from his analysis, but it was entirely impossible. "Thanks very much, Ramesh."

"I mean it in the nicest possible way!"

"Anyway, why are you scared? I hope no one told you a ghost story. I still haven't forgotten the time that you watched 'Scooby-Doo Meets the Boo Brothers' and had to sleep at my house for a week."

"This is completely different. And, in my defence, that cartoon was a lot scarier than the Universal certificate suggested." He managed to look surprisingly serious considering the topic of the conversation, and the fact he was wearing Backstreet Boys pyjamas. "I'm scared because I'm getting married tomorrow… and I think you might be right."

"You mean my theory that married people's skulls start to change shape so that they end up looking alike?"

He crossed his arms, and I knew that wasn't what he had in mind. "No. The thing you said about this not being the wedding I should have planned. It's true. This place is beautiful, but it's not me."

He sat down on my bed where Nigel had already fallen asleep and was apparently snoring out the tune of 'My Heart Will Go On' from Titanic.

Ramesh looked so miserable that I had to shove Nigel over a bit and sit down beside him. "Don't worry about anything I say, mate. I came to your wedding with a man who thinks that the zenith of human civilisation was the day that the Gameboy was invented. What do I know?"

He put his head in his hands, and I thought he might cry. "There is one thing you know, Izzy. You know me. In fact, of everyone on this planet, – with the possible exception of my exquisite fiancée – you know me best of all. Even Patricia doesn't know how freaked out I was by 'Scooby-Doo Meets the Boo Brothers'."

I laughed at this and put my arm around him. "Thank you. That means a lot. But I'm sure you've got nothing to worry about. This wedding is going to be fantastic and Anfony, Nigel and even Sindy won't be able to spoil that."

"I hope so, but I just don't know if I'm being true to what nine-year-old Ramesh wanted when he started planning this weekend. It's not just about having the greatest wedding since Grace Kelly and Prince Rainier's. It should be a reflection of who we are as a couple."

I squeezed him a bit tighter because he was a soppy so-and-so, and I loved him to bits. "You're not nine anymore, Ra. The things you wanted back then were always going to change."

He pulled in half the air in the room and let it out in one long breath. "You, more than anyone, know that I'm not as brave as people think. It took me years to stand up to our evil old boss, even when his bullying almost killed me. Instead of revealing who I really am to my family and friends, I've always gone along with what they expected."

He looked so fragile just then that I wasn't sure what else I could say, and so he kept talking. "Did I ever tell you that Patricia wouldn't date me when we were at school because she thought I was too macho?" It was good to see his smile take possession of his face once more, and I probably laughed a little harder than I should have. "It wasn't until I moved to Croydon that I found the confidence to be myself. This weekend should be a celebration of Patricia and Ramesh." It had always surprised me that he hadn't landed on a couple's name for the two of them. Raticia, perhaps? "It's the only time in our lives when people will come together for the sole purpose of saying, *Look at those two. Aren't they great?* But it's not me they're going to get, and I don't have the courage to do anything about it."

I took a moment to think about my answer before replying. "You have to do what's right for you. I'm not saying that you shouldn't have already told everyone that you find football less interesting than videos of women talking about photographs of cats, or that you'd prefer a trip to a Judy Garland memorabilia convention to a night out in a strip club, but perhaps your wedding isn't the time to make such a big announcement."

He sighed again. "It's just a shame I didn't head home a few months ago and break the news, as I actually don't feel so nervous anymore. If Gaz, Tog and Wazza were here right now, and not lying drunk outside in the rose garden, I think I'd probably come right out with it."

I punched him affectionately on the arm, because, weirdly, I'm not always as good with my feelings as he is. "The wedding will be amazing, Ra. I've got no doubt about it. And, when you come back from your honeymoon to wherever it is you're going and still haven't told me, you'll have plenty of time to reveal the truth."

At least I'd made him smile. "I hope you're right. I've never seen Patricia so nervous. She barely said a word all night which, as she was sitting next to my parents, led to a very quiet dinner on one half of the table and an endless stream of nonsense from Sindy on the other."

"I can't promise that will be any different tomorrow, but I'm sure you'll all have a good time. Just because Bette Midler isn't on the guest list – and you'll be wearing a black suit instead of the cloak and crown that I'd always imagined you walking down the aisle in – the most important thing is that you're marrying the right person."

I watched the little lines around his eyes crinkle together as he smiled. He was the best friend I'd ever had. Another jag of emotion surged up within me, so I kept talking to paper over it. "And I'm absolutely sure that Patricia is the right person, even if I think she's mad to marry you."

"You're so right. She's perfect in every possible way except for her apparent face blindness and very poor judgement when choosing a potential husband." He stifled a small sob. "I love her so much, Iz. I can't wait to see what our babies look like… I've already chosen their names."

"I'm sure you have." I rested my head on his shoulder. "Just as long as your brand of crazy fits with hers, that's all that matters." I pulled away so that I could have a really good look at him whilst he was still a young, single, completely unique human. "Tomorrow is going to be the greatest day of your life and most likely mine too. I can't wait."

He grinned at me, I grinned at him, and Nigel kicked me in the back. I think he must have been having night terrors.

"Izzy?" Ramesh began, peering at me through his long fringe. "Can I ask you something?"

"Of course you can. Anything."

"Can I go and get Elton and Kiki? They'll be lonely in my room without me."

From laughter to tears and back again in the space of thirty seconds was fairly standard practice in our friendship, and I couldn't help snickering as I nodded my head and he rushed off to get his erstwhile feline companions.

And that is how I spent his last night of bachelordom: squashed into the most comfortable bed I'd ever slept in, between Ramesh (a man with a life-sized, officially licensed, sleeping mask depicting Barbra Streisand's face), Nigel, (a bloke who once told me that he didn't think the north of England actually existed) and a couple of very purry cats.

Chapter Nine

When I woke up the next morning, I had a day of responsibilities ahead of me. To avoid the risk of any accidental glimpses of Patricia in her dress, the bride's side of the party would be kept separate from the groom's. This meant that I would act as an essential envoy between the two groups and would have to do a lot of running up and down stairs.

Though Ramesh donned his neat black suit as soon as he was awake, he still wouldn't show me the dress he'd chosen for me, and so I schlepped about all morning in my penguin pyjamas and matching dressing gown. Yes, I admit, I was schlepping about in undoubtedly the ritziest castle I'd ever been to, but it was Saturday morning! I'd normally be curled up on my sofa watching kids' TV programmes. They were lucky I was up at all.

After a lengthy breakfast, I joined the other key members of the wedding party in the chapel, where the drama had already begun.

"I can't believe she's not here yet." Gemma, the previously placid bridesmaid, practically screeched at her colleagues as I entered. "Some maid of honour she turned out to be. I'd do a much better job…"

The three bridesmaids who had made an appearance were wearing different coloured dresses in a similar style. On the other side of the church, Tog and Gaz were there, along with Danny as the head groomsman. They were dressed in pale blue suits, which would not bake them if the weather turned hot, but they were hardly up to my friend's usual idiosyncratic sartorial standards. Standing between the two groups, like referees at a boxing match, were an Anglican priest and a Hindu pujari to reflect the two sides of Ramesh's family. They both looked a little confused by the situation.

I didn't even have eyes for my ***once*** true love at that moment, as I was transfixed by the most beautiful bride I could imagine. Her hair and makeup hadn't been done yet, but Patricia was the kind of girl who didn't need such embellishments and looked at her best first thing in the morning (not that I'm jealous).

Her dress was simple in its shape and ornate in the delicate lace overlay. It had a low back and a short train, and I ignored whatever Gemma was fussing about and ran down the aisle to say, "Patricia, you look incredible… breathtaking… phenomenal and plenty of other words I can't think of right now."

She smiled and looked up at the stained-glass windows for a moment, to hide her shyness. "Thank you, Izzy. I appreciate it. But if you could go and get Sindy so that we can start this rehearsal, I'd like that even more."

Awww! Patricia's so nice, she didn't even tell you off for your flightless-bird-themed loungewear.

I was happy to be of service. I said just that and walked back towards the hotel to look for…

"Sindy!" A gasp went up around the church as all eyes turned to the large wooden door that the missing bridesmaid had just stepped through.

Even the hungover groomsmen were shocked at what they saw.

"What the hell is she wearing?" It was Gemma who uttered the words, but we were all thinking them.

Sindy marched down the aisle with a smile the size of London on her face. The off-white wedding dress she wore swished noisily with every step she took. I couldn't get my head around the idea that someone would do such a thing. If she was trying to outdo Patricia, she'd be sorely disappointed. With its puffy sleeves and enormous skirt, her outfit made her look like she was about to marry Prince Charles.

"Take it off, you demon." To be honest, Gemma was the one who seemed possessed.

Patricia still hadn't said anything when her three friends stepped away from the altar to form a protective barrier around her.

"I don't see what the problem is," throwing back her long veil, Sindy spoke in a convincingly innocent tone. "Patricia said we could choose a dress that expressed our personality, and this seemed like the obvious choice for me."

Gemma took a few paces forward to meet her head on. "Just because your fiancé left you waiting at the church, you reckon that means you can ruin Patricia's day. Is that it?"

I don't know where this ballsy lady had been at dinner last night. She'd seemed all meek and mild when making small talk with Anfony, but that mask had slipped. As the two women stared one another down, I felt like I'd walked into a gang fight.

"I'm not trying to hurt Patricia." Sindy turned to her old friend, and it was hard to know whether to believe a word she uttered. "I mean it. This isn't about you. I just wanted my chance to wear this dress, and I didn't think you'd mind."

The boys looked as though they wanted to do something to resolve the situation but couldn't quite decide what. The three of them hung in space, like coats on a rack. Tog let out a whistle of air through his teeth, but Gemma had more to say.

"Get out this minute or I'll call the hotel staff and have you removed."

Cheryl poked her head through the door at this moment, in case she would be needed, but decided to watch what would happen rather than interfering.

"I'm here for the rehearsal!" Sindy's voice reverberated around the church, rattling candlesticks and windowpanes and bouncing back to us twice over.

Full of her usual arrogance, she walked to the altar and stood at Patricia's side. I hadn't noticed until this point that a few friends and future-in-laws were sitting in the front row. Ramesh's parents looked as puzzled by the strange goings on as ever, whereas Julia Green was so unnerved that Deidre had to put an arm out to stop her marching to the front and strangling the fake-bride.

It's not really surprising, Patricia's mum is half French.

Are you saying that all French women are prone to throttling?

No. I just mean that they have big personalities, don't they? They're passionate.

There are sixty-five million people in France. Do you seriously… Oh, forget it.

I thought Patricia might finally say something against her belligerent friend, but she remained silent, and the run-through of the ceremony began. My friend Dean (did I mention that he's a tech genius millionaire?) was there in place of the groom. He wasn't a fan of the limelight, unlike the man he was standing in for, and kept pulling at his collar as though his shirt was trying to strangle him.

And yet it was the woman of the day who seemed the most despondent. Patricia barely made eye contact with the priest as he explained the order the service would take, and I thought she might cry when her mother stepped forward to walk through the first reading. Patricia was normally such a cheerful, confident person, and I couldn't wait to get the morning over with so that she could have a respite from the drama her maid of honour had brought about.

As soon as Father Michael had concluded his advice, Sindy strutted from the room with a smile on her face, and the recriminations began.

"What the hell is wrong with that girl?" Gemma asked, before catching the priest's eye. "Sorry, Father. I didn't mean to–"

"That's alright, my dear," he interrupted, sending a glare of his own after Sindy. "I'll let you off this time." He put his arm around his Hindu colleague, and they wandered off for an ecumenical chat before the big show.

"Wearing white as a bridesmaid would have been bad enough but coming here in her own wedding dress!" Danny was uncharacteristically het up on the happy couple's behalf.

"Why didn't you say anything, Patricia?" I didn't mean for my words to come out so cold, but that's what happened, and everyone turned to look at the poor woman who was suffering more than any of us.

"I…" she began, but when no more words would come, she ran from the church.

"You should have done something!" Gemma yelled at Ramesh's dopy friends, who pulled back in defence, as though each of the words was a tiny fist.

Tog and Gaz did not like her unveiled criticism and marched off outside with Danny following in their wake. As we poured from the church, and the different members of the wedding party dispersed about the hotel, I tried to make sense of it all. It was hard to tell whether Sindy brought chaos raining down around her out of spite or misadventure. The night before, it had really felt like she had a plan to enact but, after the rehearsal, I was no longer certain who her target was. The bigger question was why the bride still hadn't banished her from Hartford House entirely.

I wandered back to the west tower with a dilemma to solve. I couldn't decide whether it would be best to tell Ramesh what had happened in his absence or keep it to myself. This one doubt, at the very least, was resolved when I went into his suite to hear the song he was singing.

"I'm getting married today,
Life is going my way.
Everyone say hurray,
I'm getting married today."

I opened my mouth to tell him, but I just couldn't do it. Revealing to Ramesh that his wedding was about to be upstaged by a psychotic marshmallow in her own bridal outfit would have been like stealing a bone from a puppy… and then beating the puppy about the head with it.

"What's the matter?" he said as he placed his bowtie around his neck and did a surprisingly good job of tying it.

"Nothing whatsoever. Everything is great. The run-through went perfectly, and everyone looked amazing in their wedding outfits." I wasn't entirely convinced by my acting and so I added a quick, "Nothing unusual happened whatsoever," to seal the deal.

Great work, Izzy. He doesn't suspect a thing.

He did, of course, but shrugged and went back to admiring himself in the mirror. It wasn't every day he got to wear a classic black suit and so, inevitably, he put his hands together in the shape of a gun and pretended to be James Bond for a while.

"Oh, no. My cufflinks!" he soon yelled. "These are the wrong ones."

He was suddenly distressed as he noticed the small silver studs in the mirror.

"What's the problem with those?" I stupidly asked.

"I was supposed to wear the ones my dad lent me. Patricia must have them."

"Does it really make any difference?"

He turned on me then, his eyes burning like the fiery pits of the underworld. "Yes, it makes a difference, Izzy! I need something old…" He pointed to his wristwatch. "…something new…" He pulled up one trouser leg to show me his socks. "…something borrowed, i.e. the cufflinks, and something blue." He pulled his waistband down an inch to reveal his navy boxer shorts. It was far more than I needed to see.

"That's the bride, Ra. Not the groom."

"Isobel Palmer!" he crooned. "You sexist creature. Are you saying it's only women who should be allowed to enjoy wedding traditions?"

There wasn't much I could say to that.

"No, exactly. So get me my cufflinks, posthaste. Oh, and a glass of champagne. It's ten o'clock and I haven't had a drink yet!"

Inevitably, Cheryl knocked on the door at this moment with a bucket of ice and a bottle of Dom Pérignon from the year Patricia and Ramesh had first met. I suppose the hotel might have placed microphones all over the place to always be aware of their guests' desires, but that didn't explain how she could just materialise in the right spot each time. I finally settled on my earlier assessment that the woman was psychic.

"What are you waiting for, Izzy?" Ramesh wafted his hands in my direction as I was staring into space. "Shoo!"

As his best woman, I could only hold out for so long and scampered off down the staircase of the immense tower. I cantered through the lush hotel (still in my dressing gown, which, it should be noted, drew a number of admiring looks from a new influx of early arriving guests) to spiral back up the equally immense east tower to the bridal suite. I was a tad out of breath as I knocked on the door. I couldn't make out what Patricia shouted in reply, so I assumed the best and ploughed on in.

"Izzy, it's not how it looks."

It looked as though she was standing over her maid of honour's dead body with a bloody samurai sword in her hand, but I was willing to hear her out.

Her voice was coated with dread, and she took tiny gulps of air between each word. "I didn't kill Sindy. You have to believe me!"

Chapter Ten

It wasn't the body that so shocked me, or even the amount of blood, but the sight of perfect Patricia there as the main suspect in Sindy's murder. I let out a sound like a magpie throwing a tantrum and it must have carried to the neighbouring suites as, in the silence that followed, I could hear feet stamping towards us and raised voices. Patricia crashed down on a sofa with the sword still at her side.

"What's happened now?" the mother of the bride demanded as she bundled through the door with Deidre in tow.

I watched the pair of them to catch their reactions. There was a moment of shock, but Julia immediately hid her emotions behind a steel mask. "This wasn't my daughter." She picked her way past me to stand closer to the body. "I did this. I was tired of the way that Sindy treated everyone, and I ended her life."

I didn't answer at first but crouched down to look at the dead woman. She was still in her wedding dress, which now had a large red stain in the middle, where the sword had gone through her. This involuntary redesign looked very modern, and I could imagine some uber-fashionable film star in a glossy magazine celebrating the daring designer who had thought up such a look.

You never know whether dead bodies will have their eyes open or closed, but it turned out that Sindy was a peeper and stared out vacantly through her veil. She was lying on her front in the middle of the lounge, just beyond the two armchairs that divided the room. She had a bottle of champagne at her side, and you'd have been forgiven for thinking that she'd collapsed there after one swig too many. Her fingers had black smudges upon them, and I wondered if she'd been reading a newspaper with just her right hand. They were splayed out in front of her, like she'd tried to break her fall when she fell to the floor.

There were white flowers strewn across the carpet and, under a coffee table covered with cards and presents, a figurine of two embracing lovers lay on its side. By kneeling down, I'd noticed something else too. Beneath the green leather chesterfield sofa, there was a small bundle of clothes. Since it was in the same shade of purple as the housekeeping staff's outfit, I had to assume it was a cleaner's smock. It was easy to imagine why they'd been stuffed there and, sure enough, there were rusty red stains visible upon them.

I didn't want to draw attention to any of the evidence if I could help it, but Deidre was doing some detective work of her own. Dressed in yet another floral combo, she tiptoed around the perimeter of the room, her eyes scanning for clues. "I killed Sindy, and I hid the clothes I wore right here." Clever old biddy, she'd found the purple overalls and used them as evidence of her guilt. There was also a colourful glass bowl on the table filled with transparent sweet wrappers, but she ignored them entirely.

It was at this moment that Gaz and Tog crashed in to make the place even cosier.

"Oh my…" Tog uttered. Of Ramesh's loutish friends, he was the quietest and, without his Oompa Loompa makeup, looked quite presentable. What was more surprising, though, was just how distraught he looked at the scene before him. His mouth hung open, and he had turned the colour of my mum's ill-chosen, approximately white sofa in our living room.

"You'd better call the police and lock me up," Deidre demanded. "It wasn't Julia. I'm to blame."

"No, I did this," Gaz shouted from the entrance parlour. "I killed Sindy. It was me."

"Don't be an idiot," Tog berated him. "You don't have to lie for me."

I was losing count of the number of people who had confessed to the killing. Patricia had dropped the sword by this point, and so the boys couldn't have been covering for her. Maybe one of them really was to blame.

"Stuff and nonsense," Julia took this moment to defend her own claim. "And don't listen to Deidre, either. She had nothing to do with the murder; she's covering for me. They're all lying. I killed Sindy Braithwaite. She was a stirrer and would have ruined the wedding. I followed her here from the church in an attempt to reason with her, but she wouldn't listen."

My eyes studied the other suspects before responding. "That's a nice story, but why would you have killed her to save the wedding when this could mean the whole thing will be called off? And, more to the point, where did you get the sword?" I thought this was a key point, as I couldn't imagine where you'd find a samurai sword lying about in Hertfordshire.

Sadly, I was way off. It turned out that everyone else knew the answer, and they responded as one. "Ramesh brought it to cut the cake."

That certainly sounds like something he would do. Next question!

"Deidre, don't touch that," I called, as she was about to pick up the stained clothing. "In fact, all of you, get back by the door. This is a crime scene." There was some mumbled disagreement, but they began to shuffle away. Only Patricia remained. She looked stunned and peered down at the blood on her hands in disbelief. I noticed that there was no sign of any stain on her beautiful dress, though that might make sense if she'd worn the overalls to protect her outfit. It made me wonder how many brides over the centuries had ended up cleaning blood from their lace and tulle ensembles on their wedding days – outside of Westeros, I mean.

There was a lag, like we were talking over Skype, but she finally realised what I'd said and wandered over to stand with the others. The gang still wasn't all there, though. Anfony was the next to enter, but he could only stand staring at his girlfriend's prone form. There was still room in the entrance parlour for more suspects, too, which really is a testament to the spaciousness of Hartford Hall's bridal suite.

"I am Spartacus!" Wazza claimed as he poked his head around the door. Well, not really, but he might as well have done. "I killed her, and I'd do it again. I followed her up here and murdered her… with the sword over there that Ramesh brought to cut the cake." The lanky former banana had looked uncertain for a moment but recovered well.

"You're not listening to me," Julia Green was becoming increasingly upset. There was a tone of anguish in her voice as she begged me to believe her. "No matter what anyone else says, on the matter, I'm to blame and I'm going to call the police to confess."

An argument broke out as four… no, sorry, five of the suspects laid out the evidence for what made them the real murderer. Anfony's grating voice rose above all of them.

"Well, I'd like to take this moment to point out that I definitely did not kill that woman."

There was just time for one more entry in the *I-Killed-Sindy Sweepstakes.* "It was me," a short, flamboyant man, who I had never seen before, pushed through the squabbling pack to declare. "I have never met such an impossible woman. She made my job impossible, so I slayed her with… the sword which the groom brought to cut the cake."

"And you are?" I didn't feel too rude for asking.

"I'm Emilio, the wedding planner. I don't care if I go to prison. I swear that I did it."

"You're a fantasist, Emilio," Deidre screamed with great enthusiasm, and I was curious why this woman was so passionate on the matter. "You're only saying you're the killer for attention. That's just your style."

"I'm actually feeling a little woozy," Emilio claimed, and he quickly averted his eyes from the body. "I think I'll have a sit down outside. Though I still say I'm the man you want."

"Why is nobody listening to me?" Gaz complained. "I really did kill her."

"It's my fault," Patricia said, finally taking in the people around her. I'm not sure if this counted as a confession, but it was a step on from her first denial of guilt. Had she accidentally murdered her frenemy?

The scene descended into chaos, and I thought Deidre might end up biting someone. Gaz and Tog seemed to have fallen out, too. They were shouting back and forth at one another, and I heard the odd P-word dropped.

I'm pretty sure that you are the first person in history to feel the need to euphemise the word 'plonker'.

"Can you all calm down!?" My voice was so loud that I had to close my eyes to bear it. I think they were as surprised as I was. "Thank you. Now, I'm sure you're all guilty and you queued up to stab her one by one, but could you please wait in the hall until the police come?"

Like true Brits, they grumbled under their breath but complied with the request.

"Has anyone actually called the police?" Julia asked, and I realised we were getting ahead of ourselves.

"I'll do it," ever-efficient Cheryl called from out in the corridor. Surely she would be indispensable in a murder investigation. In fact, with the skills she'd already shown that weekend, I could only assume she had already identified the killer.

I was feeling more competent myself by now and issued another instruction. "Deidre, take Patricia into her room. She might need a drink of water."

"But the stylist will be here any moment," the flower-bedecked friend fussed in reply.

I placed a hand on Patricia's shoulder to reveal a sad truth. "The wedding will have to be delayed. You've got the place for the whole weekend and most of the guests will stick around, but a one o'clock kick-off is out of the question."

"That bloody Sindy Braithwaite," Julia Green began, before realising that this was more than a little insensitive. "I'm sorry, it's just… well, she's still messing things up from beyond the grave."

The two of them meandered away, but I didn't want Julia going with them, so I called her back. "I'll need you to stay here, I'm afraid." I could see how desperate she was to accompany her daughter, but I couldn't have them all together, getting their stories straight. What I needed was a room to keep each suspect in, but where would I find so many… "Cheryl, I need your help."

Having finished on the phone, Hartford House's own Houdini popped into the bridal suite. "How can I be of assistance?"

She quickly set about assigning the various liars to some empty bedrooms. Anfony was the only one who objected. He stormed off, saying, "I told you; I didn't kill her." It turned out that being a guest liaison assistant at a fancy hotel did not come with powers of arrest. Cheryl could do nothing to stop him.

After another quick scan of the crime scene, there was a task I needed to complete. I had to tell my best friend that his bride-to-be was a murder suspect. I was half-tempted to break an ingrained habit and interfere with the evidence. If I'd cleaned Patricia's fingerprints off the sword, it would have increased her chances of getting married that weekend. Sadly, my stupid *morals* wouldn't allow anything so obviously *illegal!*

I left Cheryl in charge of the scene and returned to the groomal (is that an adjective?) wing of the hotel. It was a long walk, and I had a list of questions in my head that needed putting in some kind of order.

> **Why had Patricia, the smartest person I know – okay, joint first with Dean – picked up the murder weapon?**

> **Why were the three amigos anywhere near the bridal suite?**

Why had so many people just confessed to a killing that they couldn't all have committed?

Was the killer one of the idiots who'd confessed? Or did his singular claim to innocence make Anfony the likely suspect?

How on earth did Patricia convince Ramesh to have a wedding planner? He'd been compiling a binder of wedding ideas since he was nine years old!

I reached his room and paused in the doorway. I really wasn't looking forward to telling him the bad news. When little Ramesh had laid out his plan for the big day, I very much doubt it had included a dead troublemaker and the bride being escorted from the hotel in handcuffs.

I took a deep breath and knocked.

"I'm completely naked!" he shouted back. "Come in to see my God-given beauty!"

I opened the door just a crack in case he was serious. Thankfully, he was in his wedding suit, not his birthday suit.

Such a disappointment.

"Ramesh, I need to talk to you." I thought this was a good, solid opening. I kept my face serious and my voice steady, but he was busy juggling some fake plastic fruit and didn't look at me.

"I think I got ready too early, Iz. There are hours until the wedding. I needed something to keep me busy, so I've been watching videos online to learn how to juggle. I think I'm getting pretty good." He wasn't going to make this easy.

"Really, mate. I've got something important to say. Can you stop that, please?"

"Is this a prank?" he asked, balancing on one leg to add an extra level of difficulty. Like most things he'd taught himself using video tutorials, he was clearly a natural. I felt a little guilty for interrupting. "Are you going to pretend that the hotel's on fire and we have to evacuate but then pour a bucket of glitter over my head?

"It's your wedding day, not the stag do. Stop, now."

An apple, two bananas and a pear rained down onto the carpet. Kiki and Elton dived out from under a chair to savage them.

That's some seriously impressive juggling, actually. It's not as though pears and bananas weigh the same. The difference in shape alone would make it difficult to-

And you. Stop, now.

Having tamed the two most easily distracted forces in my life, I pushed Ramesh onto the sofa and, instead of sugaring my words as I'd intended, came straight out with the truth.

"Sindy's been stabbed to death. Patricia found the body and, though I don't believe she's the killer, she will be a suspect." I'd failed to wipe the smile off his face but pushed on all the same. "This is serious. You won't be getting married until we find the culprit."

I think he was about to accuse me of playing a joke again, but he read my undaunted expression and realised it wasn't an act.

When he finally found his voice, he didn't sound anything like his usual self. "This is your fault, Izzy." It was little more than a crackly sort of whisper; a harsh, yet quiet declaration. But he might as well have thrown a punch for the impact it had on me. "I mean it. This stuff only happens when you're around."

I didn't react, I couldn't. He was suffering and it would have been wrong to blame him, but it still hurt. I stood there for a moment, blinking pathetically as my eyes began to water and I tried to pretend I wasn't upset.

"I'm sorry you feel that way, Ramesh. But–"

"I told Patricia that someone would get murdered if we invited you, and she said I was being insane." His delivery had increased in pace, but that unexpected coldness still controlled his voice. "There must be something about you that makes everyone in the vicinity lust for blood. It's amazing that I'm not a homicidal maniac after all the time we've spent together."

"Have you finished?" I asked, wiping away tears as I did my best to ignore his accusations.

"No, I haven't..." He stared at me, his lips pursed, his hands tearing at the cushions beneath him. "Wait, yes I have."

He broke down then. I'd seen Ramesh cry on countless occasions. He cried at the end (and beginning) of the Bruce Willis movie 'Armageddon', and at an episode of Sesame Street when Elmo said his best friend was a duckling. He cried one day because I wouldn't let him play with a pair of scissors, but this was different.

My beloved friend collapsed onto his side on the sofa, with his feet still dangling towards the floor. "This can't be happening, Iz. You have to make it right."

So then I forgot about the mean things he'd said, and the idea that he'd seriously considered not inviting his own best woman to his wedding because I was somehow cursed. I crouched down to comfort him, and he flung his arms around my head and pulled it in towards him. It wasn't very comfortable.

"I'm so sorry." My voice came out all muffled as I was speaking into his chest. "But we'll find the real killer. At least six people have already confessed. I'm sure the police won't hold Patricia responsible."

Pushing me away, he was suddenly all energy. "So, what are you waiting here for? Go and find the murderer. Shoo!"

"Don't you want to come with me to check on Patricia?"

He looked at me like I'd said he was dressed as a ballerina, or that Twix are better than Mars Bars. "It's our wedding day, Isobel. I can't see my future bride. It would be bad luck!"

"You don't think we're beyond that now?"

"No, I do not. Now get detecting or there won't be a wedding." He was surprisingly assertive. He sounded like the drama teacher I'd had a crush on at school.

Mr Cody? Woof!

"Yes, sir… I mean, yes."

I turned to go and had just made it to the door when he spoke again. "Izzy? Aren't you forgetting something?"

Turning to look back at him, I hadn't a clue what he meant.

"The cufflinks, Izzy. Where are my cufflinks!?"

Chapter Eleven

By the time I got back to the bridal suite, the police had arrived." A rather handsome officer blocked my entrance to the scene of the crime.

"I'm D.I. Holland." He had a flashy grey suit and neatly cropped hair in a side parting. He looked younger than me, which actually made me feel quite old for the first time in my life. I'd never had a *he looks younger than me* sort of thought before. "You're that detective, aren't you?"

I tried not to blush then as, yes; it was true. I was the world-famous Izzy Palmer.

They love you in Belgium!

He must have recognised me from the time I brought a movie star's killer to justice or the murder of a billionaire I solved in two days flat. "That's right, I'm Izzy Palmer." I used my least smug voice, (I promise). "It's a pleasure to meet you and, if there's anything I can do to help with the investigation, I'll be only too happy to pitch in."

His eyes kept jumping about the hallway in front of Patricia's room as though he had something more important to be doing. "There is one thing, Izzy."

I smiled like a grateful puppy and awaited my instructions. "Whatever you need, boss."

"You can stay well away from the crime scene. This is a police investigation, and we don't need amateurs poking around."

I literally took one literal step literally backwards. "But I know the suspects. I'm best friends with the groom."

He pulled his phone out of his pocket, as though to say, *I'm far too busy to explain the basics of policing to you.* "If you have any evidence to share, you can talk to one of the constables who are on duty. But that is as far as your involvement will go."

How very dare he! Tell him you've solved ten murders, Izzy!

Is it definitely ten though? I thought I counted twelve.

Ummm... approximately?

"I've solved over ten murders. How many have you even investigated?" I admittedly sounded like a spoilt child then and only enhanced this impression by curling up my lip and stamping one foot.

"That is not the issue, Miss Palmer. I am here in a professional capacity as an officer of the Hertfordshire Constabulary. You are a member of the public. Now, if you'll excuse me, I have far too many suspects to interview."

He disappeared into the suite, and I stood outside feeling miserable. I hated it when people played that whole *you're not a police officer* card. I preferred inspectors who ignored the *rules* and *laws* of Great Britain and let me poke around crime scenes. Luckily, there was someone coming to the wedding who could help me out.

My good friend Detective Inspector Irons was a known Izzy-enabler. On our very first investigation together, she'd been cynical of my crime-solving prowess. But, these days, she was always keen to hear my take on her cases. Admittedly, most of my experience came from reading inter-war murder mysteries by long-dead novelists, but I'd yet to meet a police officer with the same ability to construct far-fetched theories that, more often than not, turned out to be true.

Not that you're big-headed or anything.

I took my phone out and called Irons. A ringtone that sounded suspiciously like the theme from 'Hawaii Five-O' started playing nearby.

"Hello, Izzy?" I heard her voice from within the suite. "Where are you?"

"About five metres away, apparently. Come to the hall."

She sidestepped around the door to talk to me. "Nasty business," she said in her usual gruff tone. "Never seen someone murdered with a samurai sword before. Certainly not the way I'd like to go." She perked up a little then. "But aside from that, isn't this a beautiful venue?"

"Very tasteful," I replied, unable to consider the merits of Hartford House as anything other than a good spot for a murder. I filled her in on everything that had happened since I'd discovered Patricia standing over the body. "Can you convince D.I. Holland to let me help out? He says I'm just an amateur, but I've promised Ramesh I'll find the killer."

Her face turned a shade greyer, and she rocked on her heels. "No can do, sorry, Iz. You know what I think of your abilities, but I get the impression this is Holland's first murder investigation, and he does not want to mess it up." She must have seen how disappointed I was, as she kept talking. "I'll tell you what. He's happy for me to lend a hand, so I'll keep you up to date if he finds out anything that's worth sharing. I can be your eyes on the ground if you like."

I suppose this was something, though I wondered if I should give up and drink champagne with Ramesh instead.

You don't like champagne.

Fine, orange juice! But what chance do I have of solving the murder if I can't even speak to the suspects?

"There's plenty you could be doing," Irons said to anticipate my bad mood. "You could talk to any other guests and decide whether we can rule them out. Or you could get me a bacon sandwich from the breakfast buffet. I haven't eaten since I left home this morning."

"I think I'll do the former, thank you very much. The dead woman's boyfriend marched away from here earlier, claiming he had nothing to do with the killing."

She shrugged and had a bit of a sniff. "Suite yourself!" Her normally straight face was reshaped by laughter. "Ha! That was a good one. *Suite yourself,* because the murder took place in a hotel suite."

I attempted a polite laugh, but her gloomy expression soon returned.

"Do you have any theories about what went on here?" I thought I'd ask in case they'd discovered something I hadn't spotted.

"None whatsoever, but we're only getting started. Shouldn't take too long to work out which of them did it."

I liked her confidence. "My money's on… Actually, I'll get back to you on that."

I left her looking perplexed and went to find out whether Cheryl knew where Anfony's room was. I tried saying her name three times into a mirror, but that did nothing and so I went downstairs to a floor which was a little less plush than the penthouse. It looked more like a standard hotel, with a central corridor and plenty of rooms, most of which were locked. I couldn't find any staff, but I found what I was looking for.

"I'm telling you, Mum, she had a sword straight through her…" I heard him shouting from behind the first closed door. Using all the knowledge and experience I'd amassed as a detective, I concluded that he was probably on the phone. "Yes, of course that means she's dead. What did you expect?"

I listened for a while longer, but he didn't utter the words *I'm the one who killed her,* and so I knocked on his door and waited for him to open.

"What do you want?" he growled but didn't hang around for a response. He rushed back inside the room, leaving me to follow.

Anfony had remained calm when he'd first seen the body, but he was a mess now. He couldn't keep still and moved from point to point around the pale-green room, which clashed terribly with the vivid yellow suit he was still wearing from the night before.

I sat down in a large, overly firm armchair in front of an unlit fire. The fireplace had a carved stone mantel and there were porcelain spaniels standing guard on either side.

He started babbling before I could ask my first question. "I need you to help me out. You are that detective chick, ain'tcha?" He was too anxious to wait for an answer. "I need you to clear my name. The police are gonna think it was me. I swear they will, but I didn't have nothing to do with my Barbie's death."

"Her name was Sindy," I said, suddenly feeling protective of the horrid woman who was lying above us in a pool of her own blood. "And if the police suspect you, it'll be because they have a good reason."

He stopped pacing and locked his eyes on mine. "You don't get it. I've got form. Nothing major, but I ended up in prison once, and I do not want to go back there. You've got to help me."

"Panicking isn't going to help. Why don't you sit down?"

He kept looking at me as though he needed time to make sense of my words. When he finally reacted, it was not to have a nice comfy seat on the sofa opposite. He perched on a side table, his knee jigging up and down the whole time. His previously slick hair was sticking out in all directions and, though his shirt was clearly fresh, his suit bore a thousand tiny creases.

"Tell me what you were doing here this weekend," I began once a hush had fallen between us.

"What does that mean? I was invited!" He stretched out every word he spoke.

I took a few seconds before responding. I wanted to slow everything down and talk to him on my own terms. "No, you weren't. Sindy made sure of her own invitation but, as far as Patricia and Ramesh knew, the two of you weren't dating anymore. So how did you end up here?"

This was as long as he could maintain his focus. His gaze shot out of the window and across the ornate gardens to the helipad I'd seen as we arrived. I was pretty sure he would have flown away then if he could.

"What can I say? She charmed me."

It didn't take a genius to realise that he was holding back. What I didn't know was whether he was hiding his guilt or something less damning.

So I started again. "If you tell me everything you know, I'll do what I can to help you. Go back to the beginning and tell me how you met Sindy in the first place."

"I woke up in her flat about a year ago. I don't know how I got there."

I failed to hide my surprise. "She kidnapped you?"

"Nah. It used to happen a lot. I'm an alcoholic – well, five months sober. I'd go out to a club, get wasted and wake up somewhere. Sometimes I was alone, sometimes not so alone… like with Sindy."

"And so you've stopped drinking?"

He ran his hands through his messy hair. It was dyed black at the roots with bright blonde highlights. He made me think of a punk-rock badger I'd once seen on Saturday morning kids' show. "In a sense, yes." I thought back to the night before, and it was true that he'd stuck to water all evening. I was a bit disappointed in myself that I hadn't thought anything of it at the time. I genuinely believed I was more judgemental than that.

"So the two of you met… somewhere and started a relationship?"

He shook his head but meant yes. "I suppose so. Sindy had just broken up with her fiancé and she was a bit of a mess."

"So you had to chase after her?" I smiled. I was hoping to come across as a friendly, easygoing person as opposed to a woman in penguin pyjamas who was prying into his personal affairs. Speaking of which, I made a mental note to get changed as soon as the interview was over.

"No, the opposite. The girl was in such a bad way that I didn't want to see her again. She ground me down. I never meant to spend so much time with her, but she was a spider, weaving her web and I was just…"

"A fly?" I offered.

He looked back at me then and seemed to shudder at the memory. "Yeah, or one of them little spiders that the big spiders eat." I'm not sure he had much of a background in natural sciences, but I decided not to interrupt him again. "She was suffocating, and I couldn't stand it anymore."

"So you broke up with her?"

"Well, I tried. I wasn't myself when I was with her. We went out with her friends one night and I tried to kick a dog. I mean… I love dogs. I don't know what came over me." He looked at his large, calloused hands. They seemed much older than the rest of him. Anfony couldn't have been more than forty, but his hands had enjoyed a good few extra decades of use. They were strong too, and an image of them wrapped them around the hilt of the sword flashed through my mind.

"So you're saying that it wasn't your fault you kicked that dog?"

Ask him what he really thought of Lindsay Lohan!

"I didn't kick no dog, but I tried. We went to Patricia's engagement party and there was this dog and so I shouted to the others, 'Hey, watch this!' and swung my leg at it. The poor thing looked terrified, and I felt dreadful about it for weeks. I tried to apologise to Sindy's friends, but my words came out all wrong and it sounded like I was hitting on the bride-to-be.

His voice was filled with sorrow, as though it had been seeping into him since the conversation began. "It was one of the things that made me realise I needed to stop drinking. I swear, that wasn't the real me."

"And what did Sindy think of you getting sober?"

He winced a little and would no longer hold my gaze. "I think she enjoyed showing off what an edgelord boyfriend she had. It was like she cast a spell when we were together. It turned me into this disgusting creature who I could barely recognise. So, no. She didn't like it when I started ordering soft drinks instead of triple vodkas."

I bit my lip then, trying to work out whether anything he had said was true. His voice had softened, and his eyes had a sense of introspection to them that I would never have expected before entering the room.

"That brings us back to my original question," I said. "Why did you come this weekend? You claim you didn't want to be Sindy's boyfriend, and yet here you are at her friend's wedding."

He stood up again to resume his nervous wandering. "She made me."

I might have laughed just then. Well, I did. I laughed and the sudden loudness made him jump.

"I'm serious." He didn't just shake his head in despair at that moment, he swayed his whole body from one side to the other. "She made me come. She controlled me, even after we broke up. I tried to get away from her, but she said she wouldn't leave me alone until after the wedding. And that was why I gave in." He locked his muscles and wouldn't move one inch until his point was made. "I came to finally get away from her."

I knew what I would say even before he'd finished speaking. "You know that's a pretty good motive to kill someone?" I let the question sit between us for a while. I sat smiling in a perfectly cordial manner and, when I was sure he'd felt the impact of my words, I pressed him further. "Did you decide that this would be the best place to get rid of her? A big hotel is private enough not to be interrupted but still has plenty of other people around to take the blame."

"I didn't kill her," he screamed, and at least part of me believed him, but I wouldn't let up.

"You said yourself that you wanted to be shot of her. She was toxic and, for whatever reason, she had a hold over you. Everyone is desperate to claim credit for her murder, and yet you're the only one who denies it. What does that suggest?"

He threw both hands in the air and his voice climbed higher. "I don't know. That they're crazy? You tell me."

I could have kept prodding and poking, but that was what he expected. Instead, I lowered my voice and took my time. "Do you know what I think happened? I reckon Sindy had some scores to settle. I think she needed you for whatever petty plan she'd come up with. What I don't know is who she hated or why."

He looked even shiftier then, which is pretty impressive for a guy with a permanent scowl and a zigzag scar on his cheek. "As it happens, I've been thinking the exact same thing." He'd lost his anger, and his shoulders slumped once more. "But she never told me what she was up to."

"You weren't in the church this morning for the rehearsal."

"So?"

"So where were you?" I glanced about the room as I asked this. It looked as though someone had been in to clean it. The bed was made with the neat creases and tucks of a professional. There were no dirty glasses or empty crisp bags about the place, and it retained a faintly alpine smell that would have been overwhelmed by his presence there overnight.

He saw what I was implying, and I knew I'd blown my advantage. "I stayed here and, when the girl came to clean the room, I went looking for something to eat."

Ask him what he ate?

I'd learnt to trust my brain when it came to matters related to food.

"What did you eat?"

He paused to think. "Bacon and egg, why?"

Hmmm... his story checks out. There was definitely bacon and egg on offer this morning. Shame he didn't say lasagne or strawberry ice cream. We'd have known he was lying.

Very helpful.

"And then what? Why did you go upstairs to the bridal suite after Patricia found your girlfriend's body?"

"Why do you think?" I was hoping this was a rhetorical question, as I genuinely couldn't be sure. "I went looking for Sindy, of course."

I sat back comfortably in that elegant old chair. I don't know anything about furniture design, but it had scrolly feet and arms and a very high back with pointy bits on it. You know the type. Anyway, I relaxed into it because I was the one in control now, and I could tell he was nervous.

"That's exactly what I'm saying; you went looking for her. You went upstairs to the bridal suite where you knew she would be, and then you stabbed her through the heart."

"She wasn't stabbed through the– Damn! You did that on purpose, didn't you?"

I kept the angelic smile on my face as I put the accusation to him one last time. "Admit it, Anfony. You killed her."

He rushed at me then, and I thought I'd just done the number one stupidest thing in a short life filled with extremely stupid things. Buying a pair of white denim dungarees in my first term at university was pretty dumb. Eating spaghetti in said dungarees was borderline idiotic. But going into the secluded hotel room of a man I considered to be the prime suspect in a murder was beyond all conception of idiocy.

"I'm not a murderer," the creepy guy with frosted tips screamed from three inches away. "I never touched Sindy, but I have a good idea who did."

Chapter Twelve

I felt pretty stupid not to have considered it myself. The deranged window cleaner had out-detectived me.

"The ex-fiancé?" I had to check, partly because it was so obvious that I couldn't believe it hadn't occurred to me.

"That's right. Toby. He was here last night. He must still be hanging around somewhere."

"Sindy's ex-fiancé Toby is at the wedding?" I had presumably suffered some sort of mental disconnection, and it required Anfony to break things down very slowly for me before I could snap back to normality.

"That's what I'm saying. The whole plan she'd worked out. Her whole reason for having me here and biting my face off in the dining room last night. It was all for his benefit. Toby's your man. I'm telling you."

"Huh."

I would need a good half hour to get this mind-blowingly simple concept into my head. I'd been busy imagining any number of incredible scenarios in which Sindy had been blackmailing Patricia, who had engineered her hook-up with crazy Anfony in the knowledge he would one day flip out and murder her childhood friend. But, no, this was much simpler. And it fitted in with everything that had happened.

Sindy's dress alone should have been a big enough clue. When I'd seen her that morning in the church, I thought that she was trying to upstage the bride, but it wasn't for Patricia's sake that she'd taken the bizarre step of turning up to someone else's nuptials in her own under-used wedding dress. She was planning for this Toby guy to see her. It was so obvious, but I still needed one more gentle push for it to make sense.

"Do you see now?" Anfony seemed quite bemused by my intellectual deficiency. "Sindy came here to make Toby's life difficult. She muscled her way into an important role in the wedding and would have turned up at the church this afternoon for him to see her in the dress she was wearing when he left her standing at the altar. She had it in here last night and I wondered what she was up to. It's pretty difficult to hide something that flouncy; the wardrobe wouldn't close."

"So she didn't hate Patricia?"

He pulled back then and stood up to his full height. "Well, she hated most people, so it's hard to say. But not especially, no. If anything, Patricia was the only one from their schooldays who was nice to her. I think that's something Sindy was relying on. That night when we went to the engagement party–"

"The dog-kicking night?"

He perked up at that. "Yeah, that's the one. Well, that night, when Sindy took me home, she thought it was hilarious. She saw how meek Patricia had been. Ramesh had wanted to murder me for the look on the poor Dachshund's face–"

"You kicked a Dachshund!?"

"No, no," he raised one finger to clarify. "Remember, I only *tried* to kick him. There was no contact made between my Doc Martens and the tiny pooch."

"You were wearing Doc Martens?" I almost murdered him myself then.

"I think you're getting a bit distracted now, Izzy. The point is that Patricia did nothing, no matter how badly I behaved. Sindy had brought me there on purpose to test what Patricia would do. I reckon…"

He didn't finish the sentence and so I gave him a hand. "Sindy must have had something over Patricia. Is that it? I wondered the same thing last night. When Sindy was giving the speech, it was as though Patricia was afraid of being found out. I got the impression that she was expecting something nasty from her head bridesmaid, but it never came."

He clicked his fingers and jumped backed to standing. "That's exactly it. Sindy could never keep her thoughts to herself and hinted as much. So where do we go from here?" It was not the first time one of my suspects had mistakenly assumed they were now my sidekick.

I was sorry to disillusion him. "I'm going to look for Toby, and you should stay here and wait for the police. They'll want to talk to you."

"Wait, why can't I come with you?" He wore a hangdog expression, much as the Dachshund must have on that fateful night. "My girlfriend's been murdered, and even if I thought she was a manipulative succubus who brought out the worst in me, I'd still like to see her killer brought to justice."

I stood up and adopted my professional demeanour. It wasn't very different from my normal demeanour, but I was still working on it and had high hopes that it would one day improve. "I'm a private detective. Let me do my job."

Isn't that what D.I. Holland just said to you?

Shhh!

Anfony collapsed on the bed, and I strolled confidently from the room. I'd initially assumed that investigating a murder in loungewear would make me insecure. It turned out I was feeling more comfortable than ever. I couldn't say whether it was the loose fit or the soft fabric, but I felt like a hard-boiled private dick in flannel. Perhaps I would don such freeing attire for all my cases from now on.

But hopefully not.

"What on earth are you wearing?" my mother called as I walked past the room where she was rehearsing with my fathers and a group of my friends. "You're not at home now, Izzy. You do know that?"

I thought this was a bit rich coming from a woman in a tiger skin loin cloth and matching bikini top, who was being pursued by someone in a bear costume. "I appreciate your opinion, Mother. But I'm afraid I've got some bad news."

The lounge they were in had been reorganised so that the chairs were all placed around the sides and a number of coffee tables had been pushed together to form a small stage. I noticed several people from my previous cases lurking around. Apparently my mother hadn't deemed international theatrical legend Kebe Akerele as worthy of a part in the performance. Instead, she'd been put in charge of lighting; it was her job to shine a pocket torch at the real star at all times.

"Hi Izzy," the bear said, and I recognised the voice of my (comparatively) good friend (sort of) Princess Penelope. "Don't tell me… there's been another murder?" Her voice was all jolly, and I didn't like to bring the mood down, but…

"Yep! Someone killed one of the bridesmaids."

Ever the sensitive soul, my dear old mum was overjoyed. "This is fabulous. It will give us more time to rehearse. I really wasn't happy with our last run-through." She turned to her co-star. "And, Lady Penelope, I need more roaring from you. You have to think like a bear, not just act like one."

My father came out from his hiding place under the stage and shouted, "Okay, from the top, everybody. And would it kill you to put some oomph in it this time?"

"Must run, Izzy." Mum did just that and got into position at the side of the room.

You know what they say, you can't choose your family... But if you're sensible, you'll get as far away from them as possible.

By the time I'd got to Ramesh's room, he was lying on the floor with his cats on top of him. He was trying to drink champagne but mainly pouring it over his face. I knew things were bad when I heard Bonnie Tyler's 'Total Eclipse of the Heart' blaring out of the stereo. He was in a dark place.

"There's nothing I can do, Izzy!" he shouted over the song. "I should be downstairs schmoozing with guests, but instead I'm here drowning my sorrows. What justice is there in the world?"

I lay down next to him and looked up at the ceiling. Kiki Dee took this opportunity to jump onto my tummy in order to hunt the penguins on my dressing gown.

"If it makes you feel any better, I think I might have ruled out Anfony as the killer. Which means there are only about fifty people to go."

He turned on his side to look at me, causing Elton to hiss at him. "Thank you, dear friend. I don't know where I would be without you."

"Well, I say 'ruled out'. What I actually mean is that he wasn't quite as nasty as I was expecting him to be, and I fell for his act. He probably is the killer. He certainly had mixed feelings towards Sindy."

"Didn't we all." He sat up to open a new bottle of champagne and immediately tipped it down his throat. "She's ruined my wedding!" The words came out in a roar, and it was clear that he'd already drunk too much.

"Go easy, Ra. If the police catch the killer quickly, you might need to be sober at some point today."

"Don't be ridiculous, Izzy. The police couldn't catch a Pokémon. They'll just blame Patricia because she's a selfless angel who found a dead woman and removed the sword that killed her out of respect. My life is over. I'll stay in this room until the hotel kicks me out and then spend the rest of my life as a wino living under a bridge. You should get away from here before my bad juju infects you."

It was at this point I decided to slap him out of it.

"Ow! What did you do that for?"

"You were rambling."

He slapped me back.

"Ow! You're not supposed to hit girls!"

"And you're not supposed to hit men with sensitive skin!"

To prevent the argument turning any sillier, I held my tongue and waited for him to calm down. He rubbed his face for a while but appeared to be more aware of his surroundings.

"Ramesh, if I'm going to find the killer, prove Patricia's innocence and save your wedding, I need your help." I was being over-dramatic for his sake. Over-dramatising things is the fastest way to communicate information to my friend, and so I waved my hands about as I spoke. "I need to know about Toby!"

"What about him?" He sounded suspicious.

"Well, he was engaged to Sindy, wasn't he?"

"So?" He clambered to his feet and went to stand on the balcony. It was a sunny day, the sky was blue, and the temperature was just perfect for a wedding. I wondered if Ramesh had noticed this, as he let out a deep sigh before continuing. "Toby was well rid of Sindy and had no regrets about ending the relationship. He could have handled it better, of course, but breakups are like that."

I got up to join him. "Didn't he leave her standing at the altar?"

"Nope. She was halfway down the aisle when he did a runner. As I said, he could have handled it better."

"Well, Sindy wore her wedding dress to the rehearsal this morning. According to Anfony, she was planning to make a big scene this afternoon to get her revenge. You have to tell me all you know about Toby. You were at school together, right?"

He nodded. "But I really can't imagine him murdering Sindy. He's not the type."

I thought for a moment about how I might get through to him. "You've met quite a lot of murderers over the last two years."

"Yes," he replied and, in an efficient manner, added, "I've met five murderers and two attempted murderers."

See, Izzy, some people can count.

"And what would you say they all have in common?"

He looked out across the gardens. "How should I know? Did they all like The Beatles?"

"Why do you say that?"

"Because everyone likes The Beatles. Name me one person who doesn't like The Beatles!"

I'd like to put his unhelpful attitude down to the champagne he'd consumed, but I think that would be too generous. "Okay, except for liking The Beatles, what did the murderers have in common?"

"Nothing, why?"

"Precisely." I'd hoped he'd be able to join the dots for himself. "I'm trying to imply that you can't tell whether someone is a murderer based solely on their public persona. Toby could have snapped and killed his ex after he heard what she had planned."

"Honestly, I think that's unlikely. Toby is a bit of a lad, but he's a softie at heart."

I reflected on Ramesh's undying loyalty before cueing another question. "What does he look like? Was he at the dinner last night?"

He turned his head to one side to regard me from a different angle. "Of course he was. You saw him there. He's medium height with dark brown hair."

"Who was he sitting with?"

"Really, Izzy. You do ask strange questions. He was there with the other boys from school." His words dried up then as he caught sight of someone in the car park.

There were several cars arriving with overnight guests coming to check in. It made my poor friend sadder to see them, and I wished I could magically solve all his problems. Clearing his fiancée of murder would be a pretty special wedding present.

"Come on, get it together." A wave of determination crashed over me. "If Toby didn't do it, who do you think is responsible for Sindy's death?"

He didn't need long to deliver his verdict. "I think that Deidre and Julia are having a steamy sapphic affair. I reckon that middle-aged, twin-set-wearing, butter-wouldn't-melt Deidre murdered Sindy because she was ruining the wedding and Deidre couldn't stand to see her beloved Julia suffer."

"And do you have any sensible suggestions?"

He did not like my tone and collapsed to the floor again. "Oh, I don't know, Izzy. All I know is that I want to see Patricia and make sure she's okay, but I can't because it's our wedding day and I don't want to jinx us."

"Actually, there's something else." It was another sensitive issue which I was less than eager to disclose. "When we found the body, Tog, Gaz, Wazza, Julia and Deidre… oh and your wedding planner, what's his name?

"Emilio."

"That's it. Well, they all confessed to the murder. Anfony and possibly Patricia are the only ones who didn't. Do you have any idea why?"

"I told you, Iz. Deidre is hot for the mother of the bride and is covering for Julia." He sucked in an enormous gasp. "Oh my Gloria Gaynor! Julia is the killer. Patricia's own mum is behind it. I'm marrying into a murder-family." He scrambled to his knees and, looking to the heavens, held his hands in the air to demand, "What have I done to deserve this?"

I checked the messages on my phone while I waited for his melodramatic yell to die away. It took a while. "Have you finished?"

He looked rather refreshed. "I think so."

"Good, now pull yourself together. I need you to give me my dress for today."

"But the wedding might not even take place."

"It's either that or I solve this murder looking like an eleven-year-old girl on her first sleepover. You decide."

Forgetting his troubles for a moment, he clapped his hands together with glee and danced over to his wardrobe. "Hurray! It's time for my favourite thing in the world: makeover!" This made me question who was more like an eleven-year-old girl after all.

"Why does everyone keep trying to make me over?"

He raised one eyebrow in response before sliding open the wardrobe door. With a magical rippling of his fingers, he pointed to a red silk, floor-length dress with long straps that tied at the nape of the neck. It was smart, simple and elegant.

"I never expected anything so beautiful," I whispered, slowly coming to the terms with the fact that I wouldn't be dressed in drag or wearing any moving contraptions if we ever made it to the church.

"I know, right? I have such great taste!" He was over the moon that

I liked his choice, but not quite as much as I was.

I grabbed it from the hanger and dived into the bathroom to change. As much as I loved penguins, the dress was something of an upgrade. I had never found a piece of stitched-together cloth that fitted me so perfectly. It was tight where it needed to be and free-flowing everywhere else. I looked at myself in the mirror, unable to process what I was seeing. It was like Superwoman's cape or Lady Gaga's meat dress. I emerged a minute later feeling invincible.

You go, girl! Reach for the stars!

Ramesh was lost for words, and so I took charge. "Come on, you. We've got a murder to solve."

He beamed with excitement. "Do you mean it, Izzy? Can I really be your sidekick?"

"Yes, but hurry. We have to catch the suspects after that pretty boy D.I. Holland finishes with each one. I was far too efficient and put them all in separate rooms so they couldn't discuss what had happened. But that means we can't talk to them until the police have."

"Brilliant," he pulled on his suit jacket and looked instantly less slovenly. "Just one thing, though."

"What is it?"

I waited for him to make whatever ridiculous request he had in mind. My first guess was that, before agreeing to help, he would require an elaborate codename. Though bringing his cats on board to help us with their psychic abilities was another possibility.

"Can we stop off at the breakfast buffet? I have a hankering for a cheese croissant."

Chapter Thirteen

"I think we should start by ruling out Emilio, the wedding planner. As far as I could tell, he didn't have the faintest clue what had happened in that suite when he walked through the door." This is what I tried to say, but I had a mouth full of pain au chocolat, and it probably came out quite mumbly. The buffet was closed by this point, but Cheryl was on hand to provide us with a range of goodies.

Ramesh shoved a large pastry into his mouth as we took the main corridor through the hotel towards the east tower. "Emilio is a very passionate man, Iz. He makes me look comparatively demure. Perhaps all his Latin verve came pouring out of him and he couldn't control himself."

"Is he from Spain then?"

"No, Birmingham. But he's been on holiday there several times and just adores chorizo."

This was not a lot of help, though the breakfast treats did make up for it.

In the end, it wasn't the wedding planner we found, but Julia Green's friend Deidre. She was hovering around at the bottom of the great wooden staircase that led to the bridal suite. More police officers funnelled past us as we approached, and we saw two women on their way to the crime scene who were carrying fresh white overalls.

"Hi Deidre!" Ramesh said, his voice light and cheerful. "I hear you confessed to killing Sindy. What on earth did you do that for?"

Deidre fiddled with the pockets on the front of her dress. She looked rather like a cleaning lady even without the overalls we'd found near the body. "Yes… I did say that. Only, I made a mistake. It was rather silly, really. I don't know what came over me."

"So you didn't kill her?" I confirmed.

"No, no. Quite the opposite, in fact."

Ramesh looked confused. "So you did kill her?"

Deidre shook her head and emitted a flustered breath. "Sorry, I should have been clearer. It wasn't me."

Underneath a long, rectangular window at the bottom of the stairs, there was a comfy bench with a straight wooden back which was upholstered in a vaguely medieval fabric. I motioned for Deidre to sit down, and she seemed to debate with herself over whether this was a good idea before doing just that.

"Would you mind telling us why you decided to confess to a murder you didn't commit?" I tried to sound sympathetic, but the woman was either a fantasist or a time waster, and it wasn't easy to hide my irritation.

She shuffled in her seat. "Oh... well... I suppose it seemed like the right thing to do at the time. I didn't want Patricia's wedding day to be spoilt."

I couldn't help smiling. She was such a slight, unremarkable sort of person that it was hard to imagine such a scheme entering her mind. "You decided it would be better for you to go to prison instead of her?"

"No... I didn't really think of it like that." Her lip trembled and her eyes flicked between us. "I suppose I would have told the police eventually that I wasn't the killer. I just couldn't stand the thought of Patricia and Julia's big day being ruined."

Ramesh winked at me then, as if to say, *see, I told you it was a secret lesbian conspiracy,* before posing a question of his own. "But why would you put their safety before your own? If Patricia really was the killer – which is straight-up impossible, by the way – why would you cover for her?"

I thought she might jump to her feet and run away at this. There was something very rabbitish about her. She looked like she was waiting for the car that would crush her flat to come speeding around the corner at any moment.

Her response, when it came, was unexpectedly forthright. "Because we're friends and that means something to me. Julia has been my best friend for years and I'd be lost without her. This wedding is all she's been thinking about since her husband, Louis, died. I couldn't let it be destroyed because some silly girl had got herself killed."

She was a curious creature. Though somewhere in her sixties, and roughly the same age as Patricia's mother, she could have passed for ten years older. It wasn't just the style of her clothes that prematurely aged her. Her speech and mannerisms belonged to a woman from an earlier generation. She made me think of a 1940s housewife who had been transported to the present day. The only real surprise was that she wasn't wearing a hairnet.

"What happened after you left the church?" I asked in the hope of ruling out more of the suspects.

The muscles in her arm became rigid, and she held her bag tighter. "I stayed with Julia the whole time and then we went up to the east tower together."

Even Ramesh could tell she was lying. "That's not true, is it, Deidre?

At least she looked a touch guilty. "No. Sorry. I went to get a cup of tea in the hotel bar and Julia went looking for Patricia in the gardens. I don't think she can have found her because, by the time I returned to the bridal suite, I caught sight of my friend just ahead of me."

Ramesh looked at me as though this would be the moment that would blow the case open, but it fitted in with what I remembered.

"Did you know Sindy well?" I asked, moving us on.

She clutched a small bag in her lap. "No. Not well. I knew that she and Patricia had been at school together. I'd met her at the engagement party and a few other times when we were planning the wedding. Oh, and I once bumped into her in the supermarket when–"

"Thank you, Deidre. That was a very full answer." I swear I said this politely, with only a hint of snarkiness. "Changing the topic ever so slightly... do you have any suspicion of who might have killed her?"

She bit her lip as she considered the various possibilities. "It must be one of those people who admitted to it, I suppose. Not Julia. There's no way she'd do anything so cruel. She's an incredibly nice person and my best friend."

"What about Patricia then?" I asked with some hesitation, and Ramesh shot a thousand daggers at me with his eyes.

"Patricia?" Deidre sounded just as unnerved as my sidekick looked. "Surely she wouldn't have done anything like that on her wedding day? Not after all the work that Ramesh has done to organise it."

I had my answer already prepared. "Unless Sindy knew something that could have derailed the wedding itself."

"Isobel Palmer! How dare you!?" This was Ramesh, obviously, not the funny little lady with the alligator purse.

"Well, that might make sense, I suppose." Deidre ignored the groom's outburst. "Yes, if Sindy was blackmailing Patricia in some way, the murder would have been necessary to keep the wedding on track."

"Deidre O'Leary!" this was also Ramesh. "How dare you! My saintly

Patricia is a paragon of gentility. She couldn't squash a woodlouse, let alone slay a human being."

"Sorry, dear. I didn't mean anything by it. I must say this whole thing has set me on edge. It's not every day I see a dead body, you know?"

If only you could say the same, Izzy!

"So is it possible, Ramesh?" I turned to my friend and Deidre took a sherbet lemon from her bag and sucked it loudly, as though enjoying the entertainment in a cinema.

He pulled in his neck and jutted out his chin. "Possible? No it's quite the opposite of possible. It's…" It took him a moment. "It's impossible, that's what it is. My Patricia would never do such a thing."

"That's not what I meant. What I was asking was whether Sindy could have known something about Patricia that she wouldn't want anyone to find out."

He crossed his arms and pretended he hadn't heard.

"Ooh, look at that. He's avoiding the question." Deidre seized my arm with her frighteningly strong grip. It was another example of a suspect getting too big for her boots. "Have you considered that Ramesh himself could be involved? After all, if Sindy was blackmailing poor Patricia, he might have come to her rescue. He was one of the only people who didn't confess to the murder, too, which could mean…"

She didn't say the last few words of the sentence but mouthed them silently. I couldn't quite tell whether she said *he smells whiffy* or *he is guilty* – both of which had some truth to them, considering the amount of fancy cologne (and champagne) that Ramesh had doused himself in.

I regarded my friend for a moment and noticed a bead of sweat come rolling down his forehead.

"Deidre, you could be right."

"Izzy! I didn't kill anyone. You know me, I'd never hurt another soul. I once stepped on Kiki's foot, and she got in a terrible mood and scratched poor Elton. Neither of my cats would look at me for days, and I felt so bad I went out and bought them a steak dinner. Imagine how I'd feel if I'd stabbed someone to death."

"How did you know she was stabbed?" I said, taking a step closer to the groom.

"Ahhhh!" He sounded like a parrot in a flap. "I… I don't know. How did I…?"

I couldn't keep a straight face any longer. "Relax, Ramesh. I told you how she was killed. I don't think you're the killer and, if you were, you would already have given yourself away. You're useless at hiding things from me."

He seemed more offended by a minor detail than the suggestion he was responsible for Sindy's death. "I'm not so bad at keeping secrets, actually. I never told you about that dress, and I've had it for months. Every time I saw you, I wanted to scream my head off, but I waited until the very last moment to surprise you with it."

"It is a lovely dress, Izzy," Deidre agreed and took the skirt in two fingers to feel. She got to her feet and, in that slowly shuffling manner of hers, wandered away. "I'll be in the chapel checking on the flowers if anyone wants me. If I see the priests, I'll tell them they may need to clear their diaries for this afternoon."

Ramesh and I watched her disappear down the corridor, and I shook my head as I tried to make sense of the strange character. She was either a criminal genius and a master of camouflage or… well, she was the innocent, pseudo-elderly lady that she appeared to be. What I hadn't learnt from her that might have been useful was how she'd come to be friends with chic, debonair Julia Green in the first place.

I think that Ramesh was having similar thoughts as he made a clicking sound in his cheek and said, "What a strange bird she is."

"Has she been part of Julia and Patricia's life for long?" I asked him.

"She's an old friend apparently, though I've only known her since the time Patricia's dad got sick. She's been a big help in supporting Julia. To be honest, I find her a bit odd, and I think that Patricia feels the same. She wants us to call her Auntie Deidre."

I was about to ask how they met when a tall, dark and extremely handsome man came to ogle me. I didn't mind in the slightest.

"Izzy… dress… you… exquisite." There might have been some other words in between, but this was all Danny managed to get out with any clarity.

"Yes, it's so pretty," the even more beautiful girl on his arm agreed.

Lizzy was dressed in a blue satin prom dress, with a skirt that, sticking out at a forty-five-degree angle, seemed to defy gravity. She wore killer black heels that I would instantly break both ankles in if I dared put them on. And, worst of all, she didn't even seem jealous that her new boyfriend was staring at me like I was the Mona Lisa.

I longed for such confidence. Despite wearing my magic dress of power, I was swimming in vats, lakes, oceans of envy. Though I had been the one to instigate the end of my relationship with my former love, and I liked Lizzy more than I ever planned to, I was still jealous, and I wasn't entirely sure why.

Is it his muscly chest? He may kiss like your imaginary brother, but Dr Danny still has the pectoral prowess of a young Burt Reynolds.

"Where's Nigel?" Danny asked in that same disgruntled voice from the night before. He normally sounded like an infinitely peppy children's presenter, so this was quite out of character.

"Nigel?" I replied, as I'd completely forgotten who that was by this point. "Oh, yes, Nigel. He's about somewhere. We've been a bit busy investigating a murder."

"Are you serious?" Lizzy sounded quite concerned, so I tried to put her mind at ease.

"Yes, terrible business. One of the bridesmaids." I could see this only made her sadder, so I diplomatically added, "But don't worry, no one really liked her." To cover the fact I sounded like a heartless sociopath, I pretended my phone was ringing and hurried away. Ramesh had been laughing at me throughout this exchange, so I didn't feel too bad about ditching him.

Sadly for me, I needed to head back in the direction I'd come from. I finished my fake call and immediately returned to my friends, which rather undermined my plan for a cunning exit.

"Who was on the phone, Iz?" Ramesh was in the most cheerful phase of his champagne-induced drunkenness. I preferred the grumpier stages.

"That was my mum," I (obviously) lied. "She needed my opinion on something."

As this is my life I'm describing and embarrassment follows me like Wile E. Coyote chasing a roadrunner, my mother turned up at this moment holding two slightly different pairs of hot pants. "Izzy, I need your opinion on something. Rosy red or royal rouge?"

"Royal rouge, of course, mother." I tried to play it cool.

"That's what I thought. Your stepfather has lost his touch." She wandered off again and Danny and Lizzy wore baffled expressions, as if to say *why did her mother call before coming here?*

"There's something I wanted to ask you, Danny," I said to distract them, before realising it was true. "You were there at the rehearsal. Did you see where anyone went after it finished?"

He had a quick think. "Well, Patricia ran off first, and I saw her walking around the grounds a few minutes later. Tog hurried off pretty quickly into the hotel, and Gaz had a chat with me for a while and then headed towards our rooms in the west tower."

"What about the mother of the bride?"

"Julia?" He needed more time to remember. "She was still in the church when I left. But when I returned to my rooms a bit later, I saw her friend Deidre heading up the staircase to the bridal suite. Does that help?"

I hated to disappoint my dear Danny, but the truth hurts. "No, not really. Her room is in the east tower, and we know she went to the scene of the crime after the body was found. So unless you know the exact time, it's not much use." Afraid this sounded rude, I added a quick, "Thanks anyway!"

My friend Detective Inspector Irons-

Izzy, she has a first name, you know. It's... It's... I want to say Virginia. Or is it Veronica?

My friend D.I. Irons appeared at that moment, and I finally had a good reason to get away from my ex-boyfriend and his lady love.

"I'm sorry about all this," I told them. "Let's catch up at the wedding … if there is one." This made Lizzy and Ramesh look sad, but Danny was on hand to make them feel better.

"Just thought I should check in with you," Irons said in her usual brusque tone. "Holland is upstairs grilling the suspects like he's Eliot Ness. He's leaving them to sweat for the moment, so it'll be a while before you can talk to anyone."

"Then why did he let Deidre go?"

Her face went blank for a moment, but Irons is a good officer and quickly put the facts together. "You mean the woman who looks like a cleaner? She said she didn't know the victim well, hadn't seen anything useful and that she'd stay on site if we needed to ask her anything more. We can't lock up every guest, and so we let her go."

I moved on to another unlikely suspect. "I had a word with Anfony

LeQuinn, the dead woman's boyfriend. They were a strange pair, but I don't see why he'd have killed her. If anything, it makes me wonder whether someone was setting him up for the crime. He's the perfect culprit in some ways. He's in room 306 if you need to find him."

"Right." She mouthed the number to herself and let out a whistle. "I don't suppose you have any hunches, theories, vague presentiments of what might have happened?"

I was sad to admit it, but the closest I'd come to a theory was Ramesh's no doubt sensational suggestion that his future mother-in-law was a secret lesbian. As he'd made similar assertions on every other case we'd investigated, I wouldn't be presenting it to D.I. Irons.

"Nope, not a thing."

She chewed on the inside of her mouth for a moment. "That's alright. Grab Ramesh and we'll get some air. I have some thoughts of my own I'd like to put to you."

Chapter Fourteen

The first time that D.I. Irons had interviewed me (in Croydon police station for the murder of my boss – the first one, not the second) I'd been terrified and chattered away so nervously that I implicated myself in the killing. On that day, I'd been the idiot who, instead of running from the room screaming at the sight of Bob's bloody body, decided to go in for a closer look.

"I wouldn't say that Patricia picking up the sword is a sign that she's the killer." I tried to sound casual and carefree. "Accidentally interfering with a crime scene could happen to literally anyone."

They looked at me as if to say, *well, it happened to you.*

"No, really. She might have thought Sindy was playing a joke or…" This was the only reason I could come up with.

"That's not what D.I. Holland reckons," Irons told us. "He saw two women in wedding dresses and decided he knew the motive right away. Due to the fact we know Patricia held the sword and so her fingerprints will be on the weapon, he seems confident he's got the culprit."

Ramesh clearly wanted to fall to the ground and curse the skies at this moment, but we were walking down a stony path. To avoid hurting his knees, he waited until we reached the grass. "Noooooooooooo! Whyyyyyyy?"

"Did that make you feel better?" I asked, as I gave him a hand back up.

He released a melancholic sigh. "A bit."

With this brief drama over, I decided to check around the base of the east tower in case the killer had thrown something out of a window. This had provided a breakthrough on a previous case but did nothing to help us this time.

"Good, now listen," Irons said once we'd finished looking. I was expecting her to follow this up with an important declaration, but she said nothing more until we were sitting on a pair of benches, some way from the building.

We'd found ourselves in one of those gardens which would have looked ever so pretty from the air. The colour-coordinated flowerbeds were themselves arranged in the shape of a flower, and there was a fountain with a little bronze boy holding an endlessly spitting dolphin… which is pretty horrible if you think about it.

Though there was no one else around, Irons had a quick look over her shoulders before continuing the conversation. "I got the gist of what's going on up there; we've got five suspects still claiming they killed Lusinda Braithwaite; that would be the mother of the bride, three former school friends and the wedding planner. They can't all be telling the truth, so what I want to know is why they would lie about it."

"Well, the wedding planner, Emilio, is a massive drama queen," Ramesh proclaimed, with a theatrical hand to his forehead. "We only hired him because he's Patricia's cousin."

"He's Patricia's cousin?" I was more than a little annoyed that he hadn't told me this before.

"Yes, Izzy. Try to keep up. He's a useless wedding planner, and we're only paying him for the last-minute stuff, which I was too busy to do. Though I doubt he's even managed that if he was busy killing Sindy."

D.I. Irons–

Victoria! That's her name. I knew I'd get there in the end.

D.I. Victoria Irons looked typically unsettled by Ramesh's off-the-wall perspective on life. "So you think he might have killed her then?"

He didn't need long to consider the possibility. "I bet he wanted to. The two got on like a house on fire."

I had to whisper in his ear then, as he clearly didn't know how to use that expression. He nodded throughout my explanation and then uttered a correction. "Or rather, the two butted heads like billy goats. He ended up storming out each time we met to plan the wedding."

"So it's a possibility?" Irons asked again, as it still wasn't clear.

"Absolutely not. Emilio doesn't have the guts. I once saw him faint at the sight of his own paper cut. He wouldn't have been able to stand all that blood."

Irons crossed her leg over her knee. "Let me get this straight; you're saying he's staking his claim to a murder on aspirational grounds? He couldn't have killed Sindy, but he wishes that he had?"

Ramesh clicked his fingers and pointed to the inspector's nose. "Got it in one."

I decided it would be wise to move the discussion on. "I think that

Julia Green is a more likely culprit. There's something very detached about her."

"Yes, she's half French." My friend could be as big a moron as my own stupid brain sometimes.

"And so that makes her detached?"

"Yes, because she's French. Though you'd think her more exuberant Italian side would have balanced it out." He puzzled over this for a moment as I launched another question at him.

"So you're saying that all French people are aloof, and Italians are outgoing?"

He looked at me out of the side of his eyes. "Obviously not, Izzy. Only the women. The men are a totally different kettle *de poisson.*" He paused for a moment, then whispered, "I don't know the French word for kettle!"

I was tempted to contradict him further, but he must have foreseen my argument as he crossed his arms and said, "Hey, I don't make up the stereotypes. I just live by them."

Irons wisely ignored everything Ramesh had just blurted and got us back on track. "Well, if anyone was looking to keep up appearances at a wedding, it would be the mother of the bride. Clearly the victim was causing problems this morning. Perhaps Mrs Green decided to solve them in a drastic manner."

I'd had similar thoughts myself, but there was a problem with this theory. "It's possible, but I think she'd have done more to protect her daughter from suspicion. Don't forget, I was there when Julia first confessed. She came in, looked shocked at the carnage then spotted her daughter with the sword before confessing to the crime."

"But perhaps she only looked shocked because she hadn't expected her daughter to find the body. Perhaps she had no intention of admitting her guilt until Patricia got tangled up in everything."

If I had to choose my favourite part of being a detective, it was this. I loved bouncing my ideas off an assistant on each case. Whether it was Ramesh – who was guaranteed to come up with nonsense – or someone like the inspector with a true gumshoe brain, it was always a thrill.

"It's a nice idea," I conceded. "And that would explain her reaction when she got there. But there's one thing that doesn't fit. By killing Sindy in the bridal suite, Julia was guaranteed to ruin the wedding, so would she really have gone through with it?"

The two of us fell silent as we considered this, which gave Ramesh a chance to have his say. "Julia can be fierce, and she clearly didn't think much of Sindy Braithwaite, but I don't think she's a killer."

"Do you have any evidence to back that up?" Irons asked with a raised eyebrow. She was very much a fact-orientated officer, whereas Ramesh was more of a ridiculous loon who said whatever came into his over-creative mind.

"I have all the evidence I need right here…" He pointed at his tummy. I think this left Irons wondering whether he'd eaten a clue. Luckily, he soon elaborated on the matter. "Here in my gut. Because sometimes the gut knows more than the brain ever will."

In my case, at least, I thought there was some truth to this, but Irons disagreed. "Nope. You're talking nonsense. Now let's move on to the other suspects. What about your three friends who have all confessed?"

Ramesh leaned forward conspiratorially. "What about them?"

"Why do you think they're lying? If they are lying, that is."

He straightened up again and looked at the sky.

I could tell that he was about to point out the fact that one of the clouds looked like a pineapple and so I hissed in his direction. "Ra, concentrate."

Oh, wow! It does look like a pineapple!

"Fine. Gaz, Tog and Wazza do not like Sindy. There's bad blood going way back, but things have really been difficult over the last year."

"That doesn't explain why they'd all confess. Even if the three of them worked together, that's not the story they've given us. So what do you think really happened?"

It was a rare moment when two experienced detectives would look to Ramesh as the fount of knowledge. He clearly enjoyed the attention. He stretched one arm out in front of him, placed the other on the back of the bench and smiled.

"I'd say it was fairly obvious. They all think the other one is guilty. They're just as close friends as when we were five years old and swore a blood oath to never let a woman come between us. They still have each other's backs."

"You swore an oath to never let a woman come between you when you were only five?" I had to check. "It's hard to know whether to be impressed or appalled."

"It still doesn't make any sense," Irons mumbled. "I could understand one of them confessing, but all three? That seems wrong to me."

An idea shot into my head. "What we haven't considered is that they've confessed for that very reason. They could be trying to blur the picture. If we accept that one of them is the likely suspect – based on Emilio's fear of blood and Patricia and Mrs Green being unlikely to do anything that might spoil the wedding – with all three of them confessing, it becomes a lot more difficult for the police to spot the real killer."

My brilliant suggestion had stunned them into silence. Well, for about ten seconds at least, at which point Ramesh pointed to the sky and said, "That one looks like a rabbit… and up over there is a little girl skating on a frozen pond with snow-covered trees around her."

"Ramesh, I know it's your wedding day, and you must be quite distracted," Irons began, relatively politely for her, "but could you stop looking at the clouds and try to help us?"

"Yes, Ma'am!" he saluted and tried to think of something useful to say. "I'm sorry. What were we talking about?"

"Gaz, Tog and Wazza. We're trying to work out why they would have lied."

"Well, it's obvious." he sounded terribly smug before apparently changing his mind. "I'll have to get back to you on that."

I, meanwhile, had thought of something that was worth saying. "We keep talking as though our only suspects are the idiots who came upstairs to confess. People are always admitting to crimes for the attention it earns them. But what if our killer wasn't one of the eight who we know entered the bridal suite? What if it's another one of the guests?"

"Who did you have in mind?" Irons looked serious once more.

"The boyfriends. Anfony was dating Sindy at the time she died. He's an odd guy with a bad temper – he once tried to kick a dog. And though he was more sympathetic than I would have imagined when I interviewed him, we can't rule him out entirely. He even told me that he had a motive to kill her. He'd sobered up and got his life on track after breaking up with Sindy, but she'd sucked him back into her plans."

"Holland will be onto him in good time, but you said boyfriends, plural. Who's the other fella?"

"Sindy's ex-fiancé Toby, who left her on their wedding day. They clearly had unfinished business, or else she wouldn't have worn her wedding dress to spite him. Anfony was under the impression that she'd only brought him along this weekend to get under Toby's skin. At first, I thought it was Patricia she was going after, but now it looks like her ex was the target. I don't think anyone has considered interviewing him yet. He's been here since last night and, to be perfectly honest, I have no memory of meeting him."

Ramesh pulled himself away from the heavens for a moment and stuck his tongue out of the side of his mouth, like a dog trying to perform a taxing mental calculation. "Why do you keep saying that, Iz? He was there in the room with you when you found the body."

"Toby was?" I began and immediately realised something that should have hit me approximately forever ago. "Oh, I've been such an idiot." I slapped myself around the forehead again. "How could I not realise that Tog's real name is Toby?"

Chapter Fifteen

"How dare you, Izzy Palmer," Ramesh had found something else to get worked up about. "You are far from being an idiot and I will not hear such language bandied about when it comes to my best friend. You might be a little slow this morning, but you're no idiot."

"Thank you, Ramesh. But this changes everything. If Tog is Sindy's ex, it explains why his friends confessed to killing her. What we don't know is whether he really did it."

Irons had remained silent through this break in chapters… I mean, she hadn't said much for some time and broke her contemplative silence to deliver her verdict on this new bombshell. "It's the most convincing theory we've got yet." She nodded to herself and drummed her fingers on the bench. "With the ex-fiancé there in the room shortly after the killing and Sindy about to show him up at the wedding, things are starting to fall into place."

"I'm so stupid–" I began, but Ramesh did not approve of my choice of words.

"No, no, no!"

"I've been so foolish?"

"I'll allow it."

I smiled and started again. "I've been so foolish. Back in the church during the rehearsal, Tog and Gaz were overcome with rage when they saw what Sindy was wearing. The other bridesmaids shouted that the boys should have done something to stop her. I didn't understand what they meant, but they were talking about him – Toby/Tog. They were saying that he was responsible for Sindy's bad behaviour."

"Case closed." Ramesh nodded confidently. "Can I get married now, please?"

"Sorry, son. I'm afraid it's not that easy." Though she couldn't have been more than a few years older than us, D.I. Irons had a grown-up manner about her that we both lacked. The fact that I hadn't accidentally called her *Mother* at any point was the real wonder. "We need facts, proof, evidence. Without that, D.I. Holland ain't going to let your fiancée out of his sight."

"But you've already got a bunch of confessions. Can't we say it was one of them and get on with our day? The priests are only going to wait around for so long, you know."

"The scabbard!" I said as soon as I thought of it. "There's no way that you would have brought a super sharp samurai sword here without a cover. It must still be in the hotel somewhere. Perhaps there are fingerprints on it."

Irons registered this piece of information as though she were a human notepad. "Where was the sword kept before the killing? And why did you buy it in the first place?"

Ramesh looked shy for once. "What else would you cut a wedding cake with? Samurai swords are cool. Or haven't you seen that bit in "The Bodyguard' when Kevin Costner seduces Whitney Houston by cutting her scarf in half with his katana? Only the fact that his house looks like a serial killer's lair undermines what is otherwise one of the most romantic scenes in movie history."

Take that, the second highest-grossing film of 1992!

"And how did our killer get hold of your sword this morning?"

"Emilio had it. He was supposed to bring it to the dining room after the wedding feast."

Irons and I stared at Ramesh then as though *we really did despair*. It felt much better dealing out such withering looks than receiving them.

I hit his shoulder with the back of my hand to underline his mistake. "And you didn't think this counted as evidence when we were discussing the possibility that Patricia's cousin, your wedding planner, was the killer?"

"Not really, no. He told me this morning that he'd left the sword in the hall in front of the bridal suite so that people could enjoy its beauty. It's possibly the most elegant item I own, so it only made sense."

"Another damn dead end." It wasn't like Irons to show such emotion. It was rather exciting. "Alright, enough messing around. We need a plan."

Ramesh was quick to respond. "I should dress up and go undercover as a wealthy German count who just happens to be staying in the hotel for the weekend. I'll–"

"Nope!" She was all action, no nonsense, and I loved it. "I'll tell you what we'll do. You can wait by the east tower to grab the suspects when they leave. Then Izzy and I will interview them one by one in the small lounge near the chapel." I wasn't just impressed by how assertive she was being. It was really quite remarkable how well she'd familiarised herself with the layout of Hartford House. The place was massive.

"Nope!" Ramesh replied, as though his opinion counted the same as hers. "No one will go with me if I tell them they're going to be interviewed for a second time. I've got a better idea."

Five minutes later, I was wearing a red and blue curly wig, a pair of oversized comedy sunglasses and glow-in-the-dark vampire teeth.

"They'll never recognise you, Iz. This is perfect."

As the only person at the wedding over six foot two and a half (I'm six three!) I was fairly certain he was wrong. "I don't think I need a disguise, Ra. We just want to talk to each suspect, not convince them I'm a clown."

It was his turn to be assertive. "This is my wedding day, and you will wear a wig!"

We'd relocated to a hallway near the dining room where a camera tripod had been set up. There were a number of comedy backgrounds and funny props at hand for the guests to take hilarious photos with after the ceremony. I'm sure that, if I ever get married, the one thing I'll want most of all is a multitude of photos of my loved ones wearing bowler hats and monocles. Nothing could capture the most romantic day of my life better than a shot of my uncle Bradley with a speech bubble in his hand saying, 'Which bridesmaids are single?'

"You should probably work out how to use the camera if this ruse is going to work," Irons suggested and, to my surprise, she grabbed a few props and sat down in the enormous golden throne to be my first subject.

I looked through the viewfinder, remembered to take the cap off, forgot to turn the power on, turned the power on and pressed the button. "Smile!"

"I am smiling." Irons sounded a little hurt. "This is my smiling face."

It didn't look any different to her working face or her relaxing face. She was a woman who played her cards, not so much close to her chest, as stashed away in a safe somewhere. I liked her all the more for it.

A white-framed photograph came whirring out of a Bluetooth printer on a nearby table, and she pulled the Superman cape off and enthusiastically rushed over to peruse it.

"That's a good one," she announced. "Wait till my boyfriend sees it. We'll die laughing over that one."

The idea that Irons not only had a boyfriend but was capable of laughter were two facts that I often struggled to get my head around.

"Okay, I think we're ready," I said with some confidence, having made sure that the camera was in auto mode. "Ramesh, head back to the east tower and send your friends over when Holland finishes with them."

He gave another half-hearted salute and spun on his heel. There was still the risk that he wouldn't be able to convince anyone to come, or that they'd stay up in the bridal tower for hours, but at least we had a plan now.

I must confess that I was not happy being kept away from the crime scene. I preferred it when police officers were almost pathologically ignorant of standard protocol and let me bumble about the place to my heart's content. It wasn't just that I felt left out – which I very much did – but the fact that there was all that evidence up there which I couldn't examine. Based on prior experience, there would almost certainly be one significant clue hiding between the cushions on the sofa in the bridal suite or peeking out from under a rug. I'd probably have solved it by now if D.I. *Haven't I Got Great Hair* Holland had let me look around.

Izzy, do you have a crush on that smouldering hot detective?

Pfff… no. You do!

"Here we go!" Irons rubbed her hands together as she caught sight of someone coming down the hall towards us. "Our first victim."

Only, it wasn't any of the suspects we'd considered. My ex-boyfriend's eighty-three-year-old auntie Val had spotted our setup and come for a photo.

"Don't you look lovely with your funny wig on, Izzy!" she said in her wonderful Welsh accent. "I tell you what. I'll put one on myself." She did just that and Irons helped her pose for a photo with long, flowing golden locks and a firefighter's helmet on her head. By the time she was happy with the results, more guests had started queueing for their turn. Some of my old colleagues from Porter & Porter were there, along with a few friends from my Christmas trip to Scotland – Baby Amelia wasn't so much of a baby anymore and was walking alongside her family. Bless her little Nike trainers. There was a line of people waiting, and every last one of them knew it was me behind the disguise.

To be perfectly honest, it was nice to have a break from murder and suspicion. D.I. Irons was enjoying herself, too. She was surprisingly animated as she handed out props for people to make use of and shouted out a countdown for me to take the photo. She'd clearly missed her calling as a photographer's assistant in a department store – if such a job had existed at any point since 1987.

What this diversion did not provide us with was any relevant information whatsoever on Sindy's potential killers. In fact, rather than gaining information, we ended up filling everyone else in on what had happened.

"Do you think the wedding will be going ahead today?" Ramesh's Uncle Kabir enquired, though it was difficult to understand him through the fake beard he was wearing.

"Fingers crossed," I replied. "Now, smile!" I don't know why I said this, you couldn't see his mouth.

"Terrible business." With her photo in hand, Auntie Val had stuck around to have a chat. "And do you have any idea who the murderer could be?"

"Not yet, I'm afraid," I had to concede. "Though I'm sure we'll get to the bottom of things before long."

"Of course you will, my dear. Though, like I said, it's a terrible business. You can't go anywhere these days without coming across a body."

I thought I should at least try to reassure the dear old lady. "I wouldn't say that. In fact, Britain has a lower murder rate than most other nations, especially out here in the countryside."

"No, dear, you misunderstood me. I meant that *you* can't go anywhere these days without coming across a body. How many is that now? You must have lost count."

So true!

It was one o'clock already and all the guests who were coming had arrived. This meant that I got stuck there for an hour taking everyone's photos, which at least helped to pass the time. Ramesh eventually came to warn everybody that the wedding would be delayed until five in the afternoon.

"It's just a tiny misunderstanding," he told the disappointed crowd. "I can solemnly attest that my betrothed has not murdered anyone in the slightest. As soon as the police realise that, we'll get back on with the celebration. I've talked it over with Cheryl, our liaison with the hotel..." Cheryl, inevitably, popped up at this point to wave to the crowd. "...and we're going to have the post-ceremony drinks in the atrium now as opposed to ummm... post-ceremony."

I still thought this sounded optimistic, but his mum and dad and his sister's whole family were there, so I didn't like to contradict him. He led the large crowd over to the atrium (I hadn't realised such a place existed, but my photographer's assistant knew all about it) and we were left alone.

Irons was putting some props back into their box when something occurred to her. "Of course, there is one possibility that I didn't want to mention with Ramesh around." I knew what she was going to say. "It's more than just circumstantial evidence that suggests Patricia is the killer. I know he's got his heart set on marrying the woman, but I wouldn't bet my house on it."

I struggled to come up with an answer, as I'd been thinking the exact same thing. "She's a good person. I'm sure she is."

"That's what they said about John Wayne Gacy, Dennis Nilsen, Harold Shipman–"

"Yes, thank you." The men she was referring to were all serial killers. "I don't think Patricia is anything like them, though."

She leaned a little closer to terrify me a little more. "You say that, but when you think about it, it's not so impossible. We know this Sindy woman shoehorned herself into the wedding. We know her interest in being here was to cause a scene and upset people. You said yourself that Patricia looked very nervous last night when her head bridesmaid was giving a speech. The way I look at it, the most obvious solution is the most obvious solution; Sindy turned up at the rehearsal, upstaged the bride and paid the price."

I shuddered and changed the topic. "One thing I can't understand is, if our killer has confessed to the murder, why they would have hidden the evidence. The scabbard is missing and, if there are no fingerprints, we can assume that they wore gloves."

She paused what she was doing to think this over. "Perhaps they felt guilty about what they'd done."

"Perhaps." A hilarious thought occurred to me just then and I couldn't hold it in. "Hey, it's more like a *whodidn'tdunit* than a whodunit!"

Irons puffed her cheeks up in confusion.

"It's a joke," I explained. "You do know what a whodunit is, right?"

"Humour, Miss Palmer, is a subjective business." Irons nodded to me knowingly and got busy counting our tips. She hadn't called me "Miss Palmer" for years, and I decided never to make a joke in front of her again.

The place was tidy, and I was ready to pack away the camera when one last guest appeared.

"Hi Izzy," one of the blue-suited groomsmen murmured. "Ramesh told me I have to have my photo taken."

Chapter Sixteen

"Thanks for coming, Gaz." I motioned to D.I. Irons to leave us alone as, the last time I'd spent any time with Ramesh's schoolfriend, he'd called me a "top bird" and tried to lick my ear. I removed my wig and moustache, hoping to make use of my feminine wiles.

Ha! Now that is a good joke.

He didn't look quite so boisterous this time and landed down in the throne with a thud. He could barely look at me, which would make taking his photograph difficult. With his eyes on the floor, he kept stroking the short hair at the back of his neck as though he'd got chewing gum stuck in it. Incidentally, if such misfortune ever befalls you, do not let your mother put your head in the freezer in an attempt to snap off the offending substance. I had chilblains of the scalp, which rather impressed my doctor as, until that day, he hadn't believed such a condition to be medically possible.

"How are you doing?" I thought I'd start with a nice, easy question. After our first encounter at the strip club, I couldn't be entirely sure of his intelligence level, or whether he actually had one.

His reply came in a small, fragile voice. "I'm doing alright. Bit shaken up really."

"I suppose you've admitted to the police that you didn't kill Sindy then?"

His eyes locked onto mine at that moment, and his anger flashed like lightning. "Don't you start. I told them it was me, and that bloody inspector wouldn't believe a word of it. He reckoned I was doing it for attention. He said that, unless I could prove what happened, he wasn't interested."

I was surprised that he was continuing with the story but could see that confronting him over it wouldn't do any good. In my softest, sweetest, perhaps a little bit flirty voice, I said, "You can tell me all about if it would make you feel better."

He shook his head despondently. "I never meant to hurt her; you've got to believe me. I mean, no one else does, but I'd appreciate it if you'd give me the benefit of the doubt."

I didn't think it was the moment to offer him a Groucho Marx nose, moustache and glasses combo, so I stepped out from behind the camera. "Go on, I'm listening."

"I just wanted to talk some sense into Sindy. It's no secret that I've never got on with her, but I couldn't stand to see the way she'd been hurting my friends. Not just Ramesh and Patricia either, but Tog too. I mean, my friend Toby Gatling. You might remember him as an Oompa Loompa?"

Gaz didn't seem like such a bad guy right then (despite confessing to a brutal crime) and I felt a bit guilty about our previous meeting. "I'm so sorry that I stole your plastic breasts last weekend. Those cocktails went to my head and–"

His smile was just as shy as I felt. "Don't worry about it. Me and the boys act like prats when we've had a few drinks. They're not really like that, deep down. They're my best friends, you know? Me, Tog, Wazza and Ramekin: we're like a family."

Ha! How did we not know Ramesh took his nickname from a piece of crockery?

"I'd do anything for them." He peered off down the hall, looking more lost and lonely than ever.

"I suppose that's the thing, isn't it? Everyone knows what good friends you are, and so it's hard to believe that you killed Sindy when her ex is the more obvious suspect. We're bound to think you're lying for Toby."

He sat up higher in the chair, ready to argue back. "So why won't anyone believe that I killed her for him? You know, I love those boys like we're brothers. The fact we're so close should prove that I did it."

"Maybe," I said, trying desperately to keep an open mind and not dismiss the possibility outright that this slightly dopey guy was a steel-nerved killer. "You know what? I hardly know you. Why don't you tell me a bit about yourself before I decide whether you're guilty?"

"Well… I'm from Watford, so I'm a Hornets fan." He stood up from his seat at this point and, with his arms in the air, began a football chant. "We love you Watford, we do. We love you Watford, we do. We love you Watford, we do. Oh, Watford, we love you!" With this urge satiated, he sat back down as if nothing had happened and continued with his answer. "I'm a painter-decorator by trade and have my own firm."

"Do you like your job?"

He clicked his knuckles one by one as he replied. "Yeah, it's alright. Plenty of time to think about life and the universe and all that."

"That sounds nice. And what about Patricia? Do you like her?"

He was unsettled by this sudden change of focus. "I can't say she's my cup of tea. But if she makes Ramesh happy, that's all that matters."

I needed to get him back to the tougher questions. "I'm sorry. I interrupted you earlier when you were telling me what happened when you killed Sindy." It's amazing I could deliver such a truly disturbing sentence so casually. I'd clearly been spending too much time around murderers.

Shaking his head again, he let out a long breath. "Yeah, it's like I said. I got up to the bridal suite, and she really lost it. She started chucking stuff at me."

"What kind of things?"

"Flowers from one of the bouquets at first, but then an ornament of two lovers that she found on the shelf."

We were finally getting to the details that I needed to know.

"What about the sword? Where did you get it from?"

He looked around the hallway then, as though picturing the crime scene. "It was there on a low table. There were a bunch of wedding cards around it and some unopened presents. I picked it up to defend myself, but she kept coming at me and the stuff she was saying about Toby was just so evil that I couldn't take it anymore... so I stabbed her. I hadn't expected the blade to go through her so easily; it was like a knife through butter."

Oh come on! He could have come up with a better metaphor than that. Saying a sword is like a knife is like saying a horse is a bit like a pony.

Gaz looked down at his hands. He was actually a pretty good actor, but the facts were all wrong. He hadn't killed Sindy any more than I had.

"So she was walking towards you when you killed her?"

He was trembling by now, and I think he could tell which road we were walking down. "Yes... I mean, no. She was going away from me. I stabbed her through the back. She must have turned around to get something else to throw."

"And so you took the scabbard off the sword and stabbed her, just like that?"

He nodded but did not look sure of himself. "That's right."

"You didn't change your clothes, for example?"

"No, of course not. I saw red and killed her. That's how it happened. It was a stupid instinct, and of course I wish I hadn't done it. But it's over now, and I want to pay for my crime."

I held my tongue just then but, standing a few feet away, studied the wretched creature for ten long seconds. It was all lies, of course, but that didn't change the fact he was suffering. I wondered if he'd forced himself to believe his own story, or he was simply so attached to his friends that he was experiencing the pain of that morning's events on their behalf. The fact was that, if D.I. Holland had found any great evidence that Gaz was the killer, he would have kept hold of him, confiscated his clothes to check for traces of blood and, most likely, sent him to the local station with his wrists firmly cuffed.

"What did you do with the scabbard?" I asked.

"Well, I left it there, I suppose. What else would I do with it? Look down the back of the sofa or under the table."

I gave him a sympathetic smile and went over to the box of props for the funny photographs. I could easily have proven him wrong. I could have told him about the bloody overalls under the sofa that the killer must have worn to cover their clothes. I could have mentioned the fact that there was no sign of the scabbard or that the killer must have taken the sword from outside in the hall, which showed that they'd intended to kill Sindy when they entered the suite. Instead, I took a witch's hat from the box and handed them to Gaz before heading back to my post behind the camera.

"Ra will kill me if I don't get a photo of every last guest. Say *Ramesh and Patricia are getting married no matter what!*" I said, in that strangely flat voice that photographers use.

"Sure. I wouldn't want to let anyone down." He hesitated for a moment before a cautious smile formed on his lips, and I pressed the button.

Chapter Seventeen

I wasn't sure that hanging around in a corridor on the off chance that more suspects were released by D.I. Holland was the best use of my time. If Wazza came down, he would no doubt tell me much the same as Gaz had, with more or less accurate details depending on how good a view he'd had of the room where Sindy had been murdered. I couldn't rule them out just yet, but I didn't see that either one of them had a good enough motive to murder Sindy, no matter how much of a pain she was.

I hadn't eaten anything for at least an hour and, as I believe that weddings should be enjoyed with a canapé in one's hand at all times, I decided to make my way to the atrium where the other guests had congregated. On my way, I thought back to the first wedding I ever attended, which was almost as much of a disaster as this one. I was only seven at the time but found my cousin Tracy's union to her high school sweetheart Gordon to be indescribably beautiful.

Mum and Dad were still married and did a good job of pretending they didn't hate one another (for my sake). We were at the farthest table from the bride and groom, plonked there with a few other people they'd felt obliged to ask, but from the moment I sat down in that converted barn, with its chiffon curtains and fairy lights, I was desperate to express my congratulations to the bride.

After two courses and over an hour of begging, my mother relented and took me up to the top table which, in my excitement, I immediately knocked into and sent a poorly placed bottle crashing over. Three quarters of a litre of red wine went splashing all over Tracy's perfect white dress, and I have never felt so guilty in my whole life. The poor girl became as rigid as a shop dummy, her eyes burnt holes through me, and I wished I'd never been born.

But it was the aftermath that was particularly traumatic. We didn't go home for some reason but stayed there through the day so that people could send nasty glares in my direction. I will never forget Gordon and Tracy's first dance. With her dress irreparably stained, she sobbed throughout as I tried to hide a little deeper in the shadows in the corner of the barn. That was the first and last wedding my parents took me to and is still spoken of in aggressive whispers by my father's side of the family.

Tracy and Sindy's revamped dresses had merged together in my head, and I think I had started to feel responsible for the bridesmaid's death as much as my cousin's ruined dress. As a result, I knew to steer clear of red wine this time around, though I did help myself to a glass of orange juice from the tray of a circling waiter in the atrium. It was a gorgeous space and, had Ramesh and Patricia's families not been religious, would have made a good location for the wedding itself. The ceiling was made of curved glass panels which connected to the main structure of the old house with an iron frame. There were large trees in pots placed around the perimeter of the room and pretty climbing flowers covered one rounded wall.

"What a beautiful wedding," Mum's full-time stylist/chauffeur/cut-price wedding photographer, Fernando exclaimed as I passed him in the crowd. "Just perfect."

"Except for the murder," I reminded him.

"Yeah, except for the head bridesmaid's murder and the bride's apparent incarceration. Except for that, it's the perfect wedding."

I left him to photograph a posse of Patricia's work friends and continued my search for anyone useful. There were plenty of people I didn't know, a few old colleagues who would have spent the next three hours talking about finance if I'd let them see me and, standing by the drinks table, looking really quite pale, Gemma was with her boyfriend. She was still in her bridesmaid's dress, ready to take Sindy's place, and I wondered whether that could have been enough of a motive to kill the woman she clearly couldn't stand.

There was no time for small talk, so I started the interview with a nice simple, "Did you kill Sindy after she stole your place as the maid of honour?"

"I wish I had!"

Peter the boyfriend clearly felt the same way. "Yeah, I wish she had!" He was really quite aggressive on the matter.

"But actually, you didn't?" I felt I should check.

"How could I?" People were always asking me such impossible questions. I really didn't have an answer, so I waited for her to explain whatever it was she had in mind. "As soon as the rehearsal was over,

I accompanied Cheryl to the front desk to see what we could do about getting Sindy thrown out."

"Yeah, she did!" Peter added, though he wasn't the most impartial witness. Luckily, there was a more reliable figure on hand to corroborate the account.

"That's right," Cheryl said, she'd been standing behind one of the giant flowerpots for some reason. "We talked the situation through with our security team for about half an hour and then left Gemma and Peter in reception while I delivered Mr Khatri the bottle of complimentary vintage champagne he'd requested."

So that explained how Cheryl knew what Ramesh had wanted to drink, at least, though it got us no closer to finding the killer.

As she can apparently be in all places at once, isn't it possible that our guest liaison assistant herself is responsible for Sindy's death?

Hmmm.... Nope.

"Thanks for your help, Gemma, Cheryl, angry Peter. If you think of anything that might help work out what really happened, please let me know."

They nodded and chattered in reply, and I continued on my journey through the excited crowds. There must have been two hundred people there, and I was glad that the killer had so thoughtfully carried out the crime that morning before the suspect list got out of control. I caught a glimpse of my favourite police officer in one corner beneath an olive tree. She was holding court between the two priests and looked more animated than usual.

"What's the nastiest case you've ever dealt with?" Father Michael demanded with more than a hint of excitement in his voice.

"Well..." Irons began. "There was the bloke we investigated who was murdered in his office with a fruit knife." The Hindu priest oohed and grimaced appreciatively as Irons detailed the gory bits. "In fact, Izzy found him. Oh and some chap got stabbed at a children's birthday party. That was another of Izzy's cases. I was called in to help when the film star Sammy Akerele collapsed. He was frothing at the mouth, in Piccadilly Circus." She must have remembered that I'd been on the scene then too, but she kindly refrained from revealing the fact.

"Ouch!" the Anglican grimaced. "Such wickedness. Such wickedness indeed."

"But tell us more about the birthday party." Dressed in a long, white shirt, with an orange scarf hung loosely about his neck, Raviji, the Hindu pujari, was just as engaged as his Christian colleague. "That sounds like a good one."

I signalled to Irons that I needed her attention, and she made her excuses. "Sorry, gentlemen, you'll have to give me one minute."

"Ohhhh…" The two priests looked disappointed and turned to the finger-food buffet for solace.

That sounds like a joke. An Anglican priest and a Hindu pujari walk into a wedding…

Well? What's the punchline?

Ummm… Give me a minute, I'll come up with something.

While my brain was busy with this essential task, I filled D.I. Irons in on everything I'd learnt from Gaz. "He contradicted himself and the evidence we saw in the room ten times over, but it still gave me an insight into why he would have confessed in the first place. Those three lads are about as loyal as friends get. They may be a bunch of certified cretins, but they've got that much going for them."

"Shame he wasn't the killer, though. The day is ticking by and, if we don't find the culprit soon, there's no way the wedding will go ahead. The guests are getting restless as it is." I think this was an overstatement as everyone there seemed to be enjoying the libations and there were few frowns or panicked faces on display.

"I can only assume that Holland will be letting each suspect go in order of importance, from least to most. Though I do find it strange that Emilio isn't down here yet."

"I might be able to explain that." She cleared her throat a little proudly. "I ran upstairs after I left to check on things. Emilio Green is having a rest in a room beside the bridal suite. Holland took him back to the crime scene to make the chap explain how he'd killed her, and the man keeled over at the sight of the blood. He's been unconscious ever since. Dr Danny had a look at him and he's fine, but he's sleeping off the shock."

I was about to ask whether she'd been able to see Patricia, and what was happening with the other suspects, when one of them walked into the atrium.

"Perhaps you were wrong about the order of the suspects," Irons said, pointing across to the entrance. "If I had to pick a culprit, the mother of the bride would still be top of my list."

Julia Green looked as composed as she ever did. There was not a single hair misaligned on her head, and, despite everything that had occurred, her dark eye makeup hadn't run or smeared in the time she'd been away. Of all our suspects, she was the one I was most curious about. I wanted to sprint across the room to her but, halfway there, someone beat me to it.

"My dear Julia," Deidre sang, her face and voice vacillating between excitement and nerves. "I'm so glad they let you go. What on earth went on up there?"

Julia did not reply. As I closed the space between us, she waited for a black-waistcoated waiter to glide past and helped herself to a glass of champagne. She immediately knocked it back in four large gulps.

"Please tell me, dear. Is everything alright?"

"Yes, yes, Deidre," she finally responded in a lifeless voice. "Everything is perfectly fine. The police asked me what happened, and then let me go."

Presumably unconvinced by her friend's statement, Deidre began speaking incredibly fast. "I'm so sorry that I talked such nonsense up there. I don't know what came over me. I just couldn't stand the thought of you or Patricia getting into trouble, and all of this being ruined."

Deidre looked around the elegant hall and spotted me in the crowd a few metres away. She held me in her gaze, and Julia soon turned to see what she had noticed.

"I need to talk to you," I said without hesitation. I couldn't get the idea out of my head that every word Patricia's mother had uttered was a lie.

"This is my daughter's wedding," she replied, her voice as cold as a Himalayan peak. "I intend to catch up with family and old friends. This isn't the moment to dwell on misfortune."

Her face was so emotionless that she looked like a robot or a heavily botoxed celebrity. With her lips pursed together, she held the stem of her glass so tight that it looked as though she wanted to strangle it.

I tried again. "If you talk to me, then maybe there'll still be a wedding to celebrate."

She didn't say another word as she turned to leave the room. I wasn't sure at first if she wanted me to follow, but she threw a glance over her shoulder, and I rushed to catch up. Deidre kept step with me, her stubby legs speeding along like the flippers on a wind-up bath toy.

Apparently everyone there knew the hotel better than I did. Julia turned right along the corridor, then left and left again to lead us to a large, comfortable library with great beams of light crashing through tall windows into the otherwise shady space. I find it hard to enter rooms with lots of books in without having a good browse, but I managed to resist and asked my first question.

"Didn't the police believe you?"

"I beg your pardon?" Despite her continental upbringing, she sounded terribly British when her temper was up. "I spoke to D.I. Holland about what happened and, with the interview concluded, he let me return to the party."

"But you told me you were the killer. He evidently didn't believe that, or he would have arrested you."

Standing alongside me, I could tell that Deidre would like to have defended her beloved friend, but Julia raised one hand to silence her. "The situation is more complex than you might realise. Do you know how my daughter suffered as a child because of Sindy Braithwaite?" I did not, and she wasted no time before explaining. "That girl, who claimed to be Patricia's best friend, bullied and belittled her for years. The only mercy was that, when the two of them left school, their paths diverged. It was only after Sindy screwed up her own wedding that she came back into our lives. I rue that day more than anyone knows."

She still hadn't told me whether she had admitted to D.I. Holland that she was not the guilty party. I could see I would have to change tack to get anything from her. "No one particularly liked Sindy. Even her boyfriend makes it sound as though he was tricked into dating her. And from everything I've seen this weekend, I believe you're right. Sindy was a schemer, and she obviously had a plan in mind. She dated an alcoholic with a bad attitude and brought him to the wedding in the hope he'd make a scene. I thought last night that she wanted to show up Patricia. That was the only thing that made sense until I realised that the man who had left her at the altar is here this weekend."

I took a moment to study Julia. Standing beside the marble fireplace with her arm on the mantlepiece, she was watching me in the large antique mirror on the wall in front of her.

"Patricia was a patsy," I began once more, "a pawn in Sindy's game. It's not enough to know what the manic bridesmaid was up to. Almost everyone here had a reason to resent her behaviour, so that won't tell us who killed her."

"Then why not accept that it was me?" Her words were hollow and distended, her reflection in the glass a picture of distress.

"Because you still haven't spoken to Patricia and, until you know whether she was responsible, lying to save her is the only thing you can do."

This was what finally broke her resistance. Julia fell to her knees on the thick Persian hearth rug and tears came to her pretty hazel eyes. "I just want to hear that she's okay. I didn't know what else I could do, and so I said that I was the killer."

Deidre went over to comfort her. Until this moment, it wasn't clear whether Julia had much love for her overly chatty companion, but the respect that passed between them was now apparent.

"It's not so easy to convince people you're a killer," the short, mousy woman said with a sad smile. I'd dismissed Deidre as the needy hanger-on to a much more sophisticated woman, but she'd realised something that several of the other suspects had failed to. "I gave it a go, but there was too much I didn't know. There were far too many details that I couldn't explain, and I had to admit that I was lying to help my friends."

Julia pulled away and, freeing her hand momentarily, wiped a tear from her cheek. "I know you did your best, Deidre, and I appreciate it more than I can say. I discovered the same thing as you did. D.I. Holland saw straight through my story. I didn't know where the sword had come from and couldn't explain how I'd followed Sindy after the rehearsal. In fact, as soon as the inspector started interviewing me, I fell to pieces."

They shared another supportive hug, and I felt guilty for pressuring Julia, but I couldn't give up now.

"So you don't know anything that could help me find the real killer?"

When the two women looked back at me again, they appeared calmer, perhaps resigned to the new reality we were facing.

"No more than you do," Julia replied. "I saw the body. I saw the knife and the blood and, for the briefest of moments before I made sense of the scene, I feared it was my daughter who was lying there. As soon as I realised that Patricia was okay, I could only think the opposite – that she was the killer, not the victim. I thought that, after all the years she'd put up with that beastly girl, she'd finally cracked."

Deidre rose to standing and offered her friend a hand up. Their outpouring of grief and frustration had acted as a watershed and, though there were still tears in Julia's eyes, a buoyant smile bloomed across her face. They sat down on a blue velvet sofa near the fireplace, and I pulled a chair up in front of them.

"I think there is one thing you can help me with." I was trying to sound confident, though, if the truth be told, I had rarely felt so cut adrift on a case. "You mentioned the way Sindy treated your daughter, and it's never made sense to me that she was allowed to be a part of the wedding. When I saw them together, Patricia acted like a hostage who'd been allowed out for air. There must be a reason that she tolerated Sindy for so long."

"I've always said she's too nice to everyone," Deidre put in. "I told her she had to stand up for herself, but you're right, Izzy. Patricia gave in to whatever Sindy wanted."

I could see now that Deidre meant well, but that didn't stop her getting in the way. She offered me a sherbet lemon from her alligator purse. I took one, obviously, as I have something of a sweet tooth, though the regular sucking noise did limit the impact of my interviewing technique.

"What about you, Julia?" I asked. "Is there anything that you can think of that might explain it?"

She was hesitant once more and bit her lower lip before replying. "I don't know anything for sure."

"But you have an idea?"

She looked up at the ceiling, as though praying for strength, then nodded her head just a fraction. "After they finished school, Patricia and Ramesh moved to London to go to university, but they didn't meet until they were in their final years. They still didn't get on, at first, and only ever saw each other because they were living in the same town and had friends in common."

Julia's flow was interrupted, and I didn't think she would explain any further. Luckily, Deidre was there to encourage her friend with a squeeze of the shoulder, and she eventually picked up her thread. "At about the time she got together with Ramesh, something happened between Sindy and Patricia that made them fall out. Sindy was with Toby then and I don't know if it had anything to do with him, or whether Sindy was being her usual repulsive self. All I know is that, after seeming incredibly happy to get together with Ramesh, Patricia fell into a sort of depression. It was only when she cut the woman out of her life entirely that she came back to her old self."

"So the two had nothing to do with one another until Toby cancelled the wedding?"

"That's right."

I considered the various players just then and tried to keep them in focus in my mind. "Were you or Patricia at the church that day?"

"Well, yes actually. I'm still friends with Sindy's parents. They lived around the corner from us for twenty years, so it was almost inevitable that we'd be invited. They would have been here today if the police hadn't sent someone to break the bad news."

I wondered if this was a tale of two weddings, with the events of the first still playing out a year later at the second. Before I could ask the question myself, Julia confirmed what I was thinking.

"You know, it's probably a silly thing to even mention, but I've often wondered whether Toby was in love with my Patricia. It would explain why he changed his mind at the last minute and decided not to marry the girl he'd been dating for over a decade."

Chapter Eighteen

As Julia said, the very idea that Toby saw Patricia at the church and, overcome with old feelings, broke off his engagement was patently absurd. He'd been with Sindy for years, had got down on one knee to ask her to marry him and made it all the way to the church, only to run off before she got to the altar. It's a soap-opera plot if I've ever heard one and I refused to believe it was true.

Except…

Well, don't blame me! This was not a normal case. For one thing, I couldn't inspect the evidence first hand. I couldn't hunt across the carpet for a chipped false tooth that would inevitably belong to the killer, or rifle through the dead woman's possessions. I couldn't even play the suspects off one another to find out what they did and didn't know. Under normal circumstances, I would have been up in the east tower interviewing them one by one to see who was lying and why. The truth is that D.I. *Haven't I Got Lovely Smooth Skin?* Holland wouldn't let me anywhere near the crime scene, and so I was jumping to dramatic conclusions to fill in the gaps.

On the plus side, there was one man who would know more on the matter. I just wasn't entirely sure where he'd gone. I left the pair of widows behind in the library… Okay, if I'm being honest, I had a quick look at a shelf filled with old Agatha Christie novels from the sixties. They were the Fontana Books editions with the creepy covers. I couldn't just walk past them like I didn't care; it would have been rude! But then I went straight off in search of Ramesh.

Out in the corridor, I rubbed an old lamp that was resting on top of a dresser and Cheryl magically appeared. Not really. She was already out there, but she didn't know where Ramesh was, and so I moved on. In case I haven't already made this clear, Hartford House was a big place with lots of rooms, and I think I looked in every one of them.

"What are you doing here?" Nigel was sitting at a small table just within the dining room.

"What are you doing here?" I asked back, having more or less forgotten that I'd brought a stand-in boyfriend with me.

The room was ready for the wedding banquet. All it needed was guests. The chairs were wrapped in white cloth, as though they were observing some sombre religious ritual. A mirror ball spun on the ceiling and bored-looking waiters milled about the place, occasionally straightening a fork or repositioning a wine glass.

"The timetable at the front entrance said we'd be eating at three o'clock, so here I am." Nigel didn't stop shovelling mini roast potatoes in his mouth as he answered.

"Didn't you hear that there's been a murder? They've changed the running order for the day."

He sat back in his seat to wipe gravy from his mouth with the back of his hand. "Yeah, I heard, but why should that bother me? I was promised food at three o'clock and so I came down here and demanded it. It only took about five minutes before the chef surrendered. Here's a life lesson for you, Izzy; if you want something, shout about it angrily enough and someone will get so tired of you they give in."

"That's great advice. Thanks, Nigel." I was tempted to leave him there, but it was my fault for bringing him and I felt sorry for the staff. "Why don't you come with me now? There are nibbles and drinks in the atrium, and then you can enjoy a big plate of potatoes all over again this afternoon."

He looked at the potatoes and then at me before relenting. "Go on then. I am a social animal and was feeling a bit lonely." This sentiment did not chime with my memories of him refusing to let me talk whenever he was playing a computer game during the seven hundred days of our relationship.

"So, a dead bridesmaid, eh?" he asked, as we walked along.

"Yep." I figured this was as much of an answer as the question warranted.

He sighed excessively loudly, as though the effort of walking down a corridor was simply too much. "And to think, I may have been one of the last people to see her alive."

"Why do you say that?"

"Because after you so callously left me to my own devices this morning, I went for a wander about the hotel and saw her parading about the place in a wedding dress. I could only assume that the woman was insane. Is there any chance she killed herself?"

There were so many things that were wrong with what he'd just said, but there was no time to correct them all, and I focussed on the most important one. "Absolutely impossible, unless she fell backwards onto a sword and then flipped over to lie on her front. But wait a minute. Where did you see her and at what time?"

He made a clicking sound with his tongue as he considered the details. "Must have been around half ten. I remember because the breakfast buffet had just closed after you failed to wake me early enough."

The good thing about spending time with Nigel was that every minute we were together reminded me why we'd broken up. "Did you speak to her?"

"How could I?" I had no idea how to answer this question. "She was having a screaming row with some guy at the time."

We were almost at the atrium by now, and I had to grab him by the lapels to get a clear answer. He actually looked a bit scared.

"Listen to me, Nigel, this could be extremely important so think very carefully. Who did you see Sindy with?"

He looked smug then. Well, smugger than normal. "One of those idiot friends of Ramesh's with the stupid names."

My whole body gasped at this – I think I was still in soap opera mode. "Gaz, Tog or Wazza?"

"How should I know? They've all got stupid names, and they're all idiots."

I thought about how I might rephrase the question. "Was he tall, short or dopey looking?"

"Short."

"Tog!"

"Great. Now let's get a drink." He did not appear to realise the significance of this revelation.

"Where did they go after you saw them?"

He irritably waved his head from side to side in irritation that I should ask such an entirely irritating question. "I don't know…" He swayed about grumpily. "I suppose… Yes, I think that she went up the stairs to where Patricia and her people are all staying, and Tog walked back towards the church."

"And where did you go after that?"

"I went to demand some Danish pastries from the kitchen. I only had to shout at them for a few minutes and they handed them over." A smile flashed across his face as he remembered the happy scene.

"Are you sure *you* didn't kill her?" I should probably have considered this possibility before.

"Would you like me more if I did?"

I gave him a long, hard stare. "I'm not attracted to murderers, Nigel."

"Well, you spend enough time chasing them. Are you sure that's not what turns you on?" He wiggled his eyebrows at me, and I wanted to be sick. "We all have our *thing,* Izzy. I have my foot and shoe appreciation, and you enjoy pretending you're in Scooby Doo's mystery gang."

"I don't have a thing for murderers!" It was lucky my brain was still puzzling over that stupid priest joke at this moment, or it might have pointed out a flaw in this response. "Also, it's best not to mention Scooby Doo with Ramesh around."

"Short of killing another guest, how else am I supposed to get you to notice me?" He looked terribly downtrodden and, for the first time in years, I felt a bit sorry for him. "Why did I come here this weekend if it was just to be ignored?"

I really didn't have time for this, but I suppose I owed him an explanation. "I told you already, I needed you to come here because…" Ahhh! I couldn't remember the lie I'd told him. Something about Ramesh being in danger or–

"You invited me this weekend because you didn't want your ex-boyfriend seeing you without a date and you knew that, if you brought me, the worst thing you'd have to put up with is me borrowing your footwear from time to time. You see, Izzy, that's my problem. Women always find me too inoffensive."

I had to laugh at this. It was simply too hilarious. "Inoffensive is not the word I would use for you, Nigel. And in terms of what I look for in a boyfriend, it would actually be quite high on the list. Who wants to date someone offensive?"

He had a sorrowful sniff, and I was surprised he was even capable of such emotion. "Thank you, Izzy. That means a lot. I have to confess that our breakup hurt me more than I've ever realised. This weekend has given me the opportunity to heal some old wounds. I hope that, when the next girl comes along, I'll have the confidence to be myself."

We had apparently entered a new dimension where everything was backwards. I was suddenly the unreasonable one between us, and he was gently sobbing. Sadly, there was no time to unpack this strange scene. I had a murder to solve and needed to get rid of him.

"I'm glad I could be of service... mate." That word was like a mouldy grape in my mouth. "Now get in that room and find the girl you're going to marry."

He leaned in for a hug and didn't even try to look down my dress. He really was a changed man. "Thank you, Izzy. I will never forget your kindness."

I smiled for his sake and patted him on the back as I sent him into the melee. The guests had been drinking for quite some time and the vol-au-vents and cocktail sausages weren't doing enough to soak up the alcohol. A DJ in one corner was already playing dance music and a limbo competition had started up with Ramesh's Uncle Kabir calling people forward to participate. Fernando was capturing every moment of it with his camera. My friend Dean was dancing cheek to cheek with his girlfriend, Fiona, and even the priests were having a twirl. It was like a wedding in reverse, and I wondered whether everyone would have sore heads if we ever got to the church.

I've got it! A priest, a Hindu pujari and a Rabbi walk into a cinema and start arguing. The Priest says...

Nope, it's still not quite right.

There was no sign of the groom, and so I left Nigel chatting with Lizzy and returned to the east tower. Ramesh was just where he was supposed to be, which was the last place I would have expected to find him. He sat looking miserable on the lowest step of the dark wooden staircase. Danny was there next to him for moral support.

"It's taking so long, Izzy," the groom complained. "It's like that time I tried to watch the Audrey Hepburn version of 'War and Peace'. Each minute lasts an eternity."

Danny gave me a cautious smile, and I sat down between them and put my arms around two of my favourite people.

"Investigations take time, Ramesh. You know that. I'm sure D.I. Holland is just being thorough and that, before long, Patricia will come down these stairs a free woman."

"I'm surprised they haven't taken her to the police station," Danny said, most unhelpfully, before realising his negativity wasn't what our friend needed to hear. "Or rather... it's surely a good sign that they haven't taken her to the police station. If they really thought she was responsible, they would have had her in cuffs."

I considered that they might also be keeping the various suspects around to *help with enquiries* until they were certain of the facts, but I didn't want to pile any more misery on Ramesh.

He started moaning all the same. "Nobody knows what it's like to be me. I'm going to have to get married through a glass screen at Holloway women's Prison."

"That seems unlikely as Holloway closed down several years ago and… oh, yeah… your best friend is a genius."

He turned to Danny. "Wow. Have you found the real killer?"

As a loving companion to a number of idiots, I often find myself having to punch them on the arm to force some sense into them. "Not him! Me."

Ramesh managed a smile at least. "I know, I know." He even had a bit of a chuckle at his unfunny joke. "So have you then? Found the killer, I mean."

"Well… no, but I'm getting close… I think. And I have some questions for you. What is Tog's relationship with Patricia like?"

He leaned backwards to stretch out on the steps behind him. "They get on alright. To be honest, they don't have much to do with one another."

"What about back when you were kids? Did they go out or anything like that?"

His eyes flicked about for a second, as though he was reviewing pages from their end of school yearbook (not that such things exist in Britain). "No, they barely knew each other then. Patricia couldn't stand us. She used to say I was immature and forever trying to be macho. She once got me in trouble with our maths teacher because–"

"Ra, that's too much information. Focus on your friend Toby."

"Right, got it." He took in a noisy breath and let it out again as a whistle. "Like I said, back then, we didn't have much to do with Patricia or her friends. It was only after school had ended that Tog got together with Sindy, and I met Patricia in London and we realised we didn't hate each other."

"Ahh, that's such a lovely story," that softy Danny exclaimed. "You should include that in your wedding speech."

I made a locking my mouth and throwing away the key gesture to Danny as I didn't want the groom getting mushy on me.

"Why are you asking all this, anyway?" Ramesh's soulful brown eyes widened, and he looked like a needy puppy.

"Just a hunch I had. I wouldn't have said anything, but your future mother-in-law suggested it too." My words dried up for a moment. I'd already said too much. "It's just… Well, we both wondered whether Toby was in love with Patricia. Julia thought that could have been the reason why he abandoned his own wedding."

Now he really had something to laugh about. "That's too funny, Iz. If you knew the pair of them like I do, you would never say such a thing. I've barely seen Toby utter two sentences to Patricia in the last decade."

"Which could be a sign that there's something between them," Danny once more said the first thing that came into his mind.

I didn't want to agree with him, but there was truth in his words. "Think very carefully, Ramesh. Is there any moment you can remember when the two of them were acting strangely around one another, or you caught them together unexpectedly?"

His smile had disappeared, and he tipped his head back to force himself to think. "No, it just isn't possible. Patricia can't be having an affair. She spends too much time away on business trips, for one thing."

Danny grimaced but succeeded in clamping his mouth firmly shut.

"I'm telling you, Izzy. Patricia is always too busy to be secretly in love with another man. There's never any emotion coming back the other way from Tog either. No lingering looks or dramatic sighs. They've hardly seen one another for years as it is, but this is a man whose idea of a good time is watching football and spending night after night at the pub getting bladdered with Gaz and Wazza. He's not really the type to harbour a secret longing."

As much as Ramesh was saying the very thing he wanted to believe, I had no proof that he was wrong. "Fine, it was worth a shot." In my head right then, I flicked through a list of all the gaps in the case that I hadn't managed to plug. "What about Sindy? Julia told me that she and Patricia hadn't been friends for years. What happened between them?"

"That was my doing, really." He pointed at himself with both thumbs. "When we got together, I convinced Patricia that we should spend less time with our friends from back home, and that she'd have to cut Sindy out of our lives if she was ever going to be happy."

"Which begs the question: why did Patricia let that stirrer anywhere near this wedding?"

This had apparently been puzzling my friend as well. He picked tiny specks of fluff off his suit and wouldn't look at me as he replied. "It's nothing. She's just too nice to everyone. Sindy turned up in our lives last year, just after we got engaged. She told us how lonely she'd been since Toby had dumped her, and so Patricia invited her to our engagement party and tried to be a good friend. I told her that letting Sindy be a bridesmaid would cause trouble, but there was no reasoning with her."

"Are you so sure that Sindy didn't have some secret she was holding over Patricia? It seems to me that her main reason for coming here was to get revenge on Toby. It explains the wedding dress and the passive-aggressive speech she gave last night, but not why your beloved just stood by and let it happen."

His eyes were like car headlights then, and I knew I'd overstepped the mark. "You're being ridiculous, Iz. You know Patricia; she can be a doormat sometimes and that's not great, but there's no sordid conspiracy at play. You've been reading too many mysteries."

I gasped at this before remembering that, for most people, this was not a major insult. "I'm sorry, Ramesh, but–"

He'd heard enough and shot up to his feet. "Patricia is a perfect angel. The only three people who might stake a claim to higher sanctity are Mother Teresa, Princess Diana and Cher! So watch your mouth, Izzy Palmer, because I won't hear another word against her."

Chapter Nineteen

He raced off down the corridor, and I would have gone after him to make amends, but Irons peeked down from upstairs to call my name. Fortunately, Danny did his gallant knight act and went to look after Ramesh in my stead.

"Don't worry about it, Iz," my former beloved called back over his shoulder. "I'll make sure he's okay. And, as I tried to say before, that really is a great dress."

There was no time to melt at his compliment; Victoria was shouting for me again. Nope, sorry. Calling her by her first name just feels wrong.

"Izzy, come up here quick," Irons (much better!) called down.

There were a number of police officers lounging about on the first-floor landing. I had to assume they were on their breaks, as they all had glasses of orange juice and mini sandwiches cut into triangles. I could only think that Cheryl had paid a visit to provide refreshments – that woman was in all places at all times.

"I'm not allowed up here," I reminded the detective as I grumpily climbed the stairs. I'm a moody person at the best of times, but the troughs and peaks of detective work make me even worse.

"You are now. I just had a word with Holland. He wants to see you in the bridal suite." She was awfully excited about this. She actually managed a smile. "He needs your opinion on something."

I tried to play it cool but couldn't help clapping my hands, much as an over-the-top teenager or Ramesh would. "It's about time. I've been kept away from the crime scene for too long. I felt all wrong, like a penguin in the South Pole."

"Don't you mean the North Pole?"

"Not with global warming," I countered, though, admittedly I'd got the places muddled.

A couple of the uniformed officers raised their appetisers towards me in a salute and I smiled and waved back. I even heard some impressed whispers as I passed.

"That's Izzy Palmer," one portly sergeant said in quiet reverence.

"The detective off the internet?" her skinny companion responded. "The one who solved those murders at the village fete?"

"That's the one." Her reverence disappeared, and she looked a little frightened. "She's a bloody giant."

No matter how many times in my life people look past my achievements (such as my hundred per cent murder-solving success rate) to focus solely on my height, I will never get used to it.

"He's in here," Irons said and pointed me towards a door at the end of a long corridor. It opened onto a comparatively humble double room next to the main gigantic suite.

"Ah, Miss Palmer, thank you for coming." The excessively handsome officer with the baby blue eyes was sitting at a desk writing notes. Patricia's cousin Emilio, the wedding planner, was still napping on a sofa, and Wazza was lurking by the door.

Holland stared at me without saying anything, and Ramesh's gangly friend sidled out of the room with a sheepish grin.

"I'm sorry if I was too hasty before," Holland continued once the suspect had gone. "In my interviews with the various players, I've been building up a picture of what happened. There are still a lot of question marks floating over the case and, I have to admit, there was one witness I overlooked."

"Oh, yes?" I assumed he was referring to the sleepy wedding planner. "Who's that?"

"You, Miss Palmer."

I don't know if it's because of the sexy drama teacher I had in high school, but I've always thought there was something rather charming about men calling me "Miss Palmer".

Seriously, brain, this would be a good moment for you to interrupt. If you're not careful, I'll start having saucy thoughts about Mr Cody's turtlenecks. Grrrrrrrrrr!

I had evidently been staring into space, and possibly dribbling, as Holland cleared his throat and said, "Is there anything I can get you before we begin? A glass of water, perhaps?"

In response, I slapped myself about the face. I might have looked insane doing it, but it was the only thing guaranteed to pull me back to reality. Such is the power of my lifelong crush on my drama teacher.

"No, thank you. I'm absolutely fine." We all knew that this was a lie.

I sat down in an armchair without being asked. Quiet and observant as ever, Irons stayed behind in the doorway.

"I'm sure you understand that this is not a formal interview. I'm just trying to get an idea of what could have led to the tragic killing here this morning. Though my initial suspicions rested with the bride, I now believe that the dead woman's boyfriend deserves closer investigation. He's previously served time for a violent altercation and has no alibi for the time of the killing. My colleagues have taken him to the station, but before I head there to question him formally, I thought I'd better have your perspective on things."

I laughed but then tried to cover it up by faking a sneeze, which somehow triggered a real sneeze so that I appeared to be suffering from some sort of terrible allergy.

Looking more concerned about me than anyone had in hours, Holland continued his speech. "You were one of the first at the scene of the crime, and we've all heard the stories of your past success. So I'd appreciate you sharing any insights you might have for me."

I crossed my arms in front of my chest. If he read it as a hostile gesture, then he was right. "I imagine I've come to the same conclusions you have, only half an hour later each time, as I've had to wait to speak to witnesses and examine evidence because you sent me away like a naughty girl."

Brain, if you can hear me, please come back. This is going to get filthy without you around to stop me saying things like "naughty girl".

"I don't think you're a naughty girl, Miss Palmer."

Ahhhhhh, stop. His voice was just so deep and rich, and I couldn't get the memory of Mr Cody's jumper out of my head.

A priest, a pujari and a Muslim cleric walk into a bar, and the priest says... No. No. No. That's useless!

You're really not helping!

"All I want is to hear your perspective on the case." He perched on his desk and waited for me to continue.

"I don't think Anfony is to blame," I began, the words forming on my tongue before I was sure that I believed them. "I know he's the one that everyone will suspect because he's got a dodgy past and a terrible personality but, for one thing, he's too obvious."

Holland was amused by this. "I'm sorry, 'too obvious'? That's not a problem we tend to encounter in the police. I've never had to let a criminal go because I found their fingerprints on a weapon or encountered CCTV footage of them stealing from a shop."

"That's not what I mean." I wondered how I could express my thoughts without mentioning murder mysteries or Dame Agatha. "You see, the thing is, Anfony would have been a fool to kill Sindy here today." I raced on as Anfony's intelligence was not the most reliable base to build an argument upon. "Even if he was upset at the way she'd treated him, there was no reason to kill her now. There were too many people around, too high a chance of getting caught and he could have waited until the weekend was over."

"That's an interesting point." He was more relaxed than he had been that morning and gave my point some consideration. "It's hardly enough to rule him out, though. And, if it wasn't Anfony, who killed Lusinda Braithwaite?"

I wasn't used to having to give my suspicions away before the end of the investigation. Like every good (fictional) detective, I liked to keep people guessing. As a police officer was asking, though, I didn't have much option but to talk. "Toby Gatling, or Tog to his friends. He's the guy I keep coming back to. He was engaged to Sindy and did a runner from the church on their wedding day. A good number of the suspects were at school together and there's plenty of history between them, but I haven't discovered anything as significant as what happened last year."

He was unconvinced. "I just spoke to Mr Gatling, and he couldn't reproduce the slightest detail of what happened at the scene of the crime. I dismissed his confession as proof that he was covering for a friend. Do you have any evidence that can link him to the murder, rather than a vague hunch?" He delivered all this in a complacent manner. It made me wonder whether, behind his smooth exterior, he was less confident than he wanted everyone to believe.

"No, because, to reiterate, you threw me off the crime scene and Toby has been up here with you ever since. I've been hamstrung to say the least." I could tell he wanted to chip in with his thoughts, but I wouldn't let him just yet. "What I can say is that, to the best of my ability, I've been able to rule out certain suspects who previously confessed."

"Oh, yes, and–"

"For one, the mother of the bride. Julia Green is entirely guiltless. Her only crime is loyalty to her daughter and, perhaps more seriously, wasting police time. She was the first to claim responsibility for Sindy's murder, and the one with the most obvious reason to do so. She has since retracted the confession, which, in itself, does not eliminate her from the inquiry, but she went off into the gardens after the wedding rehearsal. I do not believe she could have killed Sindy and escaped before her daughter arrived back up here."

"Anyone else?"

"Yes. Deidre O'Leary ruled herself out almost as soon as she confessed to the crime. Though her behaviour this weekend has been suspicious enough that I can't say for certain she isn't to blame. Oh, and Gaz… I don't know his surname, but Gaz is clearly lying to protect his friend Toby. When I spoke to him an hour ago, he contradicted himself a number of times and failed to show sufficient knowledge of the crime to be considered a serious contender."

"Contender, Miss Palmer? It's not a competition."

"Fine. I feel confident in saying that I have ruled out Gaz Whateverhisnameis as a suspect." I rattled these explanations off at great speed, and he frowned a little and nodded, as though appreciative of my efforts.

"So you believe that you've eliminated those three suspects from the inquiry?"

I stuck my hand out to point across the room without taking my eyes off D.I. Holland. "Those three plus Emilio Green. He only claimed to be the killer because he wishes he had the stomach to have murdered the woman who had been making his life so difficult for the last few weeks. I have it on good authority that he faints at the sight of blood, as you have clearly witnessed. While that could be testament to his fine acting skills, I think it's more likely that he's simply very squeamish."

I went through the list of suspects in my head and realised I'd missed out Wazza. The only information I had on him was that he wasn't at the rehearsal, and so wouldn't have known of Sindy's outburst. To make an extremely complicated situation just the tiniest bit less complicated, I decided not to mention him.

"There is one person you appear to have overlooked." Still standing up with his legs crossed at the ankle and his pert buttocks resting just a fraction on the desk–

Izzy! Snap out of it, my brain would normally have contributed. In its continuing absence, I would have to police myself.

"Oh *really*?" Why did everything I said sound as though I'd lifted it from an erotic movie from the eighties?

"That's right. You seem to have forgotten the woman whose fingerprints are on the murder weapon who you discovered standing over the body."

"Patricia found her friend dead and did something foolish; it could happen to anyone." I moved on quickly before he contradicted me. "Have you come across a significant reason why she would have wanted to kill Sindy just hours before she was supposed to get married?"

He supported his weight on his hands behind him and raised his chin belligerently. "Not as such, though she's already confessed that she did not get on well with the deceased."

"No one liked Sindy. She was the classic guest who every wedding can do without. And besides, Patricia is clever. If she was going to murder her head bridesmaid, she would have done it before she put on her wedding dress. She would have planned out the crime, not hacked the poor woman up at the last minute."

He took a step forward and the force of this sudden movement seemed to propel his response towards me. "Unless Miss Braithwaite was holding something over her that could have endangered the wedding itself."

There was that idea again. Three different people had now reached the same conclusion. In fact, anyone who knew Sindy must have questioned how she came to be head bridesmaid, or even garnered an invitation for that matter.

"Has Patricia suggested any such thing?"

"Well… no." He looked less sure of himself for the first time. His shoulders drooped, and his determined expression was suddenly absent.

"So who else could have been involved?"

If I'd been in charge of the case, this would have been the moment for one of my helpful assistants to pull out a flip pad and pens to write up some always helpful lists. Suspects, Evidence and Hypotheses is the name of the game, and I was hopeful that D.I. Irons would step forward with the necessary equipment, but it wasn't to be. Irons stayed right where she was, so I had to do it all in my head.

Patricia Green

~~**Julia Green**~~

~~**Emilio Green**~~

Anfony LeQuinn

~~**Gaz (Gary? Gareth? Garfield?) Whateverhisnameis**~~

Wazza (I should probably talk to him at some point)

Toby "Tog" Gatling

~~**Deidre O'Leary**~~

I didn't have particularly high hopes of solving the case, considering that I still hadn't learnt all the suspects' names.

Holland soon commenced his own account. "Along with the frankly bizarre number of suspects who have laid claim to the murder, I had my constables look into the other members of the wedding party. They spoke to one of the bridesmaids…" He consulted a note on the desk behind him. "…one Gemma Robins. She was particularly vocal in her distaste for the deceased. In fact, she was so aggressive on the matter that I talked to her myself. She told me that she should have been the head bridesmaid and that Sindy had usurped her. It turns out she was disappointed not to have been the one to wield the sword, but she stopped short of confessing to the crime and, without any forensic evidence, we've no other reason to suspect her."

"I spoke to her too and she has an alibi. What about the groom?" I was well aware that Ramesh being the killer was beyond the rules of normal existence, but Holland couldn't have known this, and I thought I should take the time to point it out. "Have you considered the possibility he was involved?"

"We spoke to him, of course, but he was getting ready around the time of the murder and a photographer took some photos of his preparations. Plus, no one reported seeing him out of his suite all morning, so it seems a safe bet he's not to blame. He put forward his cats as further witnesses to his whereabouts, but I don't think we'll need to talk to them."

"If you knew some of Ramesh's more superstitious habits, you'd realise that the very idea of him going up to the bridal suite on his wedding day is categorically impossible."

"Is there anyone else we could be missing?" His voice was softer than normal, and his manner was far more collaborative than when I'd entered.

"Including staff, there were over a hundred people at the hotel at the time of the murder. But in my opinion, the main group who came to the suite after the body was found are our likely options."

He raised his eyebrows at this. "It's unusual to have a case with such a small, yet focused group of suspects. I've never come across anything like it before."

"Really?" I was as surprised as I sounded. "I find they're almost always like that."

He ignored me and focused on more important matters. "What that then means is that the killer returned to the scene of the crime, having got away without being spotted. Why would anyone do that?"

I had a genius response in mind but decided not to reveal it just yet. "How about you take me back there, and I'll give you a clue?"

Chapter Twenty

I knew that Holland would come around in the end. It must have been my feminine wiles. Perhaps I should always wear fancy dresses to investigate crimes. That or the pyjamas. It was a tough choice.

We waited for the white-suited officers to finish taking photographs and removing evidence from the bridal suite, then Holland handed me some shoe protectors and gloves.

"I bring my own," I said rather suavely, before remembering that I wasn't wearing my normal clothes and hadn't brought a bag. "Well, I usually do." I accepted his offer and slipped them on.

He cut a line into the suite, but I hung back to check a theory. "Clearly, Sindy knew the killer." I was standing by the door, which had been propped open by the police. It had a magnetic card slot and, by the look of things, a self-locking mechanism. "She must have opened the door to let her assailant in."

Irons came to see what I'd found. "Nice try, but there's a button on the back to block the catch. The other bridesmaids reported that the apartment was kept unlocked. They were all staying here last night and there weren't enough cards to go round."

I felt sulky again. I should have remembered that I'd got into the suite without a key. If only I had a functioning internal monologue to warn me about such things! But no. My brain was still working on a stand-up routine in the hope of becoming the next Bob Hope.

I shrugged off my first failure and, on entering the suite, had a question for D.I. Handsome… Holland! I mean D.I. Holland.

"So there were no other fingerprints on the sword?"

"Just Patricia Green's."

"Don't you think that's strange?"

His eyes sparkled with curiosity. "In what way?"

"Well, Ramesh must have held it at some point. He brought it with him to the wedding. And Emilio had been looking after it, so it's odd that you found no one but Patricia's prints. Surely someone wiped the handle before she touched it."

"Izzy Palmer, you clever duck," Irons practically purred, though I wasn't entirely sure that being compared to waterfowl was a compliment.

Holland was less impressed. "If we can think of such things, then so can the killer. Miss Green could have done it herself to implicate a third party. It wouldn't hold up in court."

Infuriated by his tone, though excited by his quick thinking, I had no reply for him. I walked through the small entrance parlour and into the lounge where Sindy's body had previously lain. I stopped at the point where most of the suspects had congregated, as it was only Patricia and Deidre who had gone beyond the two armchairs that divided the room. The low table was still covered with cards and presents from the night before. There wasn't an inch of space on it and so Gaz's claim that he'd found the sword there held even less weight.

Standing where I was, I could see the white roses and lilies that had been scattered across the carpet. I noticed that none of them were bent or broken, so there was no sign that Sindy had smashed the bouquet around the assailant's body, not that they would have made a particularly good weapon. I spotted the space on the far shelf where the figurine must have been plucked from, but what I couldn't see from that particular location were the blood-stained overalls. They were well hidden beneath the elegant leather sofa, and I had to wonder once more what had driven Deidre to look there.

Though desperate to defend her friends, it seemed odd that she would have thought to look for clues in just the right spot. I had only noticed them on bending down to inspect the body, but she had traversed the room in the hope of finding something which would testify to her guilt. Was she just lucky? Or had she known where to look?

I walked between the armchairs and crouched down once more to see sticky-tape crosses in place of the bloody garments. The statue of the lovers was also missing, and this triggered another question in the part of my brain that wasn't busy with other things.

"Did forensics find any fingerprints on the ornament that was under the table?"

Holland bent down to join me. "No. Why do you ask?"

I let out a breathy sigh. "I was hoping that the killer had pushed it away with their fingers when Sindy threw it. I thought perhaps it might rule out Patricia."

"Sorry, can't help you there. Though it's not a good idea to look at a crime scene and try to prove an existing theory. I know you want

Miss Green to be innocent for your friend's sake, but you should let the evidence do the talking."

He was right, but I wasn't going to tell him that. "Were there any significant footprints in this part of the room? Obviously, the women would all have been in here before Sindy died, but this was the bridal suite, and Emilio was the only man with a good reason to come inside."

"Nope. Nothing unexpected, I'm afraid." He was good at sounding sympathetic when he tried.

Irons had let us work but chimed in now with an interesting consideration of her own. "The missing scabbard is a puzzle. You have to wonder why it was taken from the room."

I considered this for a moment, then stood up because my knees were getting achy. "Unless it was never in here in the first place." It was a new idea, but it seemed to make sense. "Perhaps the killer unsheathed the sword outside and left the scabbard in the hall. When they came back out again, they picked it up so that no one would notice the sword was missing."

"We need to know where it is now, then." Holland spoke very determinedly, though I hoped the constables would already have been scouring the hotel. "I'll get someone on it."

"There's an even bigger question we haven't answered," I continued. "Those staff overalls wouldn't have done much to cover the killer's clothes. If they're the kind I've seen the housekeeping staff at the hotel wear, they barely go down to the knees. So either our culprit took the risk of blood getting onto them, or they wore something else underneath."

"She wasn't killed with a gun though," Irons contested. "When you stab someone through the abdomen with a sword, the blood would mainly go out through the exit wound. There wouldn't be great gushes of the stuff unless you pull the weapon back out again."

I peered at my trusted companion, unsure exactly how she knew such details.

"What?" She wore an offended expression. "I read a lot of true crime magazines. It helps me with my work. Not that I had many murders to deal with until you came along." Her sensitive tone disappeared, and she gave me a wink.

I managed to think up an answer. "Either way, the killer presumably wouldn't have known that and clearly tried to protect their clothes. But then, why did they take the overalls off in here? Why not wear them outside? There's a high chance that forensics could turn up evidence from them if they came into contact with their clothes."

Holland looked stumped. If he hadn't been so thoroughly decent letting me in there, I might have pointed out that, as the supervising officer on the case, he should have been the one to notice such a discrepancy.

"That has to be it." I felt increasingly sure of myself now. "I think the killer was wearing something underneath and happened to come across the overalls on their way here. Lady and gentleman, those overalls are, what we call in the private detective business, a red herring."

"Alright, Izzy. There's no need to be smug," Irons said, and Holland implied with an eye roll. "Does it bring us any closer to identifying the killer?"

"Urmmm… maybe?"

Holland laughed at me for the first time. "Well, that's encouraging. I'll tell my chief inspector that we will, at some point, know who's responsible for a crime that is already all over the internet. *Head Bridesmaid Loses Her Head*, no doubt some lazy hack will be writing somewhere. I reckon my bosses will give me a holiday if I tell them that Izzy Palmer is confident she'll eventually solve the case."

He wasn't quite finished. "You still haven't told me why the killer would have come back here. I know some sickos get a thrill from these things, but this seems different. To return before the police had even arrived is foolhardy, to say the least."

"I don't agree. I think it was very clever. For one thing, if they'd shed skin cells or left a fingerprint somewhere, it could be explained by their presence here after the act. But it also meant that the culprit could listen in to everyone else's reaction. It gave them the chance to admit to the crime and blend in with the other idiots who had come up here."

Irons crossed her arms and regarded me from another angle. "So you're saying that one of the suspects who confessed did so in order to hide their guilt?"

"I know that might sound like a contradiction, but it's really not. The killer didn't necessarily come back here to admit to the crime. But when the others claimed to be the killer, they did the same so as not to stand out. Anfony was the only one who denied it, and every last person in the room assumed he was to blame."

Holland went back to the entrance parlour to scan the scene once more. I assumed he was putting himself in the position of the killer, just as I had. "Yes, that's very clever. I think I've underestimated the person we're dealing with."

"We all have. And that's why I need to speak to Toby Gatling and Patricia too, when you finish with them."

"Patricia was the first person I interviewed," he explained, a confused look on his face. "As far as I'm concerned, she could have gone downstairs ages ago. We certainly don't have enough to charge her, and I wasn't going to ruin her wedding if I could help it."

"Then where did she go?"

Chapter Twenty-One

I found the bride-to(hopefully)-be locked away in her mother's bedroom on the floor below. She really didn't want any company.

"You have to let me in," I shouted through the door, though I was struggling to think of a reason why. "I want to help you, Patricia, but you have to talk to me." Ten seconds of silence followed, and so I tried again. If there's one thing a woman wants on her wedding day when her childhood friend has just been murdered and she foolishly handled the weapon, it's a nosy woman with a love of Agatha Christie. "The police don't think that you killed Sindy, if that's what you're worried about."

"Go away, Izzy. I just want to be alone." She sounded as though she'd been crying, so at least the trance-like detachment I'd previously witnessed in her had passed.

"You know I'm not going to leave until you talk to me. I am famed for my persistence, Patricia, and rarely give up on things. I watched every season of 'How I Met Your Mother', even after it stopped being funny."

There was another brief hush before her faint voice crept under the door once more. "I don't have the energy to talk to anyone. I'm sorry, but you'll have to tell Ramesh that I can't marry him. It's all gone wrong."

"No, nope. No chance. You're going to tell him that you will love, honour and whatever they say these days instead of 'obey' as it's not the ninth century anymore." I was hoping this would be enough to get her to open the door, but when there was still no joy, I tried one last time. "I know you didn't kill your friend. I'll do all the talking; you can just nod and shake your head."

I counted to twenty and was about to give up when there was a rustle and a click, and the door swung open.

"I suppose you can come in, but don't expect much from me." Still dressed in that beautiful white gown, her hair was dishevelled, and her light brown skin looked swollen around the eyes. She turned to go, and I caught the heavy door just in time to follow her.

The room was at the corner of the building and had two big windows overlooking the river that wound through the estate. The sun was high in the sky. It was still the perfect day for a wedding, and I had to make Patricia see that. The line between my role as detective and best woman had become blurred.

"I don't want to make you feel guilty," I began, as Patricia threw herself on the bed and her skirt fanned out around her. "But Ramesh is downstairs feeling pretty bad about life. It isn't the murder that's upset him or even the delay to the wedding, it's not being able to talk to you. He's already told me that he would marry you in prison if he had to. Do you realise what he's going through?"

She'd buried her face in the pillow and wouldn't look at me. "I told you, I don't have the energy to reply."

"Well, we both know that won't stop me."

I would have sat on the bed next to her, but there was no room, and so I balanced on the night table. That was far too high, and it would have been hard to show her much sympathy as I peered down menacingly from a metre above her, so I pulled an ottoman over and sat next to the bed.

"I don't think you killed Sindy. I think you saw the sword in her and pulled it out, but she was already dead when you got there."

Her head suddenly turned, and she locked her teary eyes on mine. "She would have ruined the wedding. That was her plan all along and, if I'd had the courage, I would never have answered her messages when she got in touch after her own disastrous day in church." She was a poorly printed photocopy of the Patricia I knew, and there was panic in her every word.

"So you killed her? Is that what you're saying?" I think I managed to put across just how hard I found this to believe. "Are you throwing your name in the hat like all the others?"

"Sure, why not?" She enjoyed a moment of well-deserved self-pity. "This day could hardly get any worse."

"Well, it could actually." I had to slow things down, as the conversation wasn't going how I'd hoped. Patricia had always been the strong, reliable one who was, almost inexplicably, marrying a loveable lunatic. I'd never seen such pessimism in her. "You could hide in this room until all your guests leave and not take the opportunity to marry the man you unquestionably adore. You could let Sindy and her killer beat you."

All I heard back was another sniff and a sigh, but I was not dissuaded from my task. "I don't know who's responsible for what happened this morning, but I refuse to believe that you are to blame. The only incriminating factor is your excessively tolerant behaviour towards Sindy, and I imagine that you'll be able to clear that up right now."

I waited. I didn't even put a question to her, as it seemed like such a logical decision for Patricia to explain her reasoning that it wouldn't need any prompting. Inevitably, I was wrong.

"Oh, come on! If anyone thinks you were involved in the killing, it's because you snapped and couldn't take Sindy's manipulation anymore, but I know that's not true. I think she had something over you, which is why you let her get away with so much. There's no way you would have put your wedding at risk by grabbing a sword and running her through. You're cleverer than that for a start."

A cold response came straight back to me. "Who's been talking?" She had cycled through every possible emotion and landed on pure fury. "Come on, Izzy. With Sindy dead, only two other people knew what happened. So who told you about it? Was it Gemma?"

"No one told me," I answered, a little defensively. "I worked it out. It wasn't particularly difficult considering that you spent most of last night looking like a shop dummy when you should have been luxuriating in the joy of the occasion. And besides, I haven't discovered what she knew about you, but it's obvious that she used it in order to become a bridesmaid."

She barely let me finish speaking before she fired another shot in my direction. "So Ramesh still doesn't know anything? You promise no one told him?"

I took my time replying because I was having trouble imagining what had got into her. "If I haven't worked it out yet, you can be sure that Ramesh hasn't got a clue."

"Good." She nodded, as though to convince herself that this was the case. "But the wedding is still off. You're his best friend. You'll have to let him down gently."

My head was spinning by now. "Seriously, Patricia? I have no idea what's going on here, but I was with you at the cake tasting. You allowed your fiancé to have quite the largest, ugliest wedding cake I have ever seen and there was no doubt in my mind that you loved him beyond all comprehension. I saw the way you looked at him last night when we arrived. I recognised the sheer relief on your face that he was there because it's the exact same expression that Ramesh wears whenever he sees you."

"It's all wrong..." she uttered, and her words faded away to nothing.

"So, no. I will not tell your fiancé that the wedding is off," I shouted this so fiercely, I almost made myself jump. "For one thing, it would eat through him like acid, and I'd have to spend the rest of my life handing him tissues and watching old musicals to make him feel better. And, for another, I know that's not what you want."

Sniff sniff sniff, sob sob sob.

"I'll tell you what I'll do instead." My voice falling softer, I waited to have her attention. "I'll find the real killer whilst the two of you get ready for the ceremony. The guests are still here. The priests are having a wonderful time and will be only too happy to do their thing. Today is your wedding day, and all the heartache and suffering that the pair of you have gone through will make what's coming next even sweeter."

Chapter Twenty-Two

Her sob sob sob turned into ha ha ha, which admittedly led to a bit more crying as the moment washed over her. At least she managed to sit up on the bed. "Oh, Izzy. I'm just like Ramesh; I can't disagree with you for long." To my surprise she launched herself forward to wrap me in a hug. "You've always had a strange power over us. I don't know why that is, but I'm glad that you're here. Even if it all goes to hell and the killer storms the wedding, thank you for trying."

I had to smile myself then. "I told you, by the time you walk down the aisle, we'll know the name of the killer. Whoever it is, they won't be sitting in the pews because D.I. Holland will have already taken them off in handcuffs. Now tell me what was really going on between you and Sindy."

After this spike of positivity, her eyes dropped to the floor, and she seemed to shrink before my eyes. The gulf between her will to put things right and the horrifying reality of actually having to do it was immense and, at first, she could do nothing but whimper.

"I hmmmm… but uuuhhhhhh, do you understand?"

"Nope, sorry, I haven't a clue what you just said." I jumped off the springy stool and went to sit next to her. It was easier said than done as she had a ridiculously wide dress on. It took some careful manoeuvring of the fabric before there was space. This made me wonder how many brides had ended up in hospital with broken noses after tripping on their trains. "Try again, and maybe this time you could use actual words. English preferably. Or Spanish at a push, but I don't speak mumbling bride too well."

She let out an airy note of laughter, rolled her shoulders and started again. "You probably know most of the story. Sindy and I were at school together." I hadn't expected her to give me such a detailed response, but I wasn't about to interrupt. "We met when we were about five years old, and she gave me a lot of confidence. Even back then, she was the bold, popular one, and being with her brought me out of myself. But as we got older, she changed. I saw real cruelty in her. She'd pick on the nerdy kids, and she was always teasing the boys. Sindy used to drive poor Tog mad with her bullying, but Ramesh would stick up for his friends, and she never got one over on him."

She looked out through the window, and I knew she was thinking about her heartbroken fiancé. I'm not psychic; it was the only thing that made sense at that moment. "I never stood up to Sindy the way he could, which made me jealous, and I liked him even less. I wished I could be brave like Ra, but I never was. Sindy controlled me; all I cared about was making it through school and going to university so that I could get away from her."

She took a pained breath before continuing. "She stayed behind in Watford and did a course to become a hairdresser. I think she resented the fact I'd managed to get into a decent university and knew what I wanted to do with my life. We only saw each other during the holidays after that, and I could just about bear her. With Ramesh gone from our lives, she hooked up with the second most popular boy from our school. Toby Gatling was told that he was going to be Sindy's boyfriend and, like me, he lacked the courage to argue back. I crossed paths with Ramesh in London that same summer and, a year later, we started going out. He convinced me that I didn't need Sindy in my life, sapping my confidence and making me feel worthless, so I simply stopped replying to her messages and answering her calls."

"You ghosted her," I said, to translate the event into modern parlance.

"Yep." She shook her head in disbelief as she recalled an event from a decade earlier. "To be honest, I never thought it would work. But with the city between us, Sindy lost the influence that she had over me. I'd been through a difficult period in my life, and I could never have broken free without Ramesh's help. I wish that had been the end of it, but even all these years later, when she invited me to her wedding, I was too polite to say no."

She came to a halt, and I knew she'd need some encouragement to continue, so I reached over to the coffee table to get her one of the little cakes (plus two for myself) that I had no doubt Cheryl had put there. She nibbled on the pink fondant fancy with a mischievous smile on her face. When there was nothing left but the wedding-themed cake case, she commenced the second half of her tale.

"Ramesh was still in contact with the boys, of course. If anything, he'd seen more of Sindy than I had over the years, but we both knew that he was immune to her charms. Gaz, Tog and Wazza are alright when they're sober, and even though Ramesh could never be himself around them, they managed to stay friends."

I got the impression that she was stretching the story out to avoid getting to the nasty part, but I tried not to put any more pressure on her than she already felt. "What happened between Tog and Sindy? Why didn't he go through with the wedding?"

She pulled her lips into her mouth for a moment before answering. "Ramesh would know more about all that than I do. I think the truth is that Gaz and Wazza tried to convince Tog not to marry her, but the more they said against Sindy, the more determined he was to go through with it. I've seen it before in other toxic relationships my friends have been in. The last thing the wronged party needs is a list of all their partner's faults. They already know all the bad stuff because they live with it every day. What would help is a solution, a way out, but only they can provide that."

"And Toby's way out came at the very last moment at the church?"

"The *very* last moment," she repeated. "I know that Ramesh had talked to him on the morning of the wedding to make sure he wanted to go through with it, but he made it to the altar. Tog stood there in his smart suit, with his buddies at his side, looking both horrified and weirdly excited by what was about to happen. The word came that Sindy's car had arrived. The organist started playing the 'Wedding March', and Tog realised it wasn't too late and went shooting out of the church through the vestry.

"Everyone laughed. The whole congregation was in fits because we thought he was playing a prank; it was just Tog's style. But when Sindy came into view, we couldn't stop. I don't know if you've ever seen a hundred and fifty people laughing their heads off as the bride takes her first steps down the aisle, only to realise that her fiancé isn't there, but it is not a pretty sight."

Despite the fact she'd been murdered in a particularly nasty fashion, I'd had surprisingly few chances to feel sorry for Sindy that day, but this was one of them. "That's horrible… No matter what else she did, she didn't deserve such humiliation. What do you think it was that made Toby run away though?"

"I suppose he realised that he was about to tie himself to a despicable person for the rest of his life. She'd never changed, you know? She was still the same catty girl she'd always been – still enjoyed making the people around her feel small. Ramesh will tell you about all the times she showed Toby up in front of their friends but, to begin with at least, the nastier she was, the more he needed her. As I said, she was toxic; that's just the word for it."

I was caught up in Patricia's version of events and pushed us on to the final stage of the story. "And after the wedding? How did you become friends again with Sindy?"

She tucked her messy black fringe behind her ear and tried to concentrate on my question. "I… It was my own fault. I tried to comfort her at the church. It was amazing how her supposed friends all disappeared. It was as if people had only gone to the wedding for the free food or to see what a train crash it would be. Even her family didn't look as though they knew what to say, and so I went to talk to her."

She looked up at the ceiling, unable to believe what she was saying as a glossy sheen coated her pretty brown eyes. "I couldn't just ignore her suffering. I couldn't be so heartless as to watch her bawl her eyes out without doing anything about it. She'd collapsed on a bench at the front of the church, and I knelt down and whispered as softly as I could that everything would be all right in the end."

This was when Patricia's tears truly came. She sputtered over the last few words of her sentence and then the normally collected businesswoman became a blubbering mess. "I lied to her. I mean, I didn't know it at the time, but that's what I was doing. I said everything would be okay and that, if Toby didn't want to marry her, he was the wrong man entirely. I told her that she'd meet someone better, and she put her arms around me and said, 'Thank you'. She said it over and over, and I felt so guilty that I'd let our friendship die. I convinced myself that she really wasn't so horrible, and that all she needed was a sympathetic friend."

I raced to the bathroom to get tissues then but couldn't find any and returned with a long, inelegant piece of toilet paper. It did the job and, with a whisk of her hand, she was back to her beautiful best.

"A week later, Sindy rang me up. It sounded like she was in a dark place, and I couldn't just abandon her. We met in London and spent the whole night reminiscing about our school days. It was nice to catch up and there was none of the bitchiness I'd been expecting. But just as we were about to head home, she said something that I hadn't seen coming. She reminded me of something I did when we were younger. She said it in a very casual, off-hand manner, but I knew exactly what she meant. Ramesh had just asked me to marry him by dressing up as a Roman centurion and re-enacting a scene from 'Ben Hur'. It's my favourite film, so I obviously said yes. And I got the clear impression from the way Sindy spoke that she wanted an invitation to the engagement party in Watford."

"The one Ramesh said it wasn't worth me going to when, in truth, it was because he'd been living a double life ever since he moved to London?"

"That's the one." She said with a smile, apparently failing to notice my glum tone. "I didn't understand it at the time, but Sindy was using me from the start. It wasn't because I'd been nice to her that she wanted to be my friend again. She was obsessed with getting even with Toby and couldn't think of another way to be in the same room as him. She showed up at the party at my future in-laws' house looking like an extra from 'Pretty Woman' and proceeded to do some 'Dirty Dancing' with the drunken weirdo she'd dragged along with her."

You can tell that someone has spent too long with Ramesh when they start casually dropping old romantic movies into the conversation for no reason.

"So whose dog did Anfony try to kick?" I'm sorry. I had to ask.

"It was my niece's puppy. A little sausage dog. And the poor thing looked so shocked."

I stuffed another cake in my mouth. It was good. But was it five-star-country-hotel good? Along with that pressing question, I had another for Patricia. "Why did Sindy bring a guy like that to your party?"

Her eyes wandered about the room to a bag hanging on the back of the door. "I don't know, I really don't. But then I've never been good at guessing what went on in her head. Perhaps she wanted to make Toby think that she'd lost her mind."

"How did he react? Presumably, it was the first time they'd seen each other since the wedding."

She hesitated then, as though she was afraid of getting good old Tog into trouble. "He took the whole thing pretty badly and dealt with it the only way he knew how. He got blind drunk and challenged Anfony to a fight. Luckily, Anfony was even more inebriated and ended up swinging his boot at the dachshund instead."

I had to suppress a laugh then, as this was actually quite funny… though not for the dog.

Presumably Patricia didn't hear as she continued in the same serious voice. "After that, I finally stood up for myself and told Sindy that there was no way I'd let her come to the wedding if she brought that psychopath with her. A couple of weeks later, she told me they'd broken up and so she remained a bridesmaid."

Her voice fell quiet again, and she looked at me like she felt she had to explain herself. "I didn't want her here; you must realise that. But I thought that if I involved her in planning the wedding, then it might help calm her down. And it worked for a while, it really did. She stopped getting drunk every night, barely talked about Tog anymore and, though she drove Emilio up the wall, one of the bridesmaids nearly quit, and my friends still won't forgive me for–"

Her explanation had been increasing in pace and volume and so she caught herself and slowed back down. "What I mean is that she was never easy-going, but I had no idea she was planning to sabotage the wedding. I knew she was bringing a boyfriend, but it was only last night that I found out it was Anfony. Then she turned up to the rehearsal in her own wedding dress, and I can't say I didn't think about murdering her because I genuinely did. If that was just the practice, I had to wonder what she had planned for the wedding itself."

She finished the sad tale of Sindy Braithwaite, but there were plenty of scenes she'd skipped over. Rather than snapping at her with a hundred more questions, I allowed a brief burst of silence to fill the room.

She must have known that everything she'd just told me added up to a motive for killing Sindy. "Wait, I didn't mean that I was glad she was killed, or that I was the one who did it. All I was trying to say was that–"

"Relax, Patricia." I put one hand on her shoulder. "I told you, I've never believed you were to blame. Just because you're better off with Sindy out of the way, that doesn't make you the killer. But there are still some things you haven't told me and, if you really want to clear your name, you'll have to trust me with the secret that Sindy knew."

She looked so faint then, I thought she might collapse back onto the bed. "I can't, Izzy. You don't understand, but I can't tell you that."

I grabbed her arm to stop her from falling. "You can trust me. I promise I won't tell anyone." There was something else I had to say, even though I wasn't sure it was true. "I'd never tell Ramesh."

Patricia shut down again. For a little while, she'd been back to her usual breezy but determined self, but as soon as I set this ultimatum, she disappeared once more.

"I don't understand what you're so afraid of," I said when she wouldn't make another sound. "There's nothing you can say to scare off Ramesh. You must know how much he loves you."

She gazed blankly through the window, and the grandfather clock in the corner of the room ticked ten times before I spoke again. "I think I know what you did. It was early on in your relationship with Ramesh. Immediately before you stopped speaking to Sindy."

She gave no hint that I was on the right track, but her pupils seemed to grow a little darker in the sunlight that was flooding in around us.

"You had an affair, didn't you? With one of Ramesh's friends."

Chapter Twenty-Three

I left the room both wiser and more in doubt than at any other point that weekend. Patricia wouldn't confess to me, but she also didn't tell me I was talking nonsense. I should have realised that there was only one person who could have convinced her to explain what had happened, and it wasn't the right moment to involve him. I slipped away, but she remained there looking just as traumatised as when I'd entered.

Poorly done, Izzy, my brain would normally have said. So that was one piece of unpleasantness I was spared. And when I got back to the bridal suite, it turned out that Holland's last suspect had been released. The police had finished with Toby, so I had to assume that the D.I.s hadn't discovered anything useful to link him to the crime.

"Where's he gone now?"

"Downstairs, obviously," the dashing young detective informed me, and I had a brief fantasy of playing Tuppence to his Tommy. It didn't last long, and I went back to barking at him.

"Fine. Then I'll go and look for him."

"Good, you do that. Why are we still shouting?"

"I have no idea." If anything, the volume of my voice increased at this point. "Good luck with your investigation. Maybe we can get a drink together if this wedding ever happens."

"That sounds nice," he bellowed back, as though we were talking across a busy motorway. "I'll look out for you later."

Feeling a little odd about the whole thing, I shrugged and sped down the stairs in search of my last key witness. There was no sign of Danny or Ramesh at the bottom of the east tower to point me in the right direction, and so I headed towards the west tower in case Toby had retreated to his quarters for the weekend. Luckily, as I didn't know his room number, I spotted him in the ballroom on the way.

Heavy blinds had been drawn over the windows, and the room had been converted into a disco for the night. Apparently ready to drown his sorrows, he had a can of Carlsberg in his hand and was swinging a lucky dance partner around to the sound of Aqua's biggest hit. Though the couple were the only guests in there, the DJ in his little booth was having a great time. He apparently knew a special 'Barbie Girl' dance, which he was encouraging the invisible crowd to join in with.

Toby's partner was tall, with long blonde hair, and wore a beige suit. It took me a moment to realise that I was looking at Wazza in a wig from the photography booth.

"Hello, boys. I need a word with you," I said, like some femme fatale from a film noir.

They didn't respond but continued spinning round and around in the beam of a flashing strobe light. Toby dipped Wazza low, and I shouted to them once more.

"I need to talk to you. Right now."

Toby must have heard this time as, holding his friend for a few more seconds, his eyes sought me out in the darkness. That was when Wazza collapsed to the floor. I suppose he must have already had a few drinks as, instead of pulling himself back up to standing, he just lay there giggling.

"Cut the music," I said with such conviction that I surprised myself. The tubby DJ with the shiny golden jacket must have mistaken me for someone with authority, as he immediately lowered the volume on his mixer.

"What do you want, Palmer?" Toby 'Tog' Gatling screamed across the floor to me. It was not the warm welcome I'd been hoping for.

I stalked across the room towards my prey. "I want to know why you stabbed your ex-fiancée to death." I wasn't sure of myself, but he didn't know that.

The muscles in his cheeks flexed nervously, and he poured beer down his shirt without meaning to. "I didn't kill Sindy. Why would I have bothered? It was over between us and, no matter what she did to embarrass me, that wasn't going to change."

"Maybe you didn't kill her for yourself. Maybe it was a favour for a friend. You and the boys are very close after all. Did you decide to do it for Ramesh, whose day Sindy planned to ruin? Is that what this was all about, taking one for the team?" He was anxious, and I knew I could get even deeper into his head. "I'm right, aren't I?"

"He's my brother," was all he could say in reply, and I thought perhaps I'd chanced upon the solution after all.

I didn't know what to say next, as I'd been planning to go off on a totally different tangent. "Urmmm… sorry, are you saying that you did kill your ex for Ramesh's sake?"

He rolled his head around his neck before replying. "You're the detective. You tell me!"

Hmmm, this was going to be trickier than I'd imagined. "So… No?" I tried, then found a dose of confidence. "In fact, I don't think you killed her at all. But you do have your suspicions of what really happened."

He looked towards the lighting rig beneath the ornate ceiling, which depicted scenes of bacchanalian excess. The bright beams shone back to me in his eyes. "I know that Sindy was here to cause trouble. She's had it in for me ever since we broke up."

"Why did you leave her?" I got in quickly. "Was it because you loved someone else?"

He sneered from a few metres away, and so I took a step closer to keep the pressure on.

"No, of course not. I've never loved any woman except Sindy, which makes it all the sadder that she could treat me the way she did." He bit the inside of his cheek, as though debating how much he should tell me. "She was my addiction, and she was hard to kick, but I managed it in the end. I was her prisoner for ten years, but I finally broke away."

His answer reminded me of what Anfony had told me earlier that day. The two sad characters who'd been with Sindy hadn't been free to make their own choices.

"But something must have changed to make you leave her on the day of your wedding. What was it?"

He scrunched his face up at this. "I left that church because I realised that I hated Sindy Braithwaite. I saw what life with her had in store for me. I saw what it would mean to marry a cruel, manipulative woman whose only pleasure came from other people's misery. I'd been with her for ten years, but I hated her with a passion."

I still wasn't convinced that this was the whole story. "What about Patricia?"

"What *about* Patricia?"

"She was there at the church, and I know the two of you had an affair at the time she was getting together with Ramesh. So is that the real reason you called off the wedding?"

Toby couldn't reply at first. He just stared at me without moving a muscle. Wazza must have heard the question. The blonde wig now askew, he sat up on the floor to listen to what his friend would say.

"I don't know what you're talking about. I don't think I've ever shaken Patricia's hand, let alone slept with her. The only reason I still know her is because she's Ramesh's girlfriend. I'd never betray him like that and, to tell you the truth, I don't think she likes me very much."

I was about to contradict him, to push him to confess, but I saw my mistake just in time. These were not the words of a man lying to protect himself. He really had no idea what I was talking about.

My mind raced with the missed connections that had racked up that day, and I tried to find a firmer footing. "What brought you four friends together? Why are you still so close? Most school friends drift apart by our age."

"We're not as close as we'd like to be. Ramesh doesn't come home so often anymore because he's busy with his posh London friends." The man had clearly never been to Croydon if he thought I was posh! "I work for Gaz, so we see each other every day, but even Wazza only comes to Watford at the weekends. I mean, we still love each other like no one else, but it's different these days." He sounded sadder about this than the death of his ex.

With no clear sense of what I should be asking him, I kept the questions coming all the same. "What did you think when Sindy brought Anfony to Ramesh's engagement party?"

He shook his head and looked away. "I thought she was mad to go out with such a nutter, and I thought that she'd only brought him to get under my skin."

I was trying to unnerve him with the pace of my questions; hoping that, in his panic, he might reveal something he didn't want me to know. "Why did you confess to the killing if you say now it wasn't you?"

"Because…" he began, and I knew I'd got him. "Because I love my friends and I didn't want to see any of them suffer."

"When you entered the room, you must have thought that there was someone obvious who killed her. Who were you protecting?"

"I thought…" He stared straight at me, his defiance now exhausted. "I thought it must have been…"

"He thought it was me," Wazza said, standing up to his full height and removing the wig from his head.

Chapter Twenty-Four

I was trying to remember the order of events that had taken place after I'd found Patricia standing over Sindy's body.

"Gaz and Tog came in first," I said to myself. "And then you were one of the last to join." I wasn't sure if this confirmed or undermined his claim.

Luckily for me, Toby had a clearer head and explained what I had failed to understand. "I saw that Sindy had been murdered, and I knew that it was my fault. I knew that she'd never have ended up like that if I hadn't broken up with her. I thought quickly and knew that, of everyone there, it was Wazza who hated her most. I didn't want to see one of my absolute best friends going to prison for my mistake, so I said that I did it."

"But before that Gaz said he was to blame. So why would he have lied?"

"You still don't get it, Izzy," Wazza said, and I couldn't entirely disagree. "The four of us, me, Tog, Gaz and Ramekin. We're family. No, we're closer than that. We're something different altogether. We're like a system of trees and when one of us is threatened, we do what's necessary to defend each other. I thought that Gaz was to blame because he never got on with Patricia."

"And, meanwhile, Gaz lied for me," Tog added. "He saw the body and thought that I had killed Sindy. He didn't want me to get into trouble. Of course, I knew I hadn't killed her and assumed that Wazza was behind it."

"We clubbed together. Our root system sent out a warning, and we all did what we had to." Wazza was taking his tree metaphor a bit too far.

"That still doesn't explain why any of you went up to the bridal suite."

Neither of them responded to this, and I thought I'd found a chink in their story.

"I had a note in my room," Tog explained. "When I went back to the west tower after the rehearsal, there was a note telling me to go up there."

"And I saw him and Gaz going along the corridor as I was wandering about the hotel after breakfast. I figured the rehearsal was over and decided to see what they were up to."

"Have you shown the note to the police?" I asked, as it all sounded a bit too convenient.

"I did eventually." Tog looked at the shuttered windows as though searching for daylight. "They didn't seem to think it was important, but I couldn't recognise the handwriting. It was in big messy capital letters. It looked like a child had written it."

"Did Gaz get one too?"

Toby thought for a moment. "No, but he was with me when I found it. I'd had that big argument with Sindy and then I went for a walk along the river to clear my head."

"Did you see anyone else out there?" I asked, as a number of the suspects claimed to have been outside at that time.

He had to consider the question for a few seconds before replying. "Yeah, Patricia was sitting on a bench in the garden, but I didn't go near her, so she wouldn't have seen me out there." This seemed an excessively convenient answer, but I held my tongue. "When I got back to our rooms, Gaz was coming out of his door, and I spotted the note. It was on the floor in front of my room."

"Was it in your name?"

He looked nervous but didn't hesitate to answer. "That's right. It was a little envelope, the kind of thing you might send as a thank you note for a wedding. It had my name on and, inside, all it said was that I should go to the bridal suite as soon as possible."

It wasn't just the wedding that felt like it was happening in reverse. The case was all backwards. A note leading to a dead body should have been the first thing I discovered, but I was only hearing about it now.

"Gaz tried to tell me it was just Sindy messing with me, but I wouldn't listen and the two of us set off. When we got there, you and Patricia and her mum and that odd lady who looks a bit like a cleaner–"

"Deidre!" Wazza chimed in. "She's nice. She gave me a scotch egg at the engagement party."

"That's the one, Deidre. Well, you were already in the room, and I didn't realise that Patricia had found the body or picked up the sword until much later when that inspector bloke interviewed me. He left us waiting for hours, and I was sure that I'd be the one to go down for the murder because of my past with Sindy and everything she'd been up to."

"My friend, Danny... well, he's more like a brother really, though he's also my ex-boyfriend..." I abandoned this sentence, then started it again with only the most essential information included. "Ramesh's other groomsman, Danny, saw you and Sindy arguing after the rehearsal."

"So? I just admitted as much."

I wouldn't let him break my concentration. "I'm not denying that. I was going to ask what you talked about. It was presumably the last time anyone spoke to her before she was killed."

He froze, and the spinning disco lights flashed across his face. Multicoloured spots washed over him in phases and, when he opened his mouth to reply, it looked as though he'd swallowed a red circle, like Pacman in a maze. "She said that she had big plans for the wedding and that the dress she'd worn was only a taster. She said it was my turn to suffer in church, and she wouldn't stop until I knew how she'd felt on her big day."

Wazza stepped forward and put his friend in a headlock. I think this is the lad version of sympathy.

Looking at me from that awkward angle, Toby had an opportunity to get his own misdeeds off his chest. "I told her that I'd murder her if she messed up the wedding for Ramesh. I told her that, no matter what I'd done, it wasn't right to take it out on our friends."

"But they weren't her friends, were they?" I said, putting myself in her shoes for a few steps.

"That's exactly what she told me. She said that no one cared about her. None of the people we'd grown up with gave a damn when we broke up."

"Patricia did," I replied in a whisper, but Toby was ahead of me.

"That's true, she did. Not that Sindy appreciated it. When Patricia tried to comfort her, all she saw was a way to get back at me. Sindy brought everything on herself. What happened this weekend was down to her." I was about to correct him when he added a caveat. "And me."

Wazza let go of his friend and, in that rather gentle manner of his, tried to comfort him. "Don't say that, buddy. You can't shoulder all the blame." He held out an unopened can of beer which magically appeared in his hand. I could only assume he'd had it hidden in his back pocket.

As Wazza comforted his friend, I tried to work out whether I was any clearer than I had been that morning on what had happened to Sindy. The boys' tungsten-strong friendships must have made her feel all the more excluded after Toby abandoned her. It wasn't just her ex she wanted revenge on, it was the whole lot of them.

If it hadn't been physically impossible, I might have imagined that she'd killed herself to unleash one last explosion of wrath upon them. It was impossible, wasn't it? Yeah, it was. Wasn't it? No, no, it definitely was. She wouldn't have been able to get the curving blade of the samurai sword all the way through her abdomen without a helping hand.

"I don't suppose you had an affair with Patricia, did you?" I asked Wazza, who almost melted at the idea.

He let out a long whistle. "I wish! Patricia was the prettiest girl in school. Which is another reason why Sindy resented her. She was a bit like the wicked stepmother in Snow White actually."

I realised at this moment that I knew literally nothing about this guy. I'd basically dismissed him as a suspect, as his name had so rarely come up in my interviews, and I hate it in mysteries when the killer turns out to be someone really unimportant. "What do you do, Wazza?"

"I suppose, based on my training, I'm a rocket scientist." He gave a typically moronic guffaw, and I thought he was trying to be funny. "Though in actual fact, I work on chemical weapons demilitarisation for the Ministry of Defence at Porton Down. My team has been working on a new enzyme that can break down the most lethal properties of weapon stockpiles after wars. It's fascinating stuff. I could go on about it for days."

This was not the answer I'd been expecting. "Of course you could. How wonderful." I was unable to squeak out much more than this. Had I massively underestimated this man? I still pictured him as the banana, sliding up and down the pole at the strip club for Ramesh's stag do. Was it really possible that he'd masterminded some terrible scheme to murder Sindy and protect his friends? "I don't suppose you killed Sindy, did you?"

He let out a few notes of his highly inane laughter then. "Nope, sorry. I can't help you there. I was having breakfast between the hours of eight and eleven. Whenever I'm in a posh hotel, I like to make the most of the continental buffet. Ask the staff if you don't believe me. They were trying to chuck me out from about ten o'clock." A conspiratorial look passed across his face then. "Have you considered Patricia's mother? I find her scary."

I stood there feeling stupid for a few minutes, by which time Gaz had shown up looking ever so excited about the private disco. The three of them boogied about together, whilst DJ Coolpants pumped out the Macarena, and the realisation of my failure sunk deep within me. I felt as though I wouldn't solve the murder even if the wedding went on for weeks.

Chapter Twenty-Five

'The day is always darkest before the dawn,' my brain would have reassured me if it hadn't been occupied trying to out-Woody-Allen Woody Allen. I also greatly doubt that saying is scientifically true, so at least I avoided another debate on its accuracy.

I drifted back to the atrium where the real party was still swinging. The priests were taking part in a twist competition – Pujari Raviji was clearly winning. Lovely, octogenarian Auntie Val and Ramesh's joyful uncle were waltzing in the middle of the room and, still with the camera around his neck, Fernando was leading a sing along of Queen songs, though the music pounding out of the speakers was 'Come on Eileen'.

None of that was of much interest to me though, as I couldn't take my eyes off a couple in the corner who were pressed up against a tree, fighting each other with their tongues. Nigel and Lizzy had connected in a big way. Not only did I feel dreadful for poor Danny who had brought his pretty date along for her to be stolen out from under him by that walking toad, I felt bad for Lizzy who, in two years' time, will realise that she's been dating a monster. I considered doing something about it, but I was fairly sure they wouldn't have heard me over the noise of all that suction.

My friends Dean and Fiona were slow dancing, and my number one dad and (not really a) Princess Penelope were having a champagne break from the rehearsals. There was no sign of Ramesh, though, so I returned to the bridal suite. I figured I'd have one last look around before I accepted the fact that I was a failure as a detective, the wedding would be ruined, and I would never find true love. There were constables on duty beside the suite, but Holland and Irons had disappeared. The uniformed officers seemed happy to wave me through, so at least I could meditate on the case for a while without interruption.

A little meditation was just what I needed. A wedding is more or less the worst place to solve a crime. There had been a thousand people in my head all day and, while it's true that there was more space in there than normal, I hadn't had a moment to concentrate. It was nice to shut the door behind me and enjoy the calm of that murder scene. The music coming from the atrium was little more than a faint thud. There was no one there to ask me stupid questions, and the puffy armchairs looked comfy enough for me to curl up in a ball and have a nap. I didn't, of course, but it was tempting.

Instead, I pulled up the list of suspects in my head and restored all the names I'd previously discarded. I think that, deep down, I'd decided early on that one of Ramesh's friends must have been responsible because they had no reason to be up in the wing of the house reserved for the bride and her entourage. With that idea now disproven, I reconsidered my options.

As D.I. Holland had suggested, it could be one of those cases where the obvious suspect really was the right choice. Sindy had messed about with Anfony's head and used him just as she had her friends. From everything I'd heard, she'd only dated him in order to disrupt first the engagement party and then the wedding itself. Was that really enough for him to have murdered her?

Patricia, meanwhile, was more entangled in the dead woman's life. Though I hadn't discovered the exact details of the secret that hung over her, it had been serious enough to ignore Sindy's misdemeanours that weekend. Surely this meant it was something that Patricia didn't want her fiancé discovering, which made me assume it was related to an affair, which, apparently, was not the right solution after all.

As I was still focussing on the likely suspects, Toby "Tog" Gatling was the obvious next name on the list. He admitted that he hated Sindy and had every reason to want her out of the picture. However, Danny had seen him walking away from the scene of the crime when Sindy was still alive, and he had a good reason to have returned there after she was dead. Had he been a master criminal in an Agatha Christie novel, he would still have found a way to kill his nemesis-ex. Tog didn't seem like an evil mastermind, but then I'd already underestimated Dr Wazza, the apparent genius. I'd have to learn my lesson at some point.

I'd assumed at first that the note Toby had found by his room was written by the killer to confuse the evidence at the crime scene but, standing in the bridal suite once more, I realised there was a far simpler explanation. Sindy had black ink on her fingers and Tog had told me that the note was written in a messy font. It didn't take a genius to work out that she had smudged the words to disguise her handwriting. It was written on a bridal note card too and there were enough of those hanging about the place to write emergency thank yous. Why she had wanted her ex up there would remain a mystery but was presumably part of her grand plan to sabotage the wedding.

Of the three amigos de Ramesh, Tog had claimed that Gaz was the least fond of Patricia. It crossed my mind that he could have mistaken the fake bride for the real one. And yet, when I'd interviewed him, he'd shown very little knowledge of what had occurred that morning. Though he was clearly desperate to believe he was responsible for the crime, he'd ended up contradicting the basic facts that the scene had revealed. I'd been wrong to rule him out so quickly, but then why would he have killed her?

Meanwhile, as the minor player in the group – the Winston to the main gang of Ghostbusters – Wazza had very little to gain from killing Sindy. He also hadn't been at the rehearsal to learn of the chaos she'd brought about and, rocket scientist or otherwise, the only motive I'd found for him to murder her was his loyalty to Tog.

There was still the possibility that the boys' friendship was so strong that they wouldn't let evil Sindy come between them, even if it meant resorting to murder. It was an enticing theory, but there were two problems. First, I didn't like demonising a woman as evil. For all her faults, Sindy was at least marginally less of a psychopath than whoever ran her through with a samurai sword. And second, I'd seen no evidence of them working together. The three of them had been off in different parts of the hotel at the time she was murdered and only came together just before the body was found.

So who did that leave me with? A wedding planner who fainted at the sight of a papercut. A middle-aged woman who dressed like a school cleaner and the mother of the bride, who presumably wouldn't have been stupid enough to ruin her daughter's big day. Yep, it was official; I didn't have a clue who the killer was.

I moved onto the list of evidence and scanned the room to remind myself of everything that the scene of the crime had offered up. There were the flowers, which had now turned brown out of water. There were the bloody overalls which I had to believe had been planted there to mess with my head – why else would a killer have got undressed before escaping? The sword itself had been taken away by the police but its presence in the room showed that it was a pre-meditated crime, unlike the story that many of the suspects had presented as proof of their guilt.

So maybe I was mistaken from the beginning. Maybe my big theory was wrong. Maybe the killer hadn't confessed in order to blend in with the other well-meaning suspects. It could have been someone else entirely – one of the bridesmaids for example. The usurped maid of honour, Gemma, would be the obvious choice if she hadn't had an alibi. Or perhaps Cheryl, the omniscient private assistant, was so tired of being ordered about by Sindy that she decided to have a quick game of stabby stabby. But where was the fun in any of that? Agatha Christie never wrote a story where the incredible, mind-blowing twist at the end was that some random bloke did it who had barely got a mention before. The very idea of such a boring conclusion made me sick!

And so, I did not give up. Examining the lounge in the bridal suite, where a bloodstain was still visible on the carpet, I looked at the room one final time. I spotted the sweet wrappers on the shelf where the statue had been thrown from and remembered Deidre sucking on sherbet lemons all day. This might have been a good piece of evidence if it weren't for the fact there were at least ten transparent wrappings there. If she was the killer, she'd have had to stick around for a long time after she killed Sindy to get through so many sweets.

There'd been a bottle of champagne by the body which I'd felt sure would turn out to be a vital clue but, unless the police came back with some significant forensic evidence, it now appeared to be meaningless. Sindy had must have been drinking from it before she died. It meant nothing more than that.

But then again, if she'd been had the bottle in her hand, why didn't she–

Ahhhhhhhhhhhhh! I've got it! my brain said, and we both felt like celebrating.

You've worked out who the killer is?

No, but I've got the punchline to my joke. A rabbi, a pujari and a priest walk into a bar. A theological discussion kicks off and the rabbi says, "I have the fairest God." The pujari says, "I have the most gods." And the priest says, "I'll have a double whisky."

You spent all day, and that was the best you could come up with?

You should have heard my first attempts.

As my brain tittered away to itself, I tried to concentrate on the case. I'd seen something before I was interrupted. The champagne bottle could be important after all, but that didn't mean I knew who was responsible for the killing. Unless…

I scanned that room one last time to be sure of the evidence. I could see the flowers and the outline of the bottle, the blood stain where Sindy had been lying and the space on the shelf where the figurine had previously stood. It was so obvious. How could I have missed it before?

I'd done it. I'd finally done it and I wanted to run and tell Ramesh the good news, but I had no idea where he was, so I went to see Patricia instead.

"I've done it," I yelled as I skipped past the officers at the door, and they replied with smiles and cheers.

"Congratulations, Miss Palmer!" the older of the two shouted after me.

"She's like a galloping cyclops!" her hairy colleague whispered, once he thought I was out of earshot.

"Patricia, listen!" I said, as I bumped up against Julia Green's door. "I know who the killer is. The wedding's back on."

"Do you really mean it?" Her tiny voice shot out to me from under the door.

"Yes, I mean it. Though I do have one question. Why did you take the sword out of Sindy's body?"

I heard her move closer to reply. "I really have no idea. I think it's because, whenever I watch a TV show where that happens, I scream at the idiot on the screen to get away from the body. I was drawn towards it and couldn't resist."

I'd finally found someone who got me. "That's exactly it! It's such a stupid thing to do that it's hard to resist." I was overjoyed, but then I remembered how little time we had. "I'll send Fernando up to do your hair and makeup, and we can still have the ceremony at five(ish) as we told everyone."

"Wait, Izzy." There was a note of distress in her voice, and she opened the door with sorrow and fear still there on her face. "I can't get married. Not without talking to Ramesh first. I've lied to him all these years, and he deserves to know the truth."

I wasn't sure what to say to that. I couldn't stand the thought of her ancient secret breaking them up now. Not after everything I'd done to keep the party going.

I nodded all the same. "Okay, I'll make sure you have time before the service. But you must start getting ready while I organise everything."

She smiled for the first time that day and it gave me the confidence for what I needed to do next. I had some orders to give and ran back to the landing.

"Constable, I need you to radio your boss and get him to bring Anfony LeQuinn back to the hotel. Tell him Izzy Palmer just solved the murder."

Chapter Twenty-Six

I was in something of a quandary. I knew who the killer was, had a pretty good idea about the motive, but I couldn't decide where the best place would be to reveal my findings.

"Cheryl!" I shouted as I got to the bottom of the stairs and, sure enough, she was on hand when I needed her.

"Yes, Miss Palmer. How may I help?"

"Cheryl, I'm about to do one of those scenes that you get at the end of a murder mystery when the detective goes through all the suspects one by one to explain how they were involved in the crime and why."

She was suddenly very chipper. "Oh, I love that bit. It's my favourite scene in every whodunit."

I might have snorted a little in reply. "I'm afraid not everyone agrees. One review I got said that my summing up was 'downright cringeworthy'."

Review? Cheryl's face said, though she remained silent.

"Yeah, there's a website where you can leave reviews for private detective agencies. Everyone's a critic these days. Anyway, there are some people who do enjoy my carefully constructed denouements, and I need somewhere dramatic for this one."

"The roof," she said without hesitation, and I wondered whether she would consider coming to work for me. She couldn't be a worse sidekick than Ramesh, and she definitely provided better snacks. "The ramparts of the east tower are particularly pretty."

"Perfect. If you could get someone to take a screen up there for me to hide one of the suspects behind, that would be really useful."

"Will you be requiring any refreshments?" she asked (because she's amazing).

"Absolutely." I only had one more question for her. "How about hot chocolate for eleven people?"

"I'll order a samovar!" She gave me a big thumbs up and scampered off to make the arrangements.

"It must be nearly thirty degrees, Izzy," Ramesh complained once I'd rounded up everyone we needed. "Why would anyone want hot chocolate?"

"Hot drinks are better at quenching your thirst, Ra," I replied a little too insistently. "Everyone knows that."

"Fine, but perhaps you can tell me why I have to be behind this screen?"

I smiled and pushed him further into the shadows. "You'll see."

We were still waiting for the last few people to appear on the roof when D.I. Holland arrived with Anfony in tow.

"One of my constables discovered the scabbard a few metres from the house. It could have been thrown from the east tower windows, including the bridal suite, though it's impossible to say exactly how it got there."

"What about the clothes the killer wore beneath the overalls?"

"Yep, they turned up in the river. Luckily, some angler found them downstream and *fished* them out." I'd known a number of detective inspectors, and this was about as good as their jokes got. "When the woman saw the news, she called it in. There are shoe protectors, overalls and gloves, much like a scene of crime officer would wear. We'll be lucky to get any forensic evidence off them after they've been in the water, though. Bloodstains, sure, but not much else."

"That's great, thanks."

He crossed his arms, and I knew he had a challenge for me. "So… how does all that fit in with your little theory?"

I couldn't help smiling. "It fits in just fine, thank you."

You tell him, Iz!

Oh, brain. It's nice to have you back.

I was pleased to see that D.I. Irons had tagged along too as, when I said that some people love my finales, I was mainly thinking of her. Once Patricia arrived, with Fernando still doing her hair as they crossed the flat stone roof, I was finally ready to begin.

I cleared my throat to get everyone's attention, and the suspects and police officers formed a circle around me in the middle of the tower. The sun was still high in the sky and beat down on us like a punishment for a really very minor offence. It sparkled along the length of the river and, as I began my tale, a helicopter touched down on the lawn.

"Normally I would go into great detail and explain why each of you could be guilty, but there's a wedding to celebrate, and I feel that most of you have done the job for me by admitting to the murder."

"I never admitted to anything," Anfony commented.

"Just to be accurate, I didn't confess either," Patricia clarified, which is good because I'd never been totally clear on the matter.

"Patricia?" Ramesh shouted. "Is that you?"

"Yes, darling. That's why Izzy put you behind a screen."

"Shouldn't Ramesh be considered a suspect himself?" Irons suggested between sips of her hot chocolate, and the group began to discuss the possibility.

Gaz seemed unhappy about something. "If Anfony, Patricia and Ramesh get to have a go, you should do me too."

"Seriously? There's only half an hour before the wedding." I was beginning to get annoyed. "I've already proved you couldn't have killed Sindy. Do I really have to go through it again?"

"Yes!" the whole lot of them sang as one.

"You can skip me if you're in a hurry," Julia kindly agreed.

"I'm easy either way." Toby didn't look particularly keen on being there in the first place, so this was hardly a surprise.

"To be perfectly honest, Izzy," the voice from behind the screen moaned, "I'm feeling a little left out."

"Oh, come on, people," I raised both hands to get them to calm down. "We've realistically got about fifteen minutes before we have to set up for the ceremony. There is no time to detail every last clue and consideration that occurred to me today." To pre-empt more complaints, I started in on a brief overview. "That being said, I'll give the potted version. Deidre, there was proof you'd been at the scene of the crime thanks to the sweet wrappers you left all over the place. Evidently this was less than damning as you presumably spent time there last night with the rest of the bridal party. You also didn't seem to know much about how Sindy was murdered, but I didn't rule you out entirely because of your close attachment to the mother of the bride."

"Ooh, me next," Gaz chirped.

"Gaz, as were alone during your photo shoot earlier, I should reveal that you ruled yourself out by giving a truly unlikely account of your supposedly savage act and detailing a version of events which was entirely implausible."

He really grinned at this. "I have to confess; I didn't have a clue where the murder weapon had been. I knew she'd get me on the details."

"I appreciate you trying to cover for me, mate." Toby punched his friend on the arm.

"It wasn't for you!" Gaz giggled and raised his fists to shadowbox for some reason. "I thought Wazza had done it. He's always hated Sindy."

"It's harder than you'd think pretending to be a murderer," Deidre pointed out, not for the first time that day, and several of the suspects had a jolly laugh.

Even trying to be quick, I was deathly slow. I was beginning to understand what the one-star review was referring to when it had criticised my technique on rate-a-detective.com.

I moved us not so swiftly onwards. "Emilio couldn't be in the same room as a dead body without feeling queasy. Wazza wasn't in the rehearsal and wouldn't have seen the chaos Sindy caused to know that she needed dealing with. And, despite his previous poor behaviour, Anfony was not as beholden to Sindy as many of her old friends were. I struggled to find a motive for why he would have killed his on-again, off-again girlfriend in such a public manner."

"Thank you so much, Izzy." The punk-rock badger's lips started trembling. "That is one of the nicest things anyone has ever said about me."

I took a deep breath, hoping we could now get on to the juicy stuff. "So how many suspects does that leave us with?"

"I count three," Wazza said. "Julia, Patricia and Tog."

"Tog! Tog! Tog!" Gaz chanted, as though this were a school competition instead of a murder investigation.

"It was supposed to be a rhetorical question, but thanks, Wazza."

He took a humble bow.

I cleared my throat and wearily continued the explanation, well aware that it wouldn't be long before someone interrupted – it was just that kind of audience. "Three suspects and three people with strong connections to Lusinda Braithwaite. Her ex-boyfriend, her ex-best friend and the mother of the bride she was planning to upstage."

I walked over to Julia Green, who had remained perfectly presented since that morning. Her fringe looked like it had been trimmed with a ruler and she wore long black gloves. I hadn't noticed it before, but there was something very Anjelica Huston-ish about her. I'm not going to deny that I was terrified of her (and Anjelica Huston ever since I saw her in 'The Witches' when I was nine).

"You were the first on the scene after I arrived, and the first to confess to murdering Sindy. With this in mind, I asked myself who, more than the mother of the bride, would want the wedding to go smoothly?"

"Ooh, ummm… What about the priest?"

"Thank you, Wazza."

He bowed his head once more and whispered to Tog who was standing next to him. "A priest would get a bad reputation if he kept giving poor services. It only stands to reason he'd want everything to go perfectly."

I turned back to Julia, but I'd lost my place by this point. "Where was I?" This was one question that Wazza didn't have an answer to. "Well, whatever. The fact is that Julia isn't the killer. Aside from her love for her daughter, who had just been humiliated at the wedding rehearsal, there was no real evidence to suggest that she was involved."

I continued walking around the circle and, despite Ramesh's prediction, I noticed a number of people with hot chocolate moustaches, including D.I. *Too Cool for School* Holland. And yes, I'm aware I hadn't learnt his actual first name.

"So then I was left with two suspects. Patricia, who was about to get married, and Toby, who had left his girlfriend at the church just moments before they were due to be wed; the very same woman who turned up dead this morning in the east tower of Hartford House."

"Clearly Patricia's innocent," Ramesh shouted around his screen. "Just tell everyone how Toby did it, and we can get on with the wedding."

I ignored him and started on the last thread of Sindy's story. "Lusinda Braithwaite was the most popular girl at…" I couldn't remember this very minor detail then, and so I went with, "…whichever school you all went to. She ruled over the other kids with fear and manipulation. But, on leaving school, she lost all that power she had possessed. Patricia and Ramesh had gone away to university, and I doubt any of the other poor souls she'd bullied all those years wanted anything to do with her. So she concentrated on her new boyfriend instead. Toby was Ramesh's right-hand man–"

"Hey, there was no hierarchy," Gaz objected. "We were all good friends. Just like the four musketeers."

"For goodness' sake!" I was really losing my patience by this point. "The next person who interrupts me will be sent back downstairs." I waited to make sure they'd got the message before continuing. "Sindy and Toby dated for years and eventually got engaged. Then, on the day of the wedding, he realised just what sort of person he was tying himself to. At first, I thought he had harboured a secret passion for another woman, but I was wrong. It's true that Toby would have seen Patricia there at the wedding for the first time in years, but that wasn't what did it. The thing that convinced him to call off the wedding was the words of his best friend Ramesh."

"Honestly," Gaz refused to leave it. "There are no *best friends*. We all get on brilliantly."

Yeah, mate. Keep telling yourself that. You're a minor character at best!

I shot my hand out and shouted across to him. "Downstairs, Gaz."

He looked like he might cry. "I'm sorry. It won't happen again. I promise."

I narrowed my eyes and I think he got the message that he was on his very last warning. When I'd calmed down, I continued the story once more. "Ramesh is like a superhero to his old school friends. The others had all tried to convince Toby he was making a mistake, but it was only when *Ramekin* did it that he finally listened."

I'd delivered this speech up close to Toby's face but decided to give him a break. I strolled around the inside of the circle and stopped to look into each person's eyes. "In fact, if there's one thing I've been impressed by this weekend, it's the strength of the friendships that I've encountered. Not just the four musketeers…" Gaz was clearly appeased by the reference. "… but Julia and Deidre, Patricia and her mother, and even Ramesh and my ex-boyfriend, Danny. But the closer we get to our friends, the more likely it is that someone will get hurt."

I took a look at my watch and decided to cut the next bit of my speech as time was running short. I was going to do this clever bit where I drew a parallel between Sindy's vicious attitude and the bond between the others around her. It would have been powerful stuff, and I'm pretty sure I would have inspired a few tears, but the minutes were ticking by.

"Lusinda Braithwaite was no angel, but she deserved some

sympathy for what Toby did to her, and Patricia provided it. Having spent a decade apart, their lives were suddenly woven together once more. But all Sindy wanted was revenge. She knew that Patricia was too nice to stand in her way, especially as she was one of the few people who knew the bride-to-be's darkest secret. And so Sindy set about plotting her grand scheme. She went to a bar and picked up the drunkest, most pathetic-looking loser she could find."

"Hey!" Anfony didn't sound too keen on my description.

That review on rate-a-detective.com was right. You're really not very good at this bit.

Shut up and think of another joke!

For the sake of diplomacy, I rephrased the sentence. "Sindy found someone that she knew would shock and disturb her ex-fiancé when they met again at Ramesh and Patricia's engagement party. She wanted Toby to think that she'd lost her mind since he dumped her, and Anfony certainly made an impression."

I heard Fernando whispering something about a dachshund just then, but I would not be distracted. "Sindy had bigger plans, though. She brought Anfony to the wedding this weekend and goaded him into greater indiscretions, plying him with drink as soon as he arrived. It might have worked if her ringer hadn't got sober over the last year. To his credit, Anfony resisted the pressure and avoided a major scene."

I gave him a smile then, to make up for calling him a pathetic loser.

"Of course, this was only part of Sindy's plan. She made a speech last night to show that she still held some power over you, after all, and turned up at the wedding rehearsal in the dress in which she should have been married. I suppose that it was these chaotic scenes which sealed her fate, but they were just tasters for whatever she had planned for the ceremony itself. I wasn't the only one to come to the conclusion that Patricia's compulsive inability to talk back to the woman intent on destroying the weekend suggested that Sindy was blackmailing the bride. That might be a good enough reason for Patricia to have killed her, or for Toby to have stepped in to save the wedding, but it missed the bigger picture.

"As Sindy proved, not all friendships are healthy. Sometimes we become so caught up in the lives of the people around us that it drives us to jealousy and obsession. What I failed to realise in this case was that it wasn't Patricia or even Sindy that this sad day revolved around. Everything that has happened here – the centre of the universe for so many of you – it all comes back to Ramesh."

"Hurray for me!" The grey office partition shook a little in the sunlight.

"Ramekin! Ramekin! Ramekin!" Wazza and Gaz both sang together. Toby still looked too nervous to celebrate the hero of the group.

"Thank you for including me, everybody," Ramesh replied (also in song form).

"Ever since you were children, Ramesh was your idol. Sindy wanted to be with him. The boys all wanted to be like him, and even the teachers admired him for his winning personality, sporting prowess and…" I really struggled over these next words. "… his classically manly demeanour. But one person took their admiration too far. There is one person here who looked up to my friend more than anyone else and whose love for him went beyond the realms of a healthy friendship."

Wazza looked nervous and sputtered out a response. "I'm sorry, Ra. I really am. I took your t-shirt from gym class when we were in the sixth form, but it was only because I like the way you smell!"

Everyone stared at the theoretically intelligent guy, and I would have to be the one to put him out of his misery. "Not you, Wazza. Though you might want to unpack some of what you just told us with a psychiatrist someday."

Looking as though he regretted his confession, he nodded, and Gaz put him in a headlock to make him feel better.

"I'm talking about a man who was so consumed with his need to be important to Ramesh that he despised Patricia and couldn't stand the thought of losing his *best friend.* I'm talking about someone who would have done anything to avoid the groom thinking badly of him, even if it meant resorting to murder."

Toby's face fell and, just then, Wazza pushed Gaz away from him. I guess that guy really was cleverer than he looked.

I waited five interminable seconds to watch the suspects' reactions and, at the very moment that Toby raised his hand to point at his friend and colleague, I delivered the name they were waiting for. "I'm talking about Gaz."

Chapter Twenty-Seven

In future cases, I must make a point of learning all names, in full, from the beginning. "I'm talking about Gaz!" Is what I said, but how much more dramatic would it have sounded if I'd been able to announce, "I'm talking about Gareth Thomas Atkinson the Third!"?

Such a simple measure would have made things so much easier. I wouldn't have spent hours of the investigation thinking that Toby and Tog were different people and, perhaps even more importantly, I wouldn't have had to use those stupid nicknames all day.

Anyway, the point is, Gaz was the killer. And, just after the reality sunk in for the assembled audience, the conversation started once more.

"You swine," Toby said, only he used a much ruder word, which I'd prefer not to repeat.

Ha, prude!

He lunged forward, and Wazza had to keep the two apart. "No matter what Sindy had done to me, she didn't deserve to die." I thought that Toby might turn to murder himself right then.

Gaz wasn't interested in either of them. "It's not what you think, Ra," he shouted across the ancient stones, his words carrying off over the tower ramparts. "I did it to protect you. I didn't want Sindy saying anything bad about Patricia. I knew how much you'd suffer, so I did what was necessary."

"He's lying," I said, barely raising my voice as he began to spit and rage.

"Don't listen to that lanky cow. What does she even know about you?" Holland and Irons moved around the circle, as Gaz continued to bellow in Ramesh's direction. "I've been your friend since we were five years old. Five! I've been here for you all that time, and nothing that happened this weekend changes that."

Rather than feeling sensitive that yet another person had mocked my height, I began to lay out the evidence against him. "Patricia told me that there were only three people who knew her secret. She mentioned Sindy and her fellow bridesmaid Gemma, and so it was obvious that the last person to know must have been–"

"Wait!" Patricia suddenly interrupted, and the two inspectors used the distraction to grab the killer by his arms. As the other suspects watched Gaz wriggling, she held one finger in the air and daintily crossed the roof of the tower to whisper to her betrothed like Pyramus and Thisbe, through the crack in their wall.

Ooh, look at Izzy, everyone! She's so cultured. She knows all about ancient Greek myths.

Everyone else was captivated by the capture of the culprit, but I kept my eyes on Patricia. I couldn't hear what she was saying, but I saw the tears forming in her eyes and a hesitant frown transform her countenance before she broke down and great sobs passed through her. Ramesh's hand reached out from behind his screen, and she took it in hers. Feeling confident that they'd be okay, I got back on with my job.

"The only other person who knew Patricia's secret was the man she had slept with soon after she'd started going out with Ramesh. Gaz hated Patricia because she'd cheated on his best friend before stealing Ramesh away from him. The fact that he was equally responsible for that drunken night didn't change anything." I had to assume she was drunk when it happened; why else would she have slept with him? "After it was clear to so many of us that Sindy was blackmailing Patricia in order to be a part of the wedding, Gaz decided to solve the problem in the most violent way imaginable."

"I did it for you, Ra," Gaz tried one last time. "It would have ruined your big day, and I just wanted you to be happy."

There were only a few minutes left now if we wanted to start the wedding on time and I didn't let up. "When we found Sindy's body this morning, I realised that I didn't just have a murder to solve, but a riddle too. The fact that the killer fled the scene showed that he didn't want to get caught, so then why confess? It took me until this afternoon to work out the answer. Gaz always planned to admit to the crime, not to assuage a guilty conscience but to distance himself from the act.

"I think he must have realised that it is much easier to give an unconvincing confession than a believable denial. He made sure to get the facts muddled to make it seem as though he was lying. The plan worked even better when the rest of you had a similar idea, and I had to sift through your well-meaning confessions. In fact, it felt like I was investigating a *whodidn'tdunit* rather than a whodunit."

I waited for the laugh which never came. Perhaps it wasn't the moment for jokes. "From what I have pieced together, Gaz went to the bridal suite shortly after the rehearsal. Sindy saw him with the sword and turned to run, but he killed her before she could get away. She didn't stand a chance."

I paused for effect this time, and the audience seemed far more receptive to my revelations than my jokes. "As a painter by trade, he'd have had overalls, gloves and shoe protectors in his van to cover his clothes when he went to do the job. But he saw a clean staff uniform in a store cupboard along the way and struck upon an idea. With the deed done, he soaked the uniform in Sindy's blood and hid it beneath the sofa where only the killer would know about them, sure that the police would require this information in order to prove he was guilty. There were other efforts he made to confuse the evidence. He threw flowers about the place and left an ornament under the table to make it look as though there had been a struggle when, in actual fact, Sindy had a bottle of champagne in her hand when she died and would have used that if she'd wanted a weapon."

"Despite his ever so clever plan, Gaz made some mistakes too. He told me about the statuette of the two lovers kissing. A statuette with no fingerprints on it, which was not visible from where he was standing in the entrance parlour after he returned. He shouldn't have known anything about it, and it took me far too long to realise that this was what I needed to prove his guilt."

"Incredible," Holland said, sounding just as impressed as that word would imply. "I'd never have thought of that."

Irons gave me a wink from behind the now docile detainee and Deidre passed the sherbet lemons around the circle as I concluded my speech.

"He killed Sindy because he didn't want the truth of his one-night stand with Patricia to be revealed. He couldn't bear the thought of Ramesh hating him and, when Sindy's behaviour got out of control and Patricia did nothing, he feared the secret would come out."

There was one part of the story I wasn't certain of, and I turned to address the culprit. "But perhaps you thought you could kill two birds with one stone. Did you wait until Sindy was in the bridal suite because you knew that, by killing her there, you would incriminate the woman she'd just humiliated? The woman who was keeping your *best friend* away from your hometown." A thought torpedoed into my brain at just the right moment. "Does that explain why you hid the scabbard in the garden near the east tower? It wasn't there when I first looked this morning, so you must have planted it later to incriminate Patricia."

He looked so proud of himself, and an unlikely volley of laughter shot out of him. "You've got it the wrong way round. I didn't go up the tower to kill Sindy."

Patricia was the only one of us brave enough to ask the question we all had in our heads. "So why were you there?"

He laughed again, really letting himself go this time, but then the creepy sound cut short just as quickly as it had started. "It was you I was after."

A repeated gasp of shock travelled across the scene. It started with the bride, who was still beside the screen she was betrothed to. This was no ruse, no red herring, no false twist in the case; the killer had been found out, and he felt no remorse for what he'd done.

"I went to the bridal suite to kill the bride, knowing that Sindy would get the blame after what she'd done. But the wrong bride was there and so I changed my plan. I went in through the door, Sindy saw me in my overalls, with the sword in my hand and ran away in a panic. So I thought, oh well, she'll do. Killing her meant that I could tidy up one loose end, and make it look as though dear Patri-tri here was to blame. You see-"

"No," I said to shut him up. "This isn't your chance to boast. We know what you did now, and I don't want to hear another word out of your disgusting mouth."

D.I. Holland whistled and two uniformed constables dashed onto the roof to take the killer away somewhere cold and uncomfortable.

You mean, Glasgow?

No, obviously not. I meant prison!

I didn't take my eyes off him as he went. He sputtered and huffed, no longer with anything to laugh about. And when he'd gone, I had some final words to offer the stunned crowd. "Gaz is a petty guy who had a petty reason to murder another human being. He was obsessed with the idea of a man who doesn't exist. A man who he idolised and turned into a hero. As Ramesh's actual best friend…"

"Awww, thanks, Iz," the soppy groom gushed. "Love you!"

"…I can tell you that he is not perfect."

"I take it back! You're horrible."

"He's a wonderful friend, and the most forgiving person I know, but he is flawed just as we all are. When we elevate a person above all others – whether it's our friends, a celebrity or even our partner – it can only end in disappointment or, in Gaz's case, worse."

The mumbling and interruptions had died away by this point, and there was a moment of silence as we reflected on what had taken place.

That was beautiful, Izzy. So wise and insightful. You didn't start too brightly, but you came into your own at the end.

Thanks, brain.

I mean it. Three stars.

Three! Out of Five?

I'm only being honest.

I shook off my chagrin at this mediocre review and looked at my watch. "That's it. We're out of time so, if anyone has any questions, you'll find me at the top table at the banquet tonight."

"If you're lucky!" Ramesh shouted. "'Not perfect' indeed!"

I suppose I hadn't been clear enough as no one moved. "Come on, we've got a wedding to get to."

The scene burst into life and Patricia was the first to descend from the roof, before Fernando went tumbling after with a comb and various clips in his hands. The other guests followed along until, finally, it was just the two police inspectors and me.

"Impressive work," Holland nodded. "But I'm afraid we'll have to hold off on that drink. I'll have a ton of paperwork this afternoon."

I smiled. "Ahh, well. An officer's job is never done."

"It is for me," Irons said. "I'm all about a work-life balance, and I took this weekend off to enjoy the wedding. If I know anything about Ramesh, it's going to be something else."

With good cheer and bonhomie, the three of us moved towards the stairs just as a small voice travelled over to us.

"Izzy, has Patricia gone? Can I come out now?"

Chapter Twenty-Eight

The ceremony didn't start on time, but that was only because Ramesh had to wait for Fernando to finish with Patricia so that he could have his hair (and subtle makeup) done to his liking. We borrowed mother's production team to get everything ready. My father was in charge of pressing Ramesh's suit, and my stepdad went from guest to guest looking for a white, sixteen-inch collar shirt. Ramesh had got ready far too early and really needed a fresh one.

The time finally came for me to thread my arm through my very best friend's and lead him to the Hartford House chapel. The florists had done a spectacular job. Boughs of ivy hung along the pews, and blooms of white flowers exploded wherever my eyes landed. The church was almost full, and nearly everyone there gave Ramesh a massive round of applause as he entered. I say nearly everyone as my date and Danny's had their mouths locked together on the back row, like young lovers in a cinema. Danny didn't seem too upset and stood at the front to welcome us to the wedding.

"I told you we'd get here in the end." Unlike Ramesh's other groomsmen, he was not averse to showing his emotions and gave our mutual friend a hug.

With Gaz otherwise occupied, Wazza had stepped in to make up the numbers, and we anxiously awaited the bride-to-be. Standing next to Ramesh, I must admit that I was nervous, jumpy and, let's be honest, close to tears.

"You are still sure about this?" I said as the congregation chattered, and bursts of laughter floated over from where the incorrigible Auntie Val was sitting.

"Of course I am." It was Ramesh's turn to give me a punch on the arm. "How can you even ask?"

I realised my mistake. "Sorry. I didn't mean, are you sure about marrying Patricia? I was trying to make sure that this traditional wedding is really what you want."

Ramesh is useless at lying to me, and so he said nothing as Cheryl ran down the right-hand aisle to tell the string quartet to start playing. Tchaikovsky's Love Theme from 'Romeo and Juliet' immediately echoed about the historic temple, and I glanced back along the aisle. Patricia couldn't have looked more beautiful in her fortunately stain-free dress. Strolling through the church, she was like a thousand-watt bulb and illuminated the world around her. Julia was at her side, looking as proud as any mother could, and the remaining bridesmaids had clearly got over the fact that they were a man down for the job.

When the slowly moving group was about halfway to us, something unexpected occurred. Cheryl darted from the back of the church to hand the bride a microphone and the music suddenly changed. Tchaikovsky's swelling opus was cut short, and Patricia raised the mic to her lips to sing in a soft, almost spoken style.

The melody sounded familiar, but I couldn't place it as she delivered the romantic opening couplet and several figures stood up around the church. I spotted Uncle Kabir first who, along with that grand dame of London theatre, Kebe Akerele, began to ooh and ahh in time with the music.

Singing sensation (and my mum) Bu-Bu La Mer fired up her famous vocal cords as Danny and no-longer-such-a-baby Amelia accompanied her. By the time we'd got to the end of the second verse, there was one person in every row providing harmony and I was trying to comprehend how Patricia had set this all up without Ramesh (or me) finding out.

Ramesh's cats ran down the aisle with little crowns and ermine-trimmed velvet robes on and, in each corner of the room, a cannon fired giant confetti hearts across the congregation. It was the cue for Patricia to start in on the chorus. It wasn't just the fact that she had an incredible voice that wowed me. She professed her love and devotion to the man who so very nearly did not become her husband with such force, and I even recognised the song before Ramesh said it.

"It's the Celine Dion version of 'The Power of Love'!" I'd rarely seen him so happy, which is really saying something. "I love her so much." I wasn't sure if he was talking about Patricia or Celine, but it didn't matter. She was his, and he would be hers. This simple fact cut through me, and I found myself tearing up. This in turn set off Danny – that big soppy puppy – and even Wazza hugged Toby, before the pair did what they could to fight off the emotion by punching one another so hard that their legs went numb.

Someone had apparently trained Elton John and Kiki Dee (the cats, not the singers) to sit beside their master near the altar and, when Patricia finished her song and got to the front of the church, she tugged off the black sleeves of Ramesh's jacket to reveal a secret, shiny gold lining that was so much more him.

Julia handed off her daughter to her almost son-in-law and Patricia mouthed a "thank you" to me, which really was the final straw. The music had died out, and the audience had fallen silent as I sobbed and blubbered away, far more loudly than was reasonably acceptable. The priest started his introduction but had to keep stopping because I couldn't control my wails of pure happy heartache. Ramesh's father passed me a handkerchief, but that did no good and so his mother offered me a cushion to bury my face in and drown out the noise.

That did the trick and, a mere ten minutes later, I'd got myself under control... Well, more or less.

It's just so beautiful, like that film with Julia Roberts!

'My Best Friend's Wedding'?

No the other one!

'Runaway Bride'

No the other one which finishes with a wedding.

You really aren't narrowing it down! 'Notting Hill'?

No, not 'Notting Hill'. 'Mystic Pizza', obviously!

The running order we'd gone through that morning was more or less maintained but, what Patricia hadn't revealed was that Cher would be calling in over Skype from Malibu to thank the manager of her British fan club and perform the first reading. The hymn was sung by Julie Andrews, who, I had to assume, had flown in on the helicopter we'd seen from the tower an hour earlier. She led a gospel choir in a version of 'Supercalifragilisticexpialidocious', not because it was in any way romantic, but because it was one of Ramesh's favourite songs.

The groom himself spent the whole service with his eyes fixed wide open in amazement, and I wondered whether he'd have the composure to say his vows. Inevitably though, when the moment arrived, Patricia and Ramesh stayed strong, whereas Danny and I went back to our ugly crying. It was lucky he was there to support me, or I might not have got through it.

"I have no idea why I'm so emotional," he whispered as I sobbed into his ridiculously muscular shoulder.

"Me neither," I replied. "But it feels so good."

And when all was said and done and the pujari had blessed the union, a rash of applause broke out around the church and the real highlight of the day could commence. My mum had a solo of her own with no accompaniment or flash mob choir. And to my amazement, she did it without costume changes or special effects. She simply stood at the lectern and sang the classic vows back to them as my newly wedded best friend took his wife's hand and led her down the aisle.

Everyone streamed outside into the evening sunlight and England looked more stunning than it ever has before or since. Fernando, in his role as the wedding photographer, positioned everyone to throw the confetti, and a positive storm of coloured paper took to the air as Patricia and Ramesh emerged from the church as one. Despite the violence and suspicion that had nearly ruined that day, it was still the best wedding I'd ever been to.

"It's just so beautiful," my mother said, as we stood with two of her husbands and my ex-boyfriend/makeshift-brother. It was her turn to cry, and we had a big group hug to comfort her before Fernando realised that he'd had the camera set to the wrong mode, and we needed to throw the confetti just one more time to get it right.

I don't think anyone minded.

Chapter Twenty-Nine

By the time our cheeks were dry, it felt as though I'd been through some kind of purge. I could only conclude that I'd lost all my water weight (whatever that is) and detoxed my spleen (if the medieval belief that it controls our emotions is to be believed). As I walked through the gardens towards the dining room, I felt like I had a cloud strapped to each foot.

"I don't know why we didn't just agree to come to the wedding together in the first place," Danny pointed out as he bounced along at my side, like a sexy bunny rabbit who I had definitely decided I could not have a relationship with.

"I'm sorry about what happened with Lizzy," I thought I'd take this happy moment and make it sad. "She obviously wasn't the one for you."

"I know she wasn't." He was still all smiles. "I've known Lizzy for years, and she's definitely not my type. I only asked her to come with me at the last minute because I'd heard you were bringing someone. I didn't want to look like a total sad sack, here on my own, all alone while you swanned about with *Nigel*." He still couldn't say my fake boyfriend's name without clenching his teeth.

"You're the lucky one. The only way I could get a date for this wedding was by promising him a pair of my slippers. Though I think that offer might have to be rescinded."

We'd made it to the elaborate dining hall, which looked just as pristine as when I'd found Nigel in there a few hours earlier. In place of a big pile of potatoes, he had Lizzy to snack on. It appeared as though the two hadn't disconnected since I'd first spotted them together in the atrium. I was trying to understand what she might see in him, but then I'd presumably experienced a similar level of infatuation when I'd first met him and could hardly criticise her.

"Poor Lizzy," I said, and an echo came back to me from my companion.

"Poor Lizzy. For her sake, let's hope it's a one-night stand."

We sat at the top table together and I took a long, hard look at the man I'd spent so much of my life in love with. It had been hard seeing him again after those months apart. There was so much that we'd left unsaid when we'd broken up the previous summer, and so much I still wanted to explain now. It didn't look like we'd get the chance anytime soon, though.

When everyone had finished taking their places and the happy couple had been welcomed to their feast with much fanfare and celebration, the real entertainment began. My mother was fortunate enough that there was already a stage – or at least a dance floor – in the middle of the room so that she could be the absolute centre of everyone's attention. Luckily for me, the waiters had already brought appetisers, as I was absolutely starving by this point and would have had to eat the floral centrepieces otherwise.

The lights fell, a moody synth started playing and my mother ran into a spotlight dressed in the cave woman outfit that I'd seen that morning. She was chased around by a bear for a bit whilst singing various notes of the melody and then four bare-chested hunks (well, my stepdad Greg, and a few of his yoga buddies) marched onto the scene with rifles and the skimpiest beefeater costumes imaginable. With the bear approaching, the royal guards took aim and there was an enormous bang. This was the perfect diversion for my mother to disappear from the stage and the trojan horse we'd towed all the way from south London was pushed over in her place. I don't know how she did it, but ten seconds later, she popped out of a hole in the top of the horse dressed in multi-coloured, tie-dyed camouflage.

My techy friend Dean had rigged some sort of mechanism in the floor, so that it rose up into the air once the main routine had started. My mother donned a headset microphone, like Britney in her heyday, and her voice boomed out of the P.A.

I was worried that she'd forgotten the words at first because all she sang for several bars was "Love love love love love" as she jumped off the horse and marched on the spot. I should have had more faith in her. Several bright spotlights scanned the audience before focusing back on her for the first verse.

> **"I'm a soldier of love,**
> **I'll shoot you in the head.**
> **I've got a lot of ammunition,**
> **Gonna love you till you're dead."**

It was quite macabre, but really very catchy, and Ramesh couldn't resist getting up to dance beside his beloved.

"I'm a soldier of love,
I'll blow open your heart,
The body count will soon rise
Though my bombs are all smart."

I wasn't convinced by the love equals war metaphor, and I'm pretty sure that, if someone had sung such a song to me, I'd have taken out a restraining order against them. But the crowd seemed to be enjoying it and, when she got to the chorus, Bu-Bu La Mer went big.

"I'm a soldier, a soldier of love!
I'm a mercenary sent from above.
I'm a warrior, I'll fight to the last.
Join my army and make it fast!"

I probably don't need to tell you, as it was the obvious next step, that members of Ramesh's amateur dramatic society filled the aisles at this point. They were dressed in cardboard boxes that had been painted to look like tanks.

Mum went through the chorus three more times and, by the end, even I was singing along. It was not her best composition, presumably because she was missing her usual collaborator, who happened to be getting married that day. But considering most of her fanbase was on TikTok these days, it was good enough for a few million hits.

"This song's for you, Ramesh and Patricia," she said, when it was over and she was being pushed about the room on the horse on wheels by the four yoga bros. "I meant every word of it. May you have a long and happy life together. I know you're going to have the most beautiful children."

Everyone was up on their feet. Every last person in that room was clapping and whistling, screaming and hollering. Tog and Wazza had even started a chant of "Bu-Bu, Bu-Bu, Bu-Bu!" as my mother took her bow.

Like Clark Kent, missing out on all the action, my mother returned a few minutes later in her guise as Rosemarie Palmer – mild-mannered former teacher – to take her place between my fathers at their table.

Like me, she was no doubt looking forward to the menu of melon soup, capon and parmentier potatoes, roast lamb, and wedding cake (obviously) for dessert.

It wasn't one of those weddings where there were loads of speeches, which dragged on for hours. Each person was limited to a tight five minutes, and they were generously spaced out between courses. There was no father of the bride to give a speech, so Julia did one of her own and told us how she knew her daughter was in love with Ramesh way back in high school, ten years before they'd said a single whispered word to one another. It was light and sweet and a welcome break from what we'd been through that day.

The further we progressed through the banquet, the closer we got to my own moment of reckoning, and the more nervous I became. But first, my dear, beloved friend had his moment to shine. He picked up his two cats from their own table nearby and approached the microphone.

"I'd like to introduce everyone to my cats." He paused and looked about the room and every face stared back at him. A hush had descended and, in an unusually calm manner, he drank it in. "Mum, Dad, I lied to you. They're not really called Rambo and Thug. This one is Kiki Dee, and this one is Elton John. And that's the first secret I have to reveal today. You see, this isn't just my wedding, it's my coming out party."

"I knew he was gay," my mother incorrectly stated, not for the first time.

"No, no," Ramesh was quick to clarify. "It's not that sort of coming out. I just want to tell everyone that... Well, there's something I should have said a very long time ago. I'd like to reveal to you all today that I..." He paused to summon up the courage, and Kiki took this opportunity to jump from his arms. "Ladies and gentlemen, boys and girls, I am here to tell you that I, Ramesh Khatri, am a peacock!"

Everyone who knew him – I mean really knew him – cheered at this moment. Those of us who'd been to see his portrayals of various minor characters in countless minor musicals put on by a number of minor amateur dramatics societies clapped and stamped our feet. The rest of the room, including Ramesh's school friends and close family, didn't know what to make of it and stayed quiet.

He pressed on regardless. "I don't want to upset my parents, but the truth is that I'm not into football or car motors. I don't watch

TV shows about barbecuing meat, and, despite the t-shirt I wore last Christmas, I've never enjoyed the Ultimate Fighting Championship. I love musical theatre and cheesy pop songs. I'm obsessed with fashion and think that the colour grey should be banned. I once stood outside a theatre in London for four hours in the hope of getting the autograph of the actress who plays Lady Edith in 'Downton Abbey', even though she's only my second favourite character on the show."

In case anyone is wondering, his absolute favourite is Maggie Smith's Dowager Countess.

He had more to confess, though, and I kept an eye on his parents to see how they were coping. "I write fan fiction of my favourite TV programmes and, no matter how hard I try, it always ends up being erotic. I run several fan clubs for some of the world's greatest divas – in case Cher's video feed appearance at my wedding hadn't given that away. Through no real skill or ability, I've become the fabulous Bu-Bu La Mer's song-writing partner, and I hope, one day, to buy a house with two swimming pools.

"All of these things may be true, and yet they don't define me. Just because I have this wide and unusual range of hobbies, it does not imply anything about my sexuality or my sanity. And yet, every little thing is a part of who I am, and I have to apologise today for hiding all that from so many of you."

He stopped again and his eyes landed on Patricia, who stretched her hand out to encourage him. "Ever since I was a child, I felt I had to conceal who I really was because it didn't fit into the idea of what a good boy or a good son or a good brother should be. Even today, I was planning to wear a disguise, and the only reason I'm up here is because of the incredible woman sitting next to me who gave me the courage to speak to you."

Danny was crying again, but I managed to hold in my tears. This was largely because I was now shaking with fear as my own speech was just minutes away.

I'm pretty sure Ramesh could still stretch this out for a couple of hours yet. Who needs a main course!?

Ramesh's family wore stern expressions and, sitting along the table from me, his school friends just looked confused. Toby appeared to have turned to stone, perhaps unsure whether the groom's continuing confessions were some form of experimental theatre piece.

My favourite groomzilla encouraged his bride to get to her feet, and there were some cheers and whistles before he spoke again. "That's who I should really be talking about this evening: my true love and now my wife, Patricia Octavia Green-Khatri." He took a step back to look at her, with their fingers still entwined. "It's been a mad old day and our lives over the last few years have been filled with highs and lows, but we've made it through and, once we've scoffed the remaining courses, and Izzy has made us all laugh and cry with the no doubt amazing speech that will follow this one, I am going to dance with the most intelligent, hardworking and beautiful person I've ever met."

He leaned in again to kiss her on the neck, and she shyly turned away from the audience. Though I was a reluctant speech giver, Patricia could barely stand the attention. She'd married a man who could barely stand to have no one looking at him, so they were a perfect match.

"I love you Patricia and I am so grateful that you feel the same way." He kissed her cheek this time and held out the mic for her to mumble a very shy, "I do. I can't help it."

"I loved you for approximately seventeen years before I had the courage to tell you and it's taken me another ten to get you here, but it was all worth it to see you so embarrassed right now that you want to throttle me."

About three quarters of the room had got behind him by this point. "Kiss! Kiss! Kiss!" they all shouted, and I was really not so surprised to see that Wazza was leading the chant.

The loving and much-loved couple's eyes locked on to one another's as they enjoyed the moment. It was Patricia, who eventually pulled her husband closer and planted her lips on his. After a good long time, they pulled away, and the microphone in Ramesh's hand just about picked up a faintly whispered, "I love you," before he made his new wife take a bow.

Chapter Thirty

"I love you, my boy," Ramesh's father told him once the next course had been consumed. "I respect everything you said up there today, but I don't understand why you would have thought we were so old-fashioned that we couldn't accept your taste in music. You know, I own a copy of Barbra Streisand's greatest hits on LP."

"Of course I know, Dad. In fact, I think of Barbra's 'A Collection: Greatest Hits…and More' as my gateway drug. You're to blame for everything that has happened since."

Mr Khatri affectionately cuffed his son around the ear. "You've always been a cheeky boy, Ramu."

"Leave him alone, dear." Mrs Khatri added. "If he can't be rude to his parents on his wedding day, when can he?"

The three had a good laugh at this before the parents went to give their new daughter-in-law a truly affectionate hug.

Ramesh sat down next to me and shrugged. "Huh. They took it pretty well. I thought Dad was sure to disown me after the erotic fan fiction thing."

I couldn't reply as my voice had gone somewhere nice on holiday. It was taking a cruise around the Mediterranean and would hopefully be back in time for work on Monday. I couldn't eat either. I just sat in my chair looking as though I didn't want anyone to know I'd spilt gravy down my dress.

Izzy! That lamb must be delicious. Eat it or I will spend the rest of your life making up bad jokes about priests!

Even this wasn't enough to knock me from my stupor and, when the plates had been cleared and Ramesh prodded me with the microphone, I just sat there.

"Ladies and gentlemen, the owner of the world-famous Private I Detective Agency, my friend and boss, Miss Izzy Palmer."

He started off the clapping, and the audience joined in surprisingly enthusiastically. I managed to control my muscles enough to look up at him and shake my head, but he wouldn't let me out of it.

"Solver of over ten murders, the woman who featured on the award-winning online exposé of the terrible killings in the picturesque village of Shackleford Rise… it's Miss Izzy Palmer!"

The applause was a little less hearty this time, and it died away much quicker when it became clear I wasn't going to stand up.

Ramesh leaned down to me and whispered in my ear. "What is the matter with you, Izzy?"

"It's my legs," I said, through closed lips, as though attempting a ventriloquist act. "They won't move, and neither will my face, apparently. I don't know what's wrong with me, but I can't do the speech."

Always happy to overlook my failings, he introduced his best woman for the third and final time. "I'm sorry everybody, she's feeling a bit shy, but I know that she would never let her best friend in the world down on his wedding day. If everyone encourages her, my partner in crime-solving will get up here and tell you how great I am. So, one last time, everybody, it's my non-sexual life companion, Izzy Palmer."

He physically placed the microphone in my hand this time so that I really didn't have a choice. That still didn't mean my body would do as it was told and, though I fought and wriggled, my legs stayed as limp beneath me as two tubes of yoghurt. I thought about getting Ramesh to haul me up and hold me there like a rag doll, but that would have looked absurd, so I remained sitting down.

"Lentils and Germans," I began, or at least that's what it sounded like through my mumbled delivery. "I first met Ramesh through our work together in a major financial services firm in the London borough of Croydon. He worked in I.T. and I–"

This is the most boring speech in the history of boring speeches. And the fact you're still sitting down makes everyone here think you've 'had a little accident'.

It's not my fault! I think a spy must have injected me with some sort of paralysis serum.

Don't be an idiot. There are no spies at Ramesh's wedding… except maybe Dean. But he hasn't injected you with anything. So snap out of it and do a good job for Ramesh's sake.

I cleared my throat, took a deep breath, thought about hiding under the table, and finally pushed myself up to standing. A couple of people looked like they'd fallen asleep by this point, Lizzy and Nigel were still making out and there was some artificially loud coughing to make the silence more noticeable but, when I got to my feet, a few people did seem to appreciate it. One man even made a *huh* noise, like he was pleasantly surprised that I had it in me.

And that's what really pushed me onwards; I was determined to do the best I could… for that guy!

"I'm so sorry. I don't know what came over me. As I was saying… Ramesh and I used to work together at the most boring office in the world and I hated every second of my job." The current boss of Porter & Porter's Croydon branch loudly cheered this statement. "But there's a reason I kept working there, and it's the man sitting next to me. From my very first day, I knew I'd met my non-sexual–"

"The word is platonic!" one grumpy woman shouted from the back of the room.

"Oh, yeah. Thanks. I knew that I'd met my platonic soulmate. We've had some unexpected moments over the last couple of years. Not least when Ramesh had to pretend he was a professional chef for the Queen's second cousin at a Christmas village in the Scottish Highlands."

"I'll never forget your Yorkshire puddings, Ra!" Lady Penelope shouted as, whatever I do in life, heckling will apparently come as standard.

Focussing on the positive, at least I hadn't put on a funny accent or pretended I had a squint. "Or the time we went on holiday and Ramesh spent the week tending bar for a group of secret Nazis."

"You still haven't paid me back for that trip, Ramu," Uncle Kabir joked, and a brief swirl of laughter spiralled around him.

"He's helped me and hampered me on countless cases now, but the charm of Ramesh is not just that he is talented in so many different ways. It's the warmth he exudes as a human being, and his ability to communicate his generosity to those around him. I know that Patricia appreciates all these things and more in her husband, and it makes me phenomenally happy to know that he has found someone equally wonderful."

Ramesh already started crying when I was sitting down spouting inanities but, as I smiled at the gorgeous, ever-so-blushing bride, the emotion finally got to her too.

"So all that leaves me to say is, Patricia, I don't feel like I'm losing a slightly deranged best friend. I feel like I'm gaining someone who can help shoulder the burden." I paused and people actually laughed this time. "I mean it from the bottom of my heart; thank you for taking him off my hands."

Chapter Thirty-One

I don't think I've mentioned this before, but I love weddings.

You see, a wedding is as much of an escape from real life as reading murder mysteries or jumping out of an aeroplane with a bit of material strapped to your back. It's like going on holiday for just one day to a place where (murder permitting) everyone is nice, the food is great and there's far too much cake to go around.

I'd like to live my life at a wedding. I don't think I'd ever get tired of the happy faces on display or the urge most people have to start dancing as soon as it's deemed acceptable. Even the occasional drunken punch-up, which British weddings can almost guarantee, wouldn't bring me down because… well… I love weddings. And, despite the cloud that would forever hang over that day – not just Sindy's murder but Ramesh's reaction when he realised he would have to use a normal kitchen knife to cut the cake – it was still an absolute fairy tale.

"Ramesh and Patricia are probably the most loved up couple who have existed since the dawn of civilisation." It might shock you to discover that this was not Ramesh talking, but Danny, who was still swooning over the romance of it all.

"I think you're probably right."

The lights were low, and we were dancing to Chris De Burgh's 'Lady in Red'. Apparently, DJ Coolpants had decided to kick things off nice and gently.

"There's something I need to say to you, Danny."

He pulled back to look me in the eye. At just a couple of inches shorter than me, he was one of the few men I'd dated who was capable of such a feat. "Wait… let me go first."

I wasn't going to give in so easily. "No chance. What if the thing I was going to say was more important than whatever you were going to say, and I ended up never saying it? I started this conversation, and I'm in charge."

He laughed with his usual beagle-like charm. "Fair enough."

"The thing is…" Having been so authoritative, I was no longer entirely sure how to phrase it. "The thing is that you're one of my favourite people and I've missed you ever since we broke up. You've been my friend much longer than you were my boyfriend, and it's stupid to let a few bad kisses get in the way of everything we've shared. And so, what I want to say is, when you're in London, I'd really like it if you could come back to Mum's house and sleep in the loft like you used to."

He let out a laugh that was as quiet as a breath and said, "Okay."

I was a little taken aback. "Is that all?"

He pulled me in again and we kept dancing. "Yep."

"You don't want to say whatever it was you previously wanted to say?"

"Nope."

I managed to sway in silence for approximately seven seconds before exploding again. "Well, now you have to tell me what it was you were going to say, or I'll spend my life worrying you should have gone first."

I could feel the skin on his cheeks stretch wider as he smiled. "I'm not going to say what I was going to say because you've already said it. I've missed you, not the person I briefly dated but the Agatha Christie-obsessed, crime-solving, hot-chocolate-loving girl who I've known since I was a kid. There was a massive great Izzy-Palmer-sized hole in my life, and I need you to fill it again."

Phwoar!

I thought about keeping my mouth shut, or thanking him for being my friend, but instead I went with, "Hey, I'm not that big."

He held me tighter and would probably have teased me back, but the music suddenly changed, the disco lights started flashing and Ramesh and Patricia ran into the room for their first dance. I'd say that I was surprised by their choice of music (and the choreography they'd clearly spent the last hour working on), but Ramesh is no longer capable of surprising me. He is a surprise. He is the living embodiment of shock and chaos (but in a good way).

What song had he chosen? 'I'm Too Sexy' by Right Said Fred? Christina Aguilera's 'Dirty'? Or what about The Cheeky Girls' eternal masterpiece 'Cheeky Song (Touch My Bum)'? No! They were all too obvious for Ramesh. That's just what everyone would have predicted, and he was a man who liked to confound expectations.

He spun his lovely dance partner across the floor, and the guests cleared a space around them as the music changed once more and a Flamenco guitar started playing. His hands a-clapping and his feet a-stamping, Ramesh circled his partner. A horn started up and then, with Patricia spinning on the spot, her hands moving speedily through the air, the singer revealed this wasn't just a flamenco. It was a 'Cheeky Flamenco'. Though it may have been one of the Transylvanian twin-sister pop act's lesser-known singles, it was the perfect accompaniment for my best friend's expression of love through the medium of dance.

I have to confess; they were pretty good – I mean Patricia and Ramesh, not The Cheeky Girls. The real miracle is that Patricia never broke a smile as she went along with Ramesh's ridiculous routine, and all thoughts that he was still the macho lad he'd made himself out to be were dispelled for good.

My mother and fathers soon took to the floor to join them, before Dean and his lovely girlfriend, Fiona, shuffled past.

"Don't you think it's a bit odd that we're all acting as though no one was murdered here today?" I heard him ask.

"No, Dean. No one but you is thinking about murder right now. Just enjoy the moment."

He wouldn't let it go. "But she was stabbed with a samurai sword! How am I supposed to pretend that everything is right with the world after that?"

Fiona shook her head and steered them away as more dancers took their place. Princess Penelope genuinely knew how to Flamenco and was putting everyone to shame, whilst Nigel and Lizzy were doing a little dance of their own under a table. To be fair, she did break away to thank me for introducing her to the man of her dreams as I shimmied by at one point, so that was… weird.

Danny grabbed me by the arm and, with a surprisingly game D.I. Irons, we did a very bad impression of Spain's greatest cultural export (after the Macarena). When the song finally changed, we strutted our stuff to Abba's inevitable 'Dancing Queen'.

Wazza and Tog no longer seemed weirded out by the transformation in their third musketeer, or even the fact that the fourth member of their posse would be spending the night (and many subsequent ones) in jail. They pulled the happy couple over and we jumped about in a circle until the song switched to something less Swedish. I can't remember another time in my life when I felt comfortable at a disco, but with all my friends there, it was just about bearable.

"Izzy," Ramesh hissed at me as he attempted a tango with Patricia. I'm not convinced that Springsteen's 'Born to Run' was intended for such a dance, but he was giving it his best shot. "Izzy, look at that."

He pointed across the crowded dance floor to where Julia Green and Deidre O'Leary had their arms wrapped around one another and were swaying to the music. Deidre looked up at her friend and the two women leaned in for a passionate kiss.

"I told you, Izzy Palmer!" I hadn't seen Ramesh so happy in literally seconds. "I told you they were secret lesbians!"

"I suppose if you predict secret lesbians on every case we investigate, a pair were bound to come along eventually."

"There's a difference between secret and discreet." Patricia pointed out, five-stepping over to us with a flick of one foot to finish. "Mum's always known she's bisexual, and Deidre's been living at her house for the last six months. Oh, and if anyone's got a problem with it, they'll have me to deal with."

She looked really very fierce just then, which didn't put Ramesh off one bit. "I love you when you talk like that."

Patricia cut across the floor to show off her moves to her mum, and I had the chance to ask Ramesh an awkward question that I'd been dying to know the answer to.

"How did you take Patricia's news up on the roof?"

He crumpled up his eyebrows, clearly unimpressed. "What? Her drunken fumble with a future murderer after we'd been on two whole dates? I think I'll get over it. For the first year we were together, I was inundated with offers from other girls. In-un-day-tid! The women of London were in agony at the thought of the capital's most eligible, musical-loving, in-touch-with-his-feelings bachelor coming off the market. I can't say I was never tempted and, to be perfectly honest, I'd have been disappointed if Patricia hadn't been in similar demand."

"How lovely." I sounded sarcastic, but there was actually something quite sweet in what he was saying. They'd chosen one another despite everything.

Ramesh lingered behind to share some more of his feelings. "I'm just so happy," he loudly whispered in my ear. "I never thought this moment would come."

"You mean because you've been waiting to marry the woman of your dreams your whole life?" I asked, as apparently the glass of lemonade I'd been drinking had turned me into a romantic.

"No, not that."

"Or because you thought you'd never get here after everything that went on this morning?"

"No, of course not. Since when has someone being murdered got in the way of our plans?" He did not wait for me to answer. "I'm happy because Patricia just announced that she's sourced me a special personalised wedding present."

"Oh right." I'm not going to lie. I was hoping for something bigger. "What is it?"

"She got us our very own couple name! You know, like Brangelina or Billary Clinton. You are now looking at one half of Pramesh, which, I have to be honest, is so much better than Raticia."

"I'm very happy for you, Ra."

"Ahem!" he fake-coughed.

"I'm sorry, I'm so happy for you, Pramesh."

"Better. Now let's keep doing exactly this for the rest of eternity and hope the night never ends."

Chapter Thirty-Two

We jumped about together for a few minutes longer, but then I got a stitch and had to sit down. I was happy to watch everyone having such a good time and didn't feel left out. Irons danced with Uncle Kabir and the ever-youthful Auntie Val. Danny convinced good old Cheryl to go for a spin with him, and then Dean and Fiona caught the bouquet as one, which showed impressive coordination at the very least.

It was the perfect wedding, right until the end of the night when I went outside for some fresh air. In the courtyard, beside the still roaring disco, I perched on a windowsill to look up at the sky. It was astoundingly clear, and the stars were as bright as torch beams shining down on me. It felt good to be alone for a few minutes with just my thoughts.

You're welcome.

It was a chance to reflect on just how lucky I was to have collected all those incredible people around me. When I was little, I'd always been jealous of kids like Tog, Wazza and (previously) Gaz who were so sure of their friendships. But now, without really trying, I'd found my own little posse, and I knew they'd stick with me no matter what.

I suppose I wasn't the only one in a reflective mood as Toby emerged at that moment and came to sit next to me on the windowsill without saying a word.

"Evening," I eventually tried, as it was clear he wanted to get something off his chest.

"Evening." Instead of using this as an icebreaker, he sat there in silence for another minute, before croaking out an "I'm sorry."

"What for?"

"For not realising who Gaz was." He let out an angry breath. "It's weird that, when I thought Wazza had killed Sindy for my sake, I would have done anything to protect him, even if it meant going to jail. But when you told me the reason that Gaz had done it, I was filled with rage."

I felt pretty bad for the poor guy. "Don't blame yourself. That's the thing about psychopaths, they don't walk around with badges declaring it."

He still hadn't looked at me at this point. "But I do. I do blame myself and I always will. Galahad was a savage."

Galahad? Gaz's real name was Galahad!

"He was a true monster and so far from the person I thought he was… and yet, I should have seen the signs."

I gave him a moment before asking the obvious question. "What were they?"

He picked at a thread on his jacket as he replied. "He had this aggressively jokey personality that wasn't really a joke at all. He was intense, you know? Like he'd always persuade us to do everything and never accept no for an answer. Compared to Sindy, I guess I didn't see it at the time, but he bullied us. And, deep down, I think I knew that was why Ramesh left Watford and why he couldn't be himself around us."

"It's hardly proof that he was evil though."

"Wait. There's more." His eyes fixed on me at last. "He loved Ramesh. I mean, he used to say we were all best friends, but he idolised Ramekin like no one else. I was at his house once and I realised he'd kept little souvenirs of our life together. I suppose we all do that in a sense, but he had a box of trinkets and I realised that there was nothing there from the things that he and I had done together, every last item in his weird wooden chest was related to Ramesh. Gaz was a nutter; I just didn't want to see it."

It's hard to know how to comfort someone at such a moment, but I had to try. "You can't think that you could have stopped him. We've all had friends that are a bit weird." Approximately fifteen names instantly came to mind. "That doesn't mean they'll turn out to be murderers."

"With Gaz, it did. When I look back through our lives together and think of all those moments that didn't make sense but we used to laugh off – when he would get ten degrees too angry at random people in a bar, or force us to go for one drink more than anyone wanted and made us feel like dirt if we dared say no – I know what they all mean now."

"That's not your–"

"I know you're trying to be nice," he interrupted, "but I've known him since we were practically babies, and I should have seen it coming." His words faded out, and he looked at the sky just as I had before him. When neither of us spoke, he stood to move off into the darkness. I thought that would be the end of it but, when I could only just make him out as a black outline in a black world, he spoke again. "Gaz always took the oath of friendship we swore as kids too seriously. I should have realised how much he despised Patricia. I should have known."

And with this, he disappeared entirely, off to sit with his thoughts or skim stones down the river in the heat of that summer night. It's not often I get to see the aftermath of my cases, and the image of him that night will stay with me for a long time. I thought about heading back inside, but something kept me there.

The steady rhythm of DJ Coolpants's bassline rumbled across the courtyard, but I still managed to catch the sound of two people talking through the cracked open window behind me. Ramesh and Patricia must have gone to catch their breath, and I didn't mean to listen in on them, but they were just so cute.

"I love you, Ramesh Khatri."

"I love you, Patricia Octavia Green Khatri. Which, I must admit, is a bit of a mouthful. I still think we could come up with a couple's surname to make it easier. How about Grhatri? I think that Pramesh Grhatri has a nice ring to it. Or what about we go by just one name each, like Madonna and Stalin?"

"It's definitely something to consider," she said in that clever way of hers, which meant she didn't say no but clearly hoped he would forget they'd ever discussed it. "Actually, there's something I have to say, and I don't know whether I'll get another chance tonight." Her words dried up and my cheeks glowed red in the darkness as I imagined her shyly searching for the right way to express herself.

"I have to say thank you for everything you've done today. If it weren't for you, the police would have arrested me, and we'd never have got married."

I felt all gooey inside to be a witness to their love, and also slightly miffed that she didn't mention the part that I'd played in saving her.

I heard a soft kiss then and Ramesh said, "Really, darling, it was nothing."

"No, my love. It wasn't nothing. If you hadn't planted the evidence and convinced Gaz to take the blame, the police would have known I killed Sindy and I couldn't let that happen. It would have ruined all our plans."

Ramesh let out a dreamy sigh. "I would do anything for you, Patricia. Anything."

It took another ten seconds for the reality of what I'd just heard to settle in. Patricia had killed Sindy and got away with it. It had been her all along. In the waves of panic that were washing over me, I had forgotten to breathe. I had to take a great gulp of air just as the window went shooting inwards and the newlyweds stuck their heads outside.

"Ahhhhhhhhhhh, Izzy! You should see your face right now."

Patricia found it difficult to speak, as she was laughing too hard. "I'm… I'm so sorry, but we saw your silhouette through the window and couldn't resist."

"You're such an easy mark," Ramesh declared, and I seriously considered pulling on his ear until he apologised.

"You're both so hilarious." I crossed my arms and wouldn't look at them.

"Don't be like that," Patricia said. "It was only a joke. I promise I have never killed anyone and that, if I ever do, you'll crack the case in record time."

"You're too kind." I ignored them and peered off into the darkness. Patricia hugged me on one side and Ramesh came to do the same on the other. I tried to pretend that I was still in a bad mood but couldn't resist a contented sigh.

"I hate weddings anyway," I lied.

"That's a shame." My best friend group-hugged me a little tighter. "We've got the Hindu ceremony next weekend. We were hoping you'd come."

I might have let out a quiet squeal of glee.

Yay, weddings!

"We really need you there, Izzy," Patricia added. "You know, just in case someone turns up dead."

The next **Izzy Palmer Mystery**
will be available in **2023** at amazon

Izzy's going to catch up with some old friends!

Find out how Izzy's adventure began...

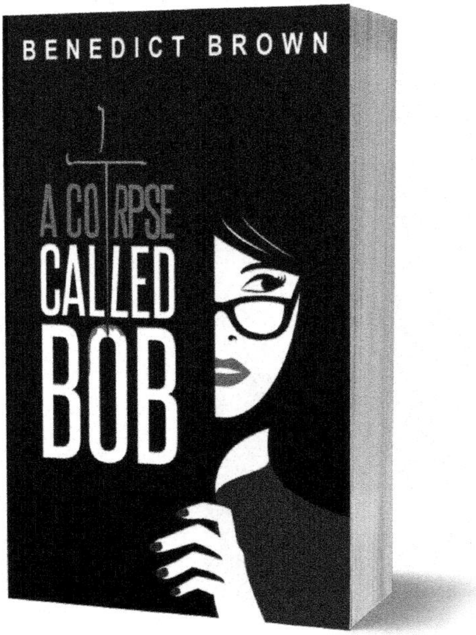

"A CORPSE CALLED BOB" (BOOK ONE)

Izzy just found her horrible boss murdered in his office and all her dreams are about to come true! Miss Marple meets Bridget Jones in a fast and funny new detective series with a hilarious cast of characters and a wicked resolution you'll never see coming. Read now to discover why one Amazon reviewer called it, "***Sheer murder mystery bliss.***"

"Lord Edgington Investigates..."

Have you discovered my new 1920s mystery series?
It's available now at amazon

Get your **Free** Izzy Palmer Novellas...

If you'd like to hear about forthcoming releases and download my free novellas, sign up to the Izzy Palmer readers' club via my website. I'll never spam you or inundate you with stuff you're not interested in, but I'd love to keep in contact.

www.benedictbrown.net

About this Book

This book is all about friendship. No, hang on a second, it's all about Ramesh. Every last word of it is about Ramesh. He's great, isn't he? And everyone loves him.

I don't think I've explained before that Ramesh – though perhaps the least likely creation in my books – is partly based on my brother Daniel. We had a pretty combative childhood, but we're good friends now and I'm a big enough person to admit that he is pretty special. He has carved out an incredible career for himself, working up from his first job as an untrained orderly to become the head of mental health nursing for a massive London hospital.

However, Daniel is also the most Rameshy person I know. He can be charming and funny, or he can be a needy and ridiculous, though rarely all at the same time. In fact, like Ramesh, he is full of contradictions. He is both flamboyant and sensible, outgoing and yet generally far too lazy to leave the house. And, oh yeah, Daniel is the biggest drama queen in Britain… and I love him for it.

So, Izzy's sidekick, and thus my dear brother, deserved a book of their own. And though I didn't go with Daniel's idea of having Ramesh as the main detective who develops psychic powers, I hope it makes him happy. We have another brother who is reserved, calm and quiet and so we are three points on a scale. We've butted heads our whole lives, but come this August, we'll all be in our forties, and we're still there for each other. Which, considering the number of times I told them as a kid that I would never talk to them again, I think is pretty good going.

However, I was telling the truth when I said that this book is also about friendship. From the wonderfully platonic relationship between my detective and Ramesh, and the fraternal love that Izzy and Danny share, to the macho bond between the four musketeers, and the toxic manipulation that Sindy resorts to, the whole plot revolves around these dynamics. The story also gets Izzy to a place where she finally feels comfortable with herself. Unlike way back in the first book in the series, she has a job she loves and is surrounded by people who she's not afraid to be herself around. She has assembled a group of friends from disparate backgrounds and, whatever happens in the remaining books, she's got them to fall back on, which is a rare gift.

I should probably mention that a lot of the details of Ramesh's wedding (not the singing, confetti cannons, or appearance by Julie Andrews) mirror my own – hang on a second, that's not totally true. I did sing "Can't Take my Eyes Off You" by Frankie Valli at my wedding! Marion and I were married in a Spanish castle eleven years ago this July and, I admit, I was a bit of a groomzilla. My poor in-laws hadn't known me long when we started planning and they must have thought I was mad to have so many opinions on everything – they know me better now and no longer have to doubt my insanity. Unlike me, Marion was pretty chilled about the wedding and, like Patricia, said to her adult bridesmaids that they could choose their own outfits – though, luckily, no one decided to wear a rival wedding dress.

We really did cut the cake with a sword, but only because the castle where we got married presented every couple with one. That influenced the cover, which in turn influenced the book, so it was nice to have Marion shaping the story a little. We had a real fairy tale wedding but there were a few things that went wrong and, if you've read this far, I figure you won't mind me getting them off my chest.

1) The photographer took so long dragging us around the castle to take overly romantic photos that we missed eating the delicious tapas appetisers! 2) On our drive from the wedding in the beautiful antique car which should have been the romantic beginning to our new life together, my brother's friend rang to ask us to stop to buy cigarettes – she didn't even smoke! 3) By the time we got back to the country house where we had the party, everyone had decided to get changed and so all the group photos feature my family in shorts and t-shirts. 4) Marion didn't want a big wedding cake so I made one out of Lego (obviously) and someone stole the bride and groom from the top!

But these were only minor issues (I promise I've forgotten all about them!) I married the most incredible, beautiful, talented woman I've ever met and continue to fall in love with her more every day.

The castle in the book was influenced by two houses in Hertfordshire where the novel is set. Hatfield House is a simply incredible building with interiors that defy belief for their rich designs and a famous portrait of Elizabeth I, holding a rainbow. She actually spent a part of her youth at Hatfield and the residence has over four-hundred years of history to investigate if you visit. Because I never make things easy on myself, I also borrowed architectural and historical features from Ashridge House, though I did make up one particular historical detail that Cheryl reveals, and I'm sure many of you will have spotted it. I have no doubt that anyone looking for a wedding venue could do a lot worse than these two incredible locations.

And so, last but not least, I will leave you with one final story of something that my terrible brother Daniel did to me. It was quite possibly the peak of his fraternal cruelty, but I can look back now and think it was funny.

I was standing at the altar in the eleventh century church in the Parador de Cardona, still waiting for Marion, who was forty-five minutes late. I spotted Daniel at the back of church, and he walked the length of the extremely long aisle with a very serious look on his face. I knew he was going to tease me because that is what he's done ever since we were little.

With that completely straight face, he said, "She's not coming," turned and walked away. I was sure he was joking, convinced in fact. But after five seconds, when he still hadn't looked back at me, my heart sunk. It was only for a moment, before he finally looked over his shoulder to stick his tongue out, but it was long enough to give me a minor heart attack. Luckily, Marion appeared a few minutes later, we got married and have been happy together ever since.

I don't think I've mentioned this before, but I love weddings.

Acknowledgements

I have to single out three people in particular for thank yous. My oldest friend in Spain Bridget is my personal cheerleader. She is always the first person to read my books in poorly punctuated scraps as I write and encourages me when I think it's rubbish and I should start all over again. The Martins in Massachusetts are my second line of defence and provide incredible analysis and insight into my books, going so far as to read them multiple times and always pushing me to improve. I'd be lost without you!

Special thanks are due to my crack team of experts – my cousin, and newly qualified doctor, Heather Elliott (**medicine**), Paul Bickley (**policing**), Karen Baugh Menuhin (**marketing**) and Mar Pérez (**dead people**) for knowing far more than me. Thanks to all my fellow writers too, especially Pete, Suzanne, Rose and (the real Izzy Palmer) Lucy.

Back before the internet helped me connect with readers, I felt quite alone in my writing, and so it is a real privilege to have met all these wonderful people and made friends with many of you. Please keep leaving positive **reviews on Amazon**. They really help!

I'm particularly grateful to my Advanced Reading team who make such a massive difference to each new book…

Rebecca Brooks, Ferne Miller, Craig Jones, Mindy Denkin, Melinda Kimlinger, Emma James, Namoi Lamont, Katharine Reibig, Linsey Neale, Sarah Brown, Karen Davis, Terri Roller, Margaret Liddle, Tracy Humphries, Anja Peerdeman, Barbara Hackel, Kathryn Davenport, Vanessa Rivington, Helena George, Marion Davis, Lori Willis, Anne Kavcic, Nancy Roberts, Pat Hathaway, Peggy Craddock, Cathleen Brickhouse, Susan Reddington, Beth Weldon, John Presler, Sonya Elizabeth Richards, Mary Harmon, Karen Alexander, Mindy Wygonik and Esther Lamin.

About Me

Writing has always been my passion. It was my favourite half-an-hour a week at primary school, and I started on my first, truly abysmal book as a teenager. So it wasn't a difficult decision to study literature at university which led to a masters in Creative Writing.

I'm a Welsh-Irish-Englishman originally from South London but now living with my French/Spanish wife and presumably quite confused infant daughter in Burgos, a beautiful medieval city in the north of Spain. I write overlooking the Castilian countryside, trying not to be distracted by the vultures, hawks and red kites that fly past my window each day.

I previously spent years focussing on kids' books writting everything from fairy tales to issue-based teen fiction. I'll be publishing those books on Amazon at some point.

"A Corpse at a Wedding" is the eighth Izzy Palmer novel and number nine **"A Corpse at a School Reunion"** will be out next year (though the novella **"A Corpse Beside the Seaside"** is out on May 31st). If you feel like telling me what you think about Izzy, my writing or the world at large, I'd love to hear from you, so feel free to get in touch via…

www.benedictbrown.net

Printed in Great Britain
by Amazon

36989885R00128